A Purrfect Date

Books by Alex Erickson

Bookstore Café Mysteries
DEATH BY COFFEE
DEATH BY TEA
DEATH BY PUMPKIN SPICE
DEATH BY VANILLA LATTE
DEATH BY EGGNOG
DEATH BY ESPRESSO
DEATH BY CAFÉ MOCHA
DEATH BY FRENCH ROAST
DEATH BY HOT APPLE CIDER
DEATH BY SPICED CHAI
DEATH BY ICED COFFEE
DEATH BY PEPPERMINT CAPPUCCINO
DEATH BY CARAMEL MACCHIATO
CHRISTMAS COCOA MURDER
(with Carlene O'Connor and Maddie Day)

Furever Pets Mysteries
THE POMERANIAN ALWAYS BARKS TWICE
DIAL 'M' FOR MAINE COON

Cat Yoga Mysteries
A POSE BEFORE DYING
A PURRFECT DATE

Published by Kensington Publishing Corp.

A Purrfect Date

ALEX ERICKSON

Kensington Publishing Corp.
kensingtonbooks.com

KENSINGTON BOOKS are published by

Kensington Publishing Corp.
900 Third Avenue
New York, NY 10022

Copyright © 2025 Eric S. Moore

All rights reserved. No part of this book may be reproduced in any form or by any means without the prior written consent of the Publisher, excepting brief quotes used in reviews.

All Kensington titles, imprints, and distributed lines are available at special quantity discounts for bulk purchases for sales promotion, premiums, fund-raising, educational, or institutional use.

This book is a work of fiction. Names, characters, businesses, organizations, places, events, and incidents either are the product of the author's imagination or are used fictitiously. Any resemblance to actual persons, living or dead, events, or locales is entirely coincidental.

To the extent that the image or images on the cover of this book depict a person or persons, such person or persons are merely models, and are not intended to portray any character or characters featured in the book.

Special book excerpts or customized printings can also be created to fit specific needs. For details, write or phone the office of the Kensington Sales Manager: Kensington Publishing Corp., 900 Third Avenue, New York, NY 10022. Attn. Sales Department. Phone: 1-800-221-2647.

KENSINGTON and the KENSINGTON COZIES teapot logo Reg. US Pat. & TM Off.

ISBN: 978-1-4967-4739-6 (ebook)
ISBN: 978-1-4967-4738-9

First Kensington Trade Edition: July 2025

10 9 8 7 6 5 4 3 2 1

Printed in the United States of America

The authorized representative in the EU for product safety and compliance
is eucomply OU, Parnu mnt 139b-14, Apt 123
Tallinn, Berlin 11317, hello@eucompliancepartner.com

A Purrfect Date

Chapter 1

A light misting rain caused me to hunch my shoulders as I hurried from my car to the doors of Market Inn. The restaurant was designed to be old-timey, with a wooden exterior, and a big wooden sign hanging above the massive barnlike doors that fronted the place. A wide awning above the doors gave me relief from the rain. I paused there, considered my next move, and then pulled out my phone.

"Uh-oh, Ash. What's wrong?" my best friend, Sierra Wahl, said by way of answer.

"Nothing's *wrong*," I said. "I'm just calling for a refresher. This was your idea, if you recall."

"A refresher, huh?" Sierra sounded skeptical. She'd set me up on this blind date, something I should have refused the moment she'd brought it up, but hadn't because, quite frankly, I could use a little romance in my life.

I stepped away from the door to let a small group of people pass. "Yeah, a refresher on . . ." I frowned. "What was the guy's name again?"

"Grady Richards," Sierra said. "He's probably already waiting for you inside. I made the reservations for you, so just go in and tell them who you are and they'll take you to him." When

I didn't say anything right away, she asked, "You're not getting cold feet, are you, Ash?"

"My feet *are* kind of cold. It's raining."

"Ha-ha. You know what I meant."

I did. And, if I was being honest, she was right; I wasn't sure I wanted to do this. The last time I went on a date was months ago and the guy had left town soon afterward. No, it wasn't my fault that he'd bolted from Cardinal Lake, but it was hard not to feel responsible. Let's just say that a lot had happened around that time and very little of it was good outside the opening of my cat yoga studio, A Purrfect Pose.

"I'll be okay," I said, huffing out a breath. "I'm just nervous."

"Don't be. He's excited about this. You should be too."

"Maybe if you told me something about him, I'd feel better about it."

Sierra tsked. "If I did that, it wouldn't be much of a blind date, now would it?"

I could have argued about that, but I'd delayed long enough. The date didn't officially begin for another five minutes, so it wasn't like I was late, but I *was* cutting it close.

"All right." I steeled myself as I turned to the door. "I'm going in."

"Good luck." Sierra sounded like a worried mother about to let her teenaged daughter leave for her first date. "Tell me how it goes."

"I will."

"Here's hoping that I won't be hearing from you until after tomorrow morning's walk of shame!"

Sierra clicked off chuckling before I could respond.

With a groan—and a bit of a smile—I pocketed my phone and entered Market Inn.

A light buzz of conversation filled the dining room of the restaurant, which was decorated much like the outside. There was a lot of rustic wood fixtures around the place. Lights that looked like old oil lamps were attached to the wall near the tables. Hanging lights of similar make hung above the central tables, casting a muddy yellow glow over the diners.

A currently unmanned podium stood just inside the doors and had a PLEASE WAIT TO BE SEATED sign written in an aged script hanging from it. I approached and waited there, eyeing the diners, searching for my date, though, thanks to Sierra's stubbornness about not telling me anything about him, I had no idea what he looked like.

"Ash?" George Wilkins's voice came from behind me. I turned to find him standing next to a man with a similar cherubic face, but with a full head of hair, rather than George's thinning pate.

"George?" I said, relieved to see someone I knew. "How are you doing?" I reached out and shook his hand. George was one of my regular yoga students. I rarely saw him outside of class. From what I gathered, he was a private man, who rarely got out.

"I'm okay." He shook and then stepped back, making room for his companion.

"Edward Wilkins." The man presented his own hand. "I'm George's cousin."

"Ash Branson," I said, shaking. His grip was painfully firm. "I run A Purrfect Pose. George is—"

"I know," Edward said with a tight smile. "George has talked at length about you. You've made quite an impression on him."

George's face flushed as he looked away, clearly embarrassed that his cousin was sharing that tidbit of information, though I was flattered.

"I'm glad he's enjoyed the classes enough to talk about them," I said. "I hope that means I'll be seeing you sometime. We'd love to have you."

"Yoga's not my thing." He made a face. "Nor are cats. But I

do appreciate all you've done for George. He could use more friends in his life."

"Three?"

I turned to find a harried-looking woman in a food-stained apron waiting with menus in hand standing next to the podium.

"No, we're not together. I'm Ash Branson. I have a reservation."

The hostess tapped the tablet on the podium. I noted the nail of her index finger was chipped, and from the redness around her cuticle, it had happened recently. "Ah. I see here you are to be seated with a Grady Richards?"

It was my turn to blush. "It's a blind date," I said, not quite sure why I was telling her. "I don't know him."

The woman nodded, set two of the menus aside, and then motioned for me to follow her.

"I'll see you in class," I said, waving to George as I was led across the dining area to a table in the middle of the room. An empty table. Apparently, Grady had yet to arrive. I sat facing the doors, hoping to catch a glimpse of him when he entered, though, as I said before, I had no clue as to what he looked like, so it wasn't going to be easy to pick him out.

The hostess returned to the front and gathered George and Edward. They were led past me and were seated in the corner behind me by the window. When I glanced back, both men were staring my way. While George hastily looked away, Edward continued to stare. He said something to George I couldn't make out, flashed me a wink, and then turned around to face his cousin.

Okay then. I settled into my seat and turned my focus toward the front door to watch for any single men entering.

The waiter approached a moment later. He appeared to be in his mid-thirties, and was of pleasant demeanor. "Hello, I'm

Alan and I'll be serving you this evening. Is there something I can get you while you look over the menu?"

"Could I get a water? I'm waiting for someone and don't know what we'll be drinking."

"Certainly." Alan bowed his head and then hurried away.

I picked up the menu and gave it a once-over. It was relatively standard fare, leaning more to the country-style side of things. I was glad Sierra had chosen Market Inn over a more expensive fancy restaurant where I knew I would have been uncomfortable. The Hop or Snoot's on the Lake would have been better choices, but they were my usual haunts, which meant I was more likely to be seen by friends and family. I was happy to avoid that sort of drama.

My water arrived. I thanked Alan, took a large gulp, and then went back to studying both the menu and the door. Every so often, someone would enter, but they were almost always accompanied by a companion or two. I checked my Fitbit and noted that it was ten past the hour, meaning my date was officially late.

A man entered alone. He scanned the restaurant, eyes passing right over me, but I noted how they'd lingered on my face for a heartbeat longer than on anyone else. His hair was close-cropped and neat. He was clean-shaven, dressed in jeans and a nice button-up shirt. He was a bit older than what I'd expected—he was maybe thirty-five or so—but I could work with that.

The hostess approached him. They spoke briefly, and then they turned my way. My heart started pounding in my chest and worked its way up into my ears. They strode across the dining room, toward where I was sitting.

And then they walked right past me, to a table in the far back of the room.

I sagged, disappointment warring with relief.

I shouldn't have come. I didn't do blind dates. I barely did *date* dates. But I was here, and I was determined to stick it out, as much as the thought of going through with it made me feel like puking.

Another twenty minutes passed. In that time, I'd ordered a Coke, drank half of it in nervous agitation, and had watched as everyone around me ordered, including those who'd come in long after me. A look back showed George and Edward were already eating, with George shooting me worried glances every few moments.

I was half tempted to call Sierra and chastise her for setting me up with a guy who seemed to have ghosted me, but I remained seated, sipping my Coke, and watching the door. It felt like all eyes were on me and I could feel my ears growing warm. My glass was soon emptied and Alan silently brought me another. The pitying look he gave me as he whisked away my empty glass told me he was thinking the same thing I was.

My date wasn't coming.

Indecision flooded me then. I was hungry and I was sitting in a restaurant, so I could order my food, eat, and then leave as if nothing had happened. I could also get up and walk out with as much dignity as I could muster and drive to Snoot's where I could drown my sorrows in one of the numerous beers they had on tap.

Or, I could just go home to my cat, Luna, and bury my head under my pillow until everyone forgot that I'd ever been there.

Before I could make up my mind about what I wanted to do, George's hissed voice came from behind me. "Edward, don't!"

A heartbeat later and Edward was standing next to me, arms crossed. His face was flushed in a way that told me he'd had something alcoholic with his dinner, and quite likely, more than one. There was anger simmering in his gaze, and for a moment, I thought he was upset with *me*.

"Who is he?" Edward demanded, biceps flexing as his fists tightened under his elbows.

Behind him, George looked on, distraught.

I knew who Edward meant, yet I found myself asking, "Who do you mean?" as if the simple question might make him less aggressive, because right then, I was kind of scared of Edward Wilkins. Unlike his cousin, who I found pleasant, despite his penchant for correcting me whenever I misspoke during one of my yoga classes, Edward exuded menace.

"You know who I mean," he said, voice slightly slurred. "The guy who stood you up."

"I don't know him. It was a blind date." When that didn't seem to appease him, I added, "My friend Sierra set it up. I don't know anything about the guy other than his name."

"See? Ash is okay," George said. "We don't have to make a sce—"

"Just a name," Edward demanded, stepping closer to me. "Tell me his name and then I'll go."

All eyes in the place seemed to be riveted to us. I wanted to sink straight through my chair, the floor, and maybe all the way down into the Earth's core, I was so embarrassed.

"Really, Edward. It's all right."

Those biceps of his flexed once again and I felt my resolve weaken and snap. I mean, why should I protect a guy who didn't have the decency to show up? I didn't want Edward to find him and beat him up or anything silly like that, but maybe a little scare would do him some good.

"Grady," I said. "His name is Grady Richards."

Edward grunted, dropped his arms. "Well, this Grady Richards character best be careful. George doesn't have many friends—"

"Edward, please!" George begged, looking around. He was as painfully aware of everyone watching us as I was. "Not here."

Edward plowed on, ignoring him. "Anyone who is George's friend, is mine. And I'm protective of my friends."

"Ash?" A man appeared at the table, dressed in faded jeans and a well-worn Cardinal Lake University T-shirt. I put him in his late twenties, which was close to my own age.

"Yes?" It came out sounding relieved. "I'm Ash."

"I'm sorry I'm late. I'm Grady." He checked his watch, pulled a face. "I got held up at work and I didn't have your number so I could call to let you know. I came as quickly as I could."

The words "Why didn't you call the restaurant?" were on the tip of my tongue, but Edward butted in before I could speak.

"You're the one who left her sitting here for over a half an hour?" He took a threatening step toward Grady, eyes narrowing.

"I am." Grady placed a hand over his heart and lowered his eyes. "And I deeply regret it. If you want me to, I can go."

Edward opened his mouth to say something, but I cut him off. "No, please, sit," I said, gesturing toward the empty chair across from me. "I haven't eaten."

Grady hesitated and then pulled out the chair. He eased down, eyes never leaving Edward.

"Come on," George said, putting a hand on Edward's bicep, which was back to flexing. "Let's leave Ash to her dinner."

Edward's nostrils flared before he leveled a finger at Grady. "You'd best not hurt her or else I will find you and make sure you never hurt anyone ever again." He then stormed toward the door.

"I'm sorry about that, Ash," George said. "Edward can be—"

I raised a hand and cut him off. "I understand. He's only trying to help."

George hesitated a moment, nodded once, and then hurried after his cousin.

"Whew," Grady said with a nervous chuckle. "I thought he was going to hit me."

I crossed my arms and sat back in my chair. Now that we were alone and most of the restaurant was no longer staring at us, some of my anger at being forced to wait had returned.

Grady saw it in my eyes and the smile faded. "Look, I truly am sorry. I should have called someone to make sure you were aware of the situation." He ran his hands through light brown hair that was a little long and unkempt. No matter how he tried to brush it away, it kept falling into his gray eyes. "I was nervous and wasn't thinking. I don't expect you to forgive me right away, but I do hope I can find a way to make amends."

The pleading look he gave me had much of the anger dissipating. There was a cute, almost boyish charm to Grady Richards that was rather disarming. The crooked smile helped.

"All right," I said. "Let's start again."

Grady's smile widened and he reached across the table. "Hello, Ash. My name is Grady." He paused briefly. For dramatic effect or nerves? I couldn't tell. "Grady Richards."

I took his hand and noted how soft his grip was. It was a stark contrast to Edward's own viselike hold. "Ash Branson."

Alan approached the table with a faint frown on his face. It was almost as if he were disappointed that I was no longer alone. He met Grady's eye and something passed between them before Alan plastered on his trained smile and took our order. He remained by the table for a heartbeat longer than he needed before he spun and hurried to the back.

As soon as he was gone, Grady heaved a sigh and then placed his elbows on the table, planting his chin in his upturned palms. "So. Tell me about yourself, Ash Branson. I know almost nothing about you."

"Join the club," I chuckled. "Sierra thought it best if we went into this thing completely blind."

"It *is* a blind date, I suppose." He laughed. It was, admittedly, a pleasing sound. "You do this often? Blind dates, I mean? This is my first."

"No. I don't really date, which I suppose is why Sierra decided to set one up for me."

Grady flashed me a smile that asked about a million questions, but I wasn't about to get into my love life . . . or lack thereof. The last time I went out on a date was almost five months ago. Before that, I'd had something of a dry spell that was more my doing than anything else. I'd had a long-term boyfriend, Drew Hinton, whom I'd been planning to marry, before I up and decided to make massive changes to my life. Those changes included breaking up with said boyfriend. Drew had been the only guy I'd ever dated up to that point, so to say my experience with dating was limited would be an understatement.

Our food arrived a short time later. Conversation was pleasant despite the rocky start to the evening, and I found myself smiling a whole lot as Grady talked. He didn't say much about himself, which was okay. I wasn't too keen on revealing too much myself at such an early stage in a possible relationship either.

By the time we were cleaning up the remains of our meals, I was starting to feel as if perhaps this might work out as something more than a one-off. Grady had a charm to him that made me almost forget his earlier gaffe.

Grady wiped his mouth with his napkin and set it aside. "I need to run to the restroom before I burst. Don't you go anywhere."

I flashed him a smile. "I'll stay right here."

Grady popped up and headed for the restrooms in the back as a rowdy group entered and were seated across the room. There were two women and a man, all in their twenties, and likely either in college, or fresh out of it. They still had that party vibe that a lot of college kids had, even though the local college here in Cardinal Lake wasn't a party school. In fact, it mostly catered to locals, though the man-made lake that gave the town its name did bring in its own collection of rambunctious kids.

"Can I get you anything else?" Alan asked as he collected our plates. "Dessert, perhaps?"

"No, thank you. I'm stuffed."

He produced the check, held it a moment, and then deposited it onto the table close to my hand. "I'll be back in a few minutes to check on you."

"Thank you."

Another long hesitation, and then he turned and walked briskly away.

I glanced back toward the restrooms to make sure Grady wasn't on the way back and noting his absence, I pulled out my phone and shot Sierra a quick text. *Grady was late, but things are looking up. Don't wait up for me.* It was followed by a winky-face emoji.

Sierra's party hat and thumbs-up response was quick to follow and had me grinning ear to ear as I repocketed my phone.

Minutes passed where I daydreamed about how the rest of my night might go. I wasn't about to go home with Grady or anything like that, but heading to a local bar for a nightcap or perhaps a drive around the lake—it was too cold and wet to walk—might put a pleasant end to the evening. I was too old—funny that I thought of being in my twenties as old—to want to park at Lovers' Perch, but the idea of finding somewhere where we could be alone and talk, somewhere where I wouldn't feel the pressure to give up too much of myself, was a pleasing one.

Of course, Grady would have to *want* to spend more time with me. Once he was back, I'd have to find out his intentions without making my own too obvious.

Speaking of . . .

I looked back at the restroom doors, which were still closed with no Grady in sight. It was followed by a quick glance at the time. He'd been gone for a little over ten minutes now. While that was a long time for a quick trip to the restroom, it wasn't unheard of. When another ten minutes passed and there was still no sign of my date, my nerves were hopping. The check lay there, almost accusingly, and I found myself snatching it up and perusing it, just so I had something to do.

Once again, I felt eyes on me, and I steadfastly refused to acknowledge them. I set the check aside, drummed my fingers on the table, and was half-ready to get up and go to the bathroom to check on Grady to make sure he hadn't fallen in.

No, Ash. He could have some sort of intestinal issue, possibly caused by nerves. You wouldn't want to embarrass him.

It took another fifteen minutes of me sitting there like a dope to realize that no matter how long I waited, Grady Richards wasn't coming back.

Frustration and embarrassment had tears forming in the corner of my eyes as I fished out my credit card and set it atop the bill. Alan appeared quietly and took my card without meeting my eye. He returned a moment later, leaned in close and said, "I'm sorry. I took a little off your bill."

Somehow, that only made me feel worse.

I gathered my things and hurried out the door. The misting rain was still coming down, but at least it concealed my angry tears as I hurried to my car. I climbed inside, feeling like a complete and utter fool, and then buried my face in my hands, fighting back a scream.

The jerk had indeed ghosted me.

I threw myself back into my seat, face wet from the rain, but my tears had dried up. There was anger, sure, and a small twinge of regret, but honestly, I wasn't all that surprised. This was why I'd never considered going on a blind date before.

You didn't know what you were walking into, and this encounter had only solidified my stance on the matter.

"Never again," I said, starting my car. Sierra could beg and plead and set me up with the best-looking guy in not just Cardinal Lake but all of Ohio, and I would refuse.

I drove home, seething. I mentally rehearsed what I was going to say to Sierra when I talked to her, how I'd explain the night to George without embarrassing myself much more.

By the time I'd parked in the lot at my apartment complex, I was feeling better about the whole situation. I fully expected to be laughing about it in the morning. These things happened all the time. There was no sense in getting bent out of shape over it.

My elderly neighbor, Edna Cunningham, was standing outside her apartment door when I ascended the stairs to the second floor where both our apartments were located. She occupied the apartment across from mine and was often found standing outside, talking to our upstairs, third-floor neighbor, Pavan Patel, though tonight, he wasn't there.

"Home early, I see," Edna said. Her eyes flickered toward the empty stairwell behind me. "And alone."

I cringed. I'd forgotten I'd told Edna about my date before I'd left. "It didn't work out like I hoped," I said as I unlocked my door.

"Oh? What happened?"

I didn't want to get into it right then, but Edna was asking because she cared, not because she was nosy, though I suppose there was a little of that involved as well.

"He was late for dinner," I said. "And then after we ate, he excused himself and never came back."

Her hand fluttered to her chest. "He didn't!"

"Oh, he did. Left me with the check and everything." I sighed. "But I'm over it." I smiled to show her that I wasn't lying.

Edna clucked her tongue and patted at her stark white hair. "I can't believe someone would do such a thing to you of all people, Ash. You're one of the most pleasant people I know. What's wrong with people these days?"

"It's all right," I said. "But thank you. I was mad at first, but right now, I just want to go to bed and forget it ever happened."

A thump came from the apartment door next to mine. I glanced that way, but my other neighbor, Leon Fitzgerald, didn't emerge.

Edna followed my gaze, then lowered her voice. "He's been acting strange as of late. Going in and out at all hours of the night. He left for work this morning looking like death warmed over, and I have a feeling he'll be doing the same tomorrow."

I hadn't had much of a chance to talk to Leon since he'd moved in four months ago. I heard him moving around his apartment every so often since we shared a wall, but I rarely saw him other than when we both were leaving in the mornings, and often, not even then.

"Maybe it's taking him time to adjust to living here," I said. "This could be the first time he's ever lived in an apartment and the noises of living so close to other people might be keeping him up at night."

"Perhaps," Edna said. She sounded unconvinced. "You know, if he had a nice young woman to show him the ropes, he might take to it quicker."

She didn't have to say it for me to know what nice young woman she was talking about. Ever since Leon had moved in, both Pavan and Edna had been hinting that I should ask him out. Pavan insisted that Leon had eyes for me and would be thrilled at the chance, though I had my doubts.

Of course, after my night tonight, I wanted nothing to do with men for the foreseeable future.

I said my goodbyes to Edna and then entered my apartment. Luna's black-and-white face popped up from where she'd been napping on the perch by the window. She stood, arched her back as she stretched, stub of a tail wagging, and then she hopped down and ran over to where I stood, eyes never leaving me.

"It's good to see you too," I said, picking her up and hugging her close.

I was convinced cats have healing properties because after only a few minutes of carrying Luna around, I felt better. No, I wouldn't give Grady a second chance, but I thought I could avoid punching him in the face if I were to ever see him again. As I readied myself for bed, I instead dedicated myself to how I was going to make Sierra pay for setting me up with the guy, and found myself grinning at the prospects.

A thump on the wall caused me to pause halfway into bed. The thump was followed by a faint curse and then a slamming door as Leon left his apartment.

Curious, I went to the window that looked out over the brightly lit courtyard. Anyone could be seen coming in and out of the four buildings that made up the apartment complex in which I lived. Security reasons, I assumed. It took less than a minute before a black-clad figure carrying a large black bag exited my complex. Leon. He hurried toward the parking lot and, I assumed, his car, without looking back.

Strange, I thought, thinking of what Edna had said, and then I dismissed it. What Leon did with his free time was none of my business.

Chapter 2

Sunday arrived with a chill that permeated my entire apartment. I woke with Luna pressed up against me, her stub of a tail pulled in close to her body. She followed me into the bathroom the moment I crawled out of bed, as was her habit. If I didn't let her in with me, she'd sit outside the door and meow and paw at the doorknob until I opened it for her.

As I ran a hot shower, I was surprised to find I wasn't as annoyed with Grady Richards as I had been last night. I wasn't thrilled about him abandoning me, nor did I appreciate the unexpected hit to my bank account, minor as it might be, but one bad night wasn't going to kill me. In fact, I could use it as a life lesson.

Once I was out of the shower and had gone through my morning routine, I ate a quick hot breakfast, and then headed to A Purrfect Pose. I didn't have classes on Sundays, but I figured I could get some other work done. The ten-minute walk was brisk and cold, yet there was something invigorating about it. I filled my lungs with frigid air and let it out in a puff of steamy breath, relishing the burn of it.

I reached the fountain-centered square on which both A Purrfect Pose and the family business, Branson Designs, sat, feeling like I could spend the entire day working and not tire. I paused long enough to look across the street at Branson Designs, noted the lights on inside, and decided to stay well clear. If Mom ever found out about my disaster of a date, she'd find some way to twist it around so that she could pressure me into coming back to work for her, as she always did when something went wrong in my life.

Instead of going for the front door of my studio, I turned down the alley that would take me to the back alleyway door of A Purrfect Pose. I always preferred to go in that way, leaving the front locked as not to give anyone the impression I was open. A half wall separated the alley from a green that was normally always busy, but this early—and with the chill on the air—there were only a couple of dogwalkers making the rounds. I expected the activity to increase as the day went along.

On the green, a Labrador puppy was running circles around a woman who clearly didn't know how to handle the energetic pup. She kept asking the dog to sit, to lie down, to do *anything* but zoom around her legs. She kept having to do one of those little half-hop steps to keep from being tripped by the leash.

I was so busy watching them that I wasn't paying attention to where I was going. When my foot landed in a puddle of icy-cold water sitting just outside my back door, it startled a yelp from me. I was wearing a pair of ratty Converse that probably needed to be replaced—and weren't thick in the best of times. They were instantly soaked through.

I leapt back, immediately thinking the worst. While it had rained last night, it hadn't been much more than a light mist, so it wouldn't have left a puddle large enough for me to step in. Did that mean the studio had sprung a leak? I feared I would open the door and find A Purrfect Pose flooded.

But then I noticed that the water wasn't clear. In fact, it had that hazy appearance that soapy water had after the bubbles had all popped. There was also quite a bit of grit and fur in it.

Dog fur.

One glance at the dog groomer beside me, and I *knew* where it had come from.

Jordan Allen Leslie, the owner of Bark and Style, the dog grooming business next door, wasn't a fan of a yoga studio full of cats. He claimed they meowed and hissed at all hours of the day, and that it caused the dogs to become agitated, which was, of course, untrue. Ever since I'd opened, he'd been doing his best to get me to pack up and move the studio somewhere else. He liked to play the innocent victim, but was often the instigator whenever trouble arose between us, hence the soapy water.

The urge to march over and pound on the door was so strong, I took a step that way, but caught myself. J. Allen—never Jordan—had a mean streak, though he did his best to hide it. If I were to confront him, he'd act offended, claim it somehow was the fault of the cats, which currently weren't even in the studio, and tell me that this wouldn't have happened if I would have taken his advice and moved elsewhere. He was also known to contact his relatives and have them harass me, all while pretending he knew nothing about it, right up until I shoved the proof of his misdeeds under his nose.

I took a deep, steadying breath, centered myself, and turned away with a muttered "Jerk" as I turned off the security system and unlocked the back door to A Purrfect Pose. I was happy to note that none of the water had seeped inside. I accepted it as a win and put J. Allen out of my mind.

There was once a time, back when I'd first opened, when my entrance would have caused the cats to erupt in excited meows, but after a bad situation where a murder had forced me to close for a few days, I realized I couldn't keep the felines in the studio when no one was here. If something were to ever happen to them, I'd never forgive myself. I did, however, miss the purrs and stampede of tiny paws that used to greet me.

I pulled my phone from my pocket, and then, hoping that it

wasn't too early on a weekend for a teenager veering into adulthood, I put in a call.

"Hi, Ash!" a chipper Tyra Potts answered. Tyra was a local teen who'd volunteered at the animal shelter from the moment she could walk. After the aforementioned murder, I'd offered her a role at A Purrfect Pose that she'd enthusiastically accepted, and would officially begin tomorrow. "What's up?"

"I'm just checking in. Tomorrow's the big day."

"It is." She paused. "I know what to do."

"I know," I said. "But I thought it would be a good idea to go over it once more, just so we both know what's happening."

In the background, a cat meowed. Tyra baby-talked to it a moment before returning. "I'll be there by six, kitties in tow. I've got the key and know the password to the security system, just in case I beat you there. I'll bring in the cats and make sure they're settled in while you get the studio ready for the day. Then you'll pay me the big bucks." I could imagine her waggling her eyebrows with a grin.

I laughed. "Something like that." I sobered. "Your parents are okay with this, right? I know I've talked to them about it, but—"

"They're cool with it. Mom told me it was about time I got paid for all the hours I put in at the shelter."

Tyra loved the animals and had always wanted to work with them more, and helping me gave her that chance. Thanks to an anonymous donor, the cats featured at the studio now had a place to stay near the shelter where they could be monitored more than when I was trying to do everything alone. The head of the shelter, Kiersten Vanhouser, was happy that it left her more room to house the multitude of other cats that came through the already overpacked shelter on a weekly basis.

"And school?"

"I have a work release. Really, Ash, it's cool. And graduation is coming up, so . . ."

"College?"

"CLU. I've already been accepted. And, sure, I could go elsewhere, but I like staying local here at Cardinal Lake. The university has what I want, so why spend more to go somewhere I wouldn't be nearly as happy?"

I squelched my way into the small bathroom near the alley door and pulled off my shoes with a grimace. "All right. If J. Allen gives you any trouble—"

"I know, I know." This time, I imagined an eye roll. "I won't engage him. I'll come right to you and you'll deal with him."

My socks came next. I set them on the edge of the sink to dry, though I doubted they'd do so before it was time to leave. "Thanks, Tyra. You don't know how much I appreciate it that you're willing to help."

"Like I said, the big bucks." She chuckled, which was accompanied by a pair of tiny meows that made me wonder if Tyra had a couple of kittens of her own or if she was at the shelter. "I should get these rascals fed. I'll see you tomorrow morning, Ash."

"I'll see you then. Tell Kiersten hi for me."

"Will do." And then she was gone.

Barefoot, I padded across the hall into the cat room and began prepping for their arrival with Tyra tomorrow morning. Food and water wouldn't be set out until the cats arrived, but I did check to make sure the litter was fresh and set out the cat toys so Tyra wouldn't have to do it. Once that was done, I headed to the front where a pair of boxes awaited me. Inside were shirts provided by Branson Designs. While Mom didn't like that I'd stopped working for her and had opened the studio, she would never say no to a commission. And for as much as I disliked working at Branson Designs, I had to admit, they did good work.

The family discount didn't hurt either.

I opened the first box with gusto, tossing the tape to the

floor to be picked up once I'd hung up the shirts. The last batch had sold out rather quickly, and I was hopeful the new ones, which ran the gamut of colors instead of only light blue, would do the same.

The logo—a silhouette of a cat doing the half-moon pose—was the first thing I saw. "A Purrfect Pose" was written in a stylish script above that. I grinned like a fool as I removed the folded shirt and held it up in front of me, which caused it to unfurl.

The smile faded fast when I saw what was emblazoned under the logo.

"A Branson Designs company?" I read aloud, brain not quite comprehending what I was seeing. I blinked a few times, read it again.

No, she couldn't have. . . . This had to be a test shirt, printed to make sure everything came out all right. Normally, Mom would keep those in reserve and would hand them out to family as cheap gifts, not include them in the purchase order.

But sure enough, the next five shirts I removed from the box all said the same thing.

Anger flared to the point where I very nearly screamed. Mom, Cecilia-*freaking*-Branson, had stamped her seal on *my* shirts, as if *my* studio was part of *her* company. I . . . she . . .

I growled as I threw the shirts back into the box. I snatched the tape off the floor and slapped it back into place. It barely clung on, but stuck. I shoved the boxes, which included the unopened one, against the wall, and then kicked them for good measure.

How could she have done such a thing? Mom had to know I would be unhappy about her slapping her company name on my shirts. What? Did she think I'd just shrug and sell the shirts anyway? That she could worm her way into my business and take over so that she could eventually shut me down and force me to come back to work for her? Was *that* her plan?

I fumed, tempted to march across the square and give her a piece of my mind. Of course, that was probably exactly what she was waiting on. Chances were good that she was currently standing by the window, staring out past the fountain, waiting for me to cross the street so she could give me whatever lecture she had prepared for me.

Like with J. Allen at Bark and Style, I refused to give her the satisfaction.

I glared at the boxes, and yeah, maybe kicked them once more, before I carried them to shelving in the back where they'd stay until I figured out how to deal with Mom. There was no way that I was going to leave them out where someone might spot them and ask to buy one.

My phone pinged and an irrational flare of irritation shot through me before I saw who the text was from: Sierra.

How did it go last night? And better question, did you get any sleep at all? It was followed by a smiley face.

It didn't go great, was my understated response. *I'll tell you about it later.*

Uh-oh. How about at Snoot's? The gang's getting together at seven.

Snoot's on the Lake was a local pub that sat, like it said in the name, on the man-made lake that gave Cardinal Lake its name. It also sounded like a fantastic idea after the last twenty-four odd hours I'd had.

I'll be there. You're buying.

Sierra shot me a thumbs-up emoji, which made me smile, before I pocketed my phone. Before I could enjoy the moment, however, there was a knock on the glass front door of the studio.

Officer Olivia Chase was standing outside the front window. She was wearing her police uniform, including her officer's cap, hands cupped around her eyes as she peered in at me. Short, with unblemished dark skin, Olivia was family. Her brother, Evan, had married my sister, Alexi, and we'd always gotten along. From her unhappy expression now, however, I realized this wasn't going to be a pleasant social call.

"Olivia?" I made her name a question as I opened the door and stepped aside so she could come in out of the cold.

Olivia hesitated on the threshold a moment before entering. "Hi, Ash," she said with a shiver. "It's frigid out there." She rubbed at her arms, and then sighed. "I saw you through the window on my way to your apartment. I'm sorry to interrupt you at work, but it couldn't be helped."

That really didn't sound good. "Is something wrong?" I asked, and then immediately followed it up with, "What did Hunter do?"

My brother often got himself into situations that put him on the wrong side of the law. Usually, it was petty stuff, though his most recent exploits had been tied to a murdered man, of which he was thankfully innocent of everything but of being an idiot.

"This isn't about Hunter." Her dark eyes found mine and I saw concern there that had my anxiety ratcheting up. "This is about you."

"Me?" came my brilliant response. "What about me?"

Olivia rubbed her gloved hands together before answering. "You need to come down to the police station with me, Ash. Chief Higgins wants to see you." She stepped back, opened the door. "And it has to be now."

The Cardinal Lake police station was only a short trip from A Purrfect Pose, especially by car, so there wasn't much time to grill Olivia about why Chief Dan Higgins wanted to see me. She took me straight through the station, past the watchful eyes of her colleagues, and deposited me in a small, stale room void of anything interesting. The desk was of plain wood. The old office chairs were uncomfortable, and likely recycled from somewhere else. A boring clock ticked away the seconds on the wall. It was as if someone intentionally made the place as depressing as possible.

As I waited for Chief Higgins, I mentally rewound my last few days, vainly trying to come up with a reason why he might want to talk to me. I hadn't done anything illegal. I hadn't talked to my brother, Hunter, who was normally the target of Higgins's ire, and Olivia had said Hunter wasn't the reason I was here, so it didn't even matter if I had.

Could it be about Lita? She was Chief Higgins's daughter, whom I'd never met. I didn't even know that she'd existed until Hunter admitted to getting her pregnant months back. The baby was due at any time, but once again, what did that have to do with me?

The door opened and Dan Higgins entered. He was a tall, bald man in his fifties with a muscular build and a perpetual frown on his face. Or, at least, the frown was always there when I saw him. Olivia claimed he could be a big old teddy bear when he wanted to be, though I had yet to see it myself.

"Ash," he said, sitting down across from me. I hoped the informal greeting meant I wasn't in *too* much trouble.

"Chief Higgins," I said. "What is this about?"

He took a moment to gather his thoughts as he spread his big hands on the table in front of him. I noted the gnarled knuckles and slight unnatural bend to his left index finger. He'd once been a football standout, and I wondered if the damage to his finger and knuckles was a result of that. The sport was hard on the body, and while he hadn't played since high school, I knew that he missed it.

He studied his hands a moment longer, and then he folded them, squeezing tightly before speaking. "I need you to tell me where you were last night."

My heart sank. Oh. That. "I went to dinner."

"Alone?" From the way he said it, he already knew the answer.

"No. I had a date." My mouth felt suddenly dry. "Can I get a water?"

Higgins sighed but didn't otherwise complain as he rose and left the room. I expected him to return with a paper cup filled with tap water, but he came back with an ice-cold water bottle. He handed it over and sat back down.

I took a large gulp and my eyes immediately watered from the cold of it. I recapped the bottle and set it aside.

"You said you had a date?" Higgins prodded.

I closed my eyes and rubbed at my temples. "Yeah." A quick mental rewind of the evening and I thought I knew what he wanted to talk about. "I know George and Edward caused a little bit of a scene, but it was nothing. My date was late and Edward got a little riled up about it."

"George and Edward?" Higgins asked, brow drawing together.

"George Wilkins and his cousin, Edward." I frowned. "You didn't know about that?"

"Pretend I don't."

I stared at him a moment, but couldn't tell if he truly hadn't heard or if he just wanted me to explain it in my own words. "George is a yoga student of mine. I guess his cousin had a few too many to drink at dinner and it caused him to get loud when it looked like I was being stood up. Grady eventually showed. Edward yelled at him. And then, both Edward and George left. I didn't think it was a big deal. No one complained, did they? I mean, if the Market Inn is unhappy about it . . ."

I trailed off when Higgins produced a notepad from his pocket and jotted something down.

"They confronted your date?" he asked when he was done.

I shrugged, already regretting mentioning it. "Edward did."

Higgins leaned forward. "What did he say?"

"Nothing much. He just warned Grady against hurting me. I was honestly surprised, since I didn't even know Edward. I guess he's protective of his cousin, and since George and I are friends, Edward thought that standing up for me would, I don't know, help George somehow. Honestly, there wasn't much to it." I tried on a smile, but it felt strained, so I dropped it.

Higgins went back to his notepad.

I chewed on my lower lip while I waited him out. I couldn't imagine how Edward's outburst would cause the police to become involved. Even if someone at Market Inn had complained, why bring me in?

"Your date was with Grady Richards, correct?" At my nod, he asked, "Did you know him well?"

"Before we met that night? No. It was a blind date."

"You went out with someone you've never met?"

I bristled at his tone. He made it sound like I'd go out with anyone who so much as glanced at me. "My friend set it up. It's not like I go out with random men all the time."

Chief Higgins jotted something else down on his notepad. I desperately wanted to know what he'd written, but didn't pry. A growing sense of dread had me eyeing the door instead.

"So, you'd never met him before last night?"

"No, I hadn't."

"Did you know anything at all about him? Where he worked? Who he spent time with? Where he grew up? Anything like that?"

"No." I crossed my arms. "We didn't get too personal with our conversation since it was our first date and all." Another thought. "He *did* leave me with the check. Is that what this is about? I paid for both meals. The waiter gave me a discount because I suppose he felt bad for me. Wasn't he supposed to do that?"

"You paid. And then you went home alone?"

Anger started simmering under the fear. "Yes, I went home alone. I spoke to my neighbor Edna when I got there." I added the last, just in case he needed a witness.

"What time was this?"

"I don't know. Before nine? I didn't check the time, but it wasn't too late. I didn't hang around too long after I realized Grady had abandoned me. I went straight home, spent some time with my cat, and then I went to bed."

Another jot in the old notebook. Then Higgins flipped it closed, stuffed it back into his pocket, and sat back to stare at me as if searching for deception.

I met his stare, though I was shaken. Why was he asking about my whereabouts *after* my date? Beforehand, I understood. There was a disturbance thanks to Edward. Alan the waiter had taken a little off my check when Grady had ghosted me. But that wasn't police business.

Oh no. Full-on panic welled up inside me. Why ask about where I was after my date?

Because something had happened afterward.

"Where's Grady," I asked, voice coming out small and frustratingly frightened.

Chief Higgins studied me a moment longer before speaking. "We got a call early this morning," he said, keeping his voice as steady as his gaze. "Officers arrived at an apartment at around six o'clock this morning and found the door to be unlocked and slightly ajar. The caller was never identified, nor were they on the scene."

Higgins licked his lips and, oddly, seemed to grow uncomfortable. We had a history, one that was often contentious, but I never got the impression that Dan Higgins didn't like me. Whatever he had to say, he knew I wasn't going to like it.

"Chief Higgins?" I asked, leaning forward. "Did something happen to Grady after our date?"

He swallowed, went on. "An open planner was found on the

scene. Your name was written on it, along with the name of a restaurant: Market Inn. Both your name and the restaurant name were circled." He paused and the look he gave me was full of pity. "I'm sorry, Ash."

He didn't have to say it. I already knew.

Grady Richards was dead.

Chapter 3

Sierra stared at me from across the table at Snoot's on the Lake, eyes wide. She'd come in looking refreshed after having the day off from work—she worked right here at Snoot's—but as soon as I opened my mouth and told her about what had happened, her entire demeanor understandably changed. "Grady's dead?"

I wrapped my hands around my beer for support when I answered. "Looks like it. I'm so sorry, Sierra."

Snoot's, like usual, was packed. The patio still had a little bit of seating available, but it was far too cold to sit outside, especially with the cold lake air blowing in. A handful of college kids were having a night of it, howling and laughing like lunatics while they leaned on the railing looking out over the lake. I expected one of them to lose their shirt by the end of the night.

"Do you think he was murdered?" Aaron Kipp asked. His long, dark hair was pulled back in its standard ponytail. His mother was Shawnee, and much of her heritage could be seen in his features. His arm was slung casually across the shoulder of his girlfriend, Henna Korhonen. She leaned into him with a sad shake of her head.

"Chief Higgins didn't say." I took a drink to gather my composure. I'd spent two hours at the police station going over my story, hoping that something I said might help catch the killer, but what did I have, really? I barely knew the guy. I turned to the one person who *had*, when I asked, "How well did you know him, Sierra?"

She blinked a few times, seemingly surprised by the question. "Honestly?" She pulled a face. "Not all that well."

My beer paused halfway to my mouth. "Wait. You set me up with a guy you didn't know?"

"I *technically* knew him," Sierra said, her expression turning to chagrin. "But only a little bit. He used to come into Snoot's every now and again and we got to talking. You know how it is? He came in alone, and since I was right there, I chatted him up."

"Hold up." I held up a hand. I couldn't be hearing her right. "You talked to a guy a few times and decided, 'Hey, I should set him up with my friend!'? What if he was some sort of psycho?" I bit my lip as instant regret flashed through me. "Sorry. That was rude."

"It's not nice to rag on a dead guy, Ash," Aaron said, earning him a shoulder punch from Henna.

"He seemed nice enough," Sierra said. "And he appeared to be pretty darn lonely. He'd come in and sit at the bar and sort of just stare into his drink some nights. I felt bad for him, hence why I decided to talk to him. I figured, 'What can it hurt?' and found him to be a decent enough guy. And since you spend most of your time locked away in your apartment—"

"I do not!" Though, I suppose as of late, I hadn't been getting out as much as I used to. I'd been so busy with the studio and worrying about Hunter's upcoming baby and the fallout that would surely result the moment Chief Higgins learned about who the father was, I'd become something of a recluse. At least, compared to what I'd once been.

"Aaron and I like to spend time inside," Henna said, snuggling up closer to him. "So, you'll get no judgment from us."

The look Aaron gave her was on the lascivious side. Across the table, the quietest member of our group, Brianna Green, mock gagged at them, drawing the hint of a smile from me.

"Yeah, but you two have each other," Sierra said, missing the whole interaction. "Ash has no one but her cat."

"Like you're one to talk," I teased.

"Yeah, but my cat Herman is about the size of a human," she shot back with a grin. "It's like having a real live person there with me." A pause. "A fluffy eat-you-out-of-house-and-home person."

"That's more than I have," Bri said, ducking her head so that her bangs concealed her brown eyes which were hidden behind the thick rims of her glasses. "And I get by fine."

"Careful, Bri," I said. "Or Sierra is liable to set you up with some guy she met on the street last week."

"Or on her way to the bathroom," Aaron added.

"Ha-ha. Very funny." Sierra stuck out her tongue before she sobered. "Do you think someone saw you with him and, I don't know, killed him because he was with you?"

"God, I hope not." I shuddered at the thought. "The only person I saw there who I knew was George. He's one of my yoga students."

"Does he have a thing for you?" Bri asked.

"No." I really hoped he didn't. "He was there with his cousin, Edward." I frowned down at my glass, which had somehow been emptied. "Edward had been drinking and had gotten loud by the time Grady showed up. He ended up confronting him in some strange defense of my honor, as if he was somehow protecting George by defending me. It was weird."

Henna pulled out of Aaron's grip so she could lean forward. "Confronted him? As in, he yelled at him? Or did he try to fight him or something?"

"Mostly just threats," I said. "I didn't think anything of it at the time. Both Edward and George left before Grady and I were done eating, so, as far as they know, we'd had a great time."

"You said Grady was found at his apartment?" Bri asked. When I nodded, she went on, "Do you think Edward could have followed him? Like, he waited around outside the restaurant and then tracked him home and killed him?"

"But why?" I asked. "Grady showed up. We had dinner. There was no reason for him to kill him."

"Other than the fact that he skipped out on you," Sierra said. "Though, I can't imagine the Grady I knew doing such a thing. He's always paid his bill here. Gave good tips, in fact."

"Wait, he bailed on you?" Aaron asked.

My face reddened in embarrassment. "He left to use the bathroom and never came back."

"What a jerk." Henna scowled. "If he wasn't already dead, I'd have a few words for him myself. No one messes with our Ash."

While the sentiment was appreciated, it didn't make me feel any better about Grady's death. I'd had dinner with the man, and honestly, had thought him to be pleasant, if not a smidge reserved when it came to talking about himself. At least until he'd snuck out on me.

"Did you do or say something to offend him?" Aaron asked, earning him a rib jab from Henna. "Hey! It's a legitimate question."

"Not that I'm aware," I said. "When he got up, I thought things were going pretty well. Maybe he ran into someone he knew and . . ." I trailed off with a frown.

"And he forgot about you?" Bri asked.

"Or he was embarrassed about going on a blind date and left me there because he didn't want anyone to know."

"Could someone have attacked him in the bathroom?"

Aaron asked. "They could have stuck a gun in his back and forced him to leave you there."

"With no one seeing?" Henna asked, skepticism dripping from her words.

Aaron merely shrugged. "It could happen."

"Seriously, Aaron?" Bri said with a roll of her eyes. "This isn't a movie." And then, to me, "Was he shot?"

"Chief Higgins didn't say," I said. "But it's possible."

We all digested that for a long moment that went on a smidge too long for my tastes.

"Refill time," I said, abruptly rising. While we did have a waitress, I desperately wanted to stretch my legs.

"I think we could all use another," Aaron said, starting to stand.

I waved him back down. "I'll order a round. I need a moment to think."

He eased back down and I headed for the bar to put in our drink order.

With Snoot's being so packed, it was tough going, but that was okay. Making sure I didn't plow into anyone or trip over a jutting leg helped keep my mind off Grady and what had happened to him. Mostly.

I kept seeing him get up and walk away. And then . . . nothing. No one followed him. I didn't see him leave out the front door, which I was facing at the time. Could he have managed to slip out without me noticing? Sure. But I was starting to wonder if perhaps he'd snuck out the back. Through the kitchen? Somewhere else? I didn't know Market Inn well enough to know if there *was* another exit.

I put in our drink order, making sure to get a couple of pitchers, rather than just simple refills. I had a feeling we'd be needing them by the end of the night.

When I returned to the table, a new thought had taken hold. "I think our waiter saw him leave," I said, sitting.

"Why do you say that?" Aaron asked. "Did he say something to you?"

"Not so much," I admitted. "But he did take a little off the bill and avoided meeting my eye. It was like he knew what had happened."

"He didn't appear alarmed?" Sierra asked.

"No. He apologized when he left the bill." I sighed. "Maybe he didn't see him leave, but was able to figure it out since I'd been sitting there alone for a while."

"Could your date have gotten a call that made him leave?" Aaron asked. "Like, something had come up and he had to rush home?"

"A call from the killer?" This from Henna, who looked at Aaron askance. "Why would he go rushing straight to his death without telling anyone where he was going?"

Aaron shrugged. "Hey, I'm just throwing ideas out there."

"We still don't know for sure that he was murdered," I said, though I was pretty sure he had been. Why else would Chief Higgins have wanted to talk to me? "I just wish I knew something about him that would help the police identify whoever did it if he *had* been."

Our pitchers arrived and we took the next few moments to refill our glasses. Mine was half-empty before everyone else finished pouring.

"Now that I think about it," Sierra said, "Grady didn't talk about himself too much to me, either. He came in here every other week or so, two or three nights straight, and then he'd be gone again for a week."

"That sounds to me like someone with something to hide," Bri said. I nodded in agreement.

"Or maybe he just had a busy life that he wanted to forget," Henna added.

"Could he have lived outside of town?" Aaron asked.

"Higgins said he was found at an apartment here in town," I

said. "I assumed it was Grady's." Though, now that I'd thought about it, Chief Higgins hadn't actually said whether it was Grady's place or someone else's.

Sierra shook her head as she studied her beer. "I feel terrible. I should have looked into the guy more before setting you up with him."

"It's all right," I said. "You couldn't have seen this coming."

"I'm just glad you're okay, Ash," Aaron said, lifting his glass. "I think it's safe to say that it wouldn't be the same around here if something were to happen to you."

"Here, here," Henna said, raising her own glass in salute.

Bri and Sierra followed suit. I rolled my eyes, even as I grinned like a fool.

The sound of our glasses clinking together was swallowed by the noise of the bar, but the sentiment remained.

"Thanks, Alexi," I said as I collapsed into the front seat of her car a few hours later. "I didn't interrupt you, did I?"

My sister, Alexandra Lee Branson, sat in the driver's seat, looking as prim and proper as ever. Four and a half years my senior, Alexi had dealt with our family drama for longer than I had, which meant she took the brunt of our mother's wrath when things didn't go Cecilia Branson's way.

Considering Hunter and me, that was often.

Alexi had decided to dedicate her life to Branson Designs, and had chosen to follow in the family naming policy, where the women kept the Branson name through marriage. It's why Alexi and I were Bransons and Hunter was a Daniels. Yes, it was often confusing, but so was my family.

Yet, despite her following in Mom's footsteps, Alexi was the best sister a girl could ever want. She wasn't strict like Mom, didn't belittle everyone else for her own personal benefit. If Alexi was the future of the Branson legacy, then it was in good, capable hands.

It was why I didn't hesitate to call her once I realized driving myself home was not happening.

"No," she said. "I was just puttering around the house." She looked me up and down, eyebrows raised. "Looks like you had a good time."

I flopped my head against the headrest. It felt like my neck had turned into a loose spring. "I did. I may have overdone it."

She studied me a moment longer before starting the car. "Care to talk about it?" she asked. When I didn't answer right away, she pressed. "It's not like you to drink too much, Ash. Something's up."

"Hunter?" I ventured. "And the baby." As if my brother's predicament served as the perfect scapegoat as to why I'd drunk more than I had in years.

"He's not in trouble yet," Alexi said. "The moment Dan Higgins finds out about him, however . . ." She sighed. "I've already started planning his funeral."

My woozy mind tried to imagine how that would go, but I only managed a handful of broken images. Hunter holding a bundle. Lita Higgins—who in my mind looked exactly like Chief Higgins with long hair and makeup since I'd never met her or seen a photo of her—lying in bed, sweat beading her brow.

And then, Dan Higgins, wearing a football uniform styled to resemble his police chief outfit, barging through the door, steam coming from flaring nostrils pierced like a bull's.

I giggled.

"Oh boy," Alexi said, shaking her head as she pulled out onto the road. "Something really is up. Spill."

My laughter dried up as I pouted out my lower lip. "My date died."

Alexi took her eyes off the road briefly to glance at me. "Your what now?"

Slowly, and in a very meandering way, I told her about my

date with Grady Richards and his subsequent death-that-was-likely-a-murder. I finished with my trip to Snoot's where I'd spent the last couple of hours unsuccessfully trying to forget all about it.

"My car's still there," I said.

"That's a good thing, Ash," Alexi said. "We can pick it up tomorrow if your head doesn't explode." She paused, added, "I'm sorry about your date."

"It's okay. I didn't really know him."

Thankfully, Alexi didn't comment on that. Maybe it was overindulgence in drink, but I was feeling rather melancholy about Grady. Sure, he'd shown up late. Yes, he left me to pay for the check without so much as a "see you later." But what little I'd seen of him made him seem like a decent enough guy. He hadn't acted as if he'd feared for his life. So what had happened?

"Mom branded my shirts," I said, mind doing a detour midsulk.

"She did what?"

"Branded my shirt with a Branson Designs thing-a-ma-boobie. You know the shirts I ordered?"

Alexi nodded. "I helped put them together. What do you mean she branded them?"

"Says Branson Designs company or something like that on 'em. Right on the front." I held up my hands, framing the imaginary shirt in front of me.

"I didn't know," Alexi said, scowling. "But I'm not surprised. You want me to talk to her about it?"

I sighed. "No, I'll do it."

"No wonder you tried to drink yourself into oblivion. Mom does that to a person."

Understatement of the year, that was.

"I'm afraid one of my yoga students might be involved," I blurted.

"With the shirts? How so?" We were stopped at a red light so she was able to give me a good looking over. From her grimace, she didn't much care for what she saw.

Admittedly, I wasn't feeling too great myself. I should have known better than to have the last couple of rounds, but someone was dead and I felt somehow responsible. It was no excuse, but sometimes you had to make a mistake to learn from it.

"Not the shirts, but with Grady's death. He got into it with my date." I frowned. "No, wait. It wasn't George. It was Edward who did it. George has a cousin named Edward. Who knew?"

"I see." Alexi eased the car forward, somehow following my jumbled ramblings. We were reaching the square, which meant we were minutes from home. "Do you think this Edward guy killed . . . what was his name again?"

"Grady. And I don't know." I crossed my arms as I stared out the window. "I hope not. It would suck for George."

Once again, Alexi wisely didn't comment on my less than stellar evaluation of the situation.

We pulled into my apartment complex's parking lot a few minutes later. The sky was clear of clouds, and I found myself leaning against the cold window, staring up into the stars as we rolled to a stop. If we'd had much farther to go, I would have fallen asleep.

"Are you going to be okay, Ash?" Alexi asked. "I haven't seen you like this since . . ." She trailed off, but I knew what she was thinking, so I said it for her.

"Since Drew."

"Yeah."

Drew Hinton and I had dated since we were kids in middle school. We'd had plans to get married, to have kids, and had already moved in with one another, fully expecting to live our lives together right up until the very end.

And then I broke up with him, moved out, and started my life over from scratch. Those first few weeks, single for the first time since I could remember, had hit me hard. I still cared about Drew and never wanted to hurt him. He understood why I did it, has even supported me since, but hurt him, I had.

I'd spent those first few days at Snoot's more than I cared to admit. If it wasn't for my friends, there was no telling what would have happened to me.

"I'll be fine," I said, rubbing at my eyes. It might have been my imagination, but I could already feel the headache coming on. "Thanks for picking me up, Alexi. I appreciate it."

"No problem. Call me anytime." She drummed her fingers on the wheel. "Do you want me to come up with you? I could make us some coffee and we could talk things through if you want?" She made it a question.

I considered it briefly before saying, "No, I'll be all right. I just need to lie down and maybe take a shower. I'll be as good as new by morning." And then, despite not really feeling it, I said, "I didn't really know the guy."

Alexi looked skeptical as I climbed out of her car. I closed the door, patted the hood, and then waved, before I staggered my way to the door to my building. I hated to admit it, but I had to pause once to double-check to make sure I had the right one before I stepped inside.

A short man, built like a bowling ball, with thick, hairy arms that looked too short for his body was standing in the lobby with my neighbor Leon Fitzgerald, who was cradling a bandaged left hand. "It's been taken care of. Get a grip, Leon. There's nothing to worry about any—" the man cut off as I entered.

I paused just inside the door, both because I felt like I'd just intruded on something and because if I took another step, I thought I might fall over.

"Are you all right, Ash?" Leon asked, confirming that, yep, I looked as bad as I felt.

"I'm fine." I frowned as my stomach did a flip. "Ish."

The short man looked from Leon to me and back again before saying, "I'm going now. Just . . . don't do anything rash, okay?" And then he turned, nodded to me once, and then hurried out the door I'd just come in.

"Who was that guy?" I asked, belatedly realizing that I was being rude.

Leon stared after the man before shaking his head. "Just someone I know."

We headed for the stairs at the same time. Leon kept his pace slow so that he could walk up beside me, which I appreciated. Right then, I could use the extra support, especially since chances were fifty-fifty that I was going to lose my balance at some point along the way. I regretted not asking Alexi to accompany me inside, though I supposed Leon would do in a pinch.

I found myself glancing at him side-eyed, wondering if Pavan was right and Leon had an interest in me. He was good-looking. No, check that, he was stunning. He had the sort of face that belonged on a movie star, one, on a purely aesthetic basis, I wouldn't mind waking up to in the morning.

My gaze dropped from his face to that bandaged hand of his. He was also limping ever so slightly.

I blurted, "What happened?" once again, realizing I was being rude too late to stop myself.

Leon looked down at his hand, shrugged. "It's nothing. I managed to sprain my wrist and twist my ankle. It was an accident."

"Fall out of the bathtub?" I asked, and then flushed when my mind provided an image of a naked Leon sprawled across the floor of his bathroom.

His chuckle sounded forced. "Something like that."

We reached the second-floor landing to find Edna standing outside her door with our upstairs neighbor Pavan Patel. The two had been talking—gossiping most likely—but stopped the moment Leon and I stepped into view.

As soon as she saw us together, Edna's eyes lit up. I knew what she was thinking and decided it best to nip those thoughts in the bud before her imagination could run wild.

"We ran into each other in the lobby," I said. Leon went straight for his door with only a cursory wave before he stepped inside his apartment.

"Looks like it was a rather rambunctious meeting," Pavan said with a waggle of dark eyebrows. Of Indian heritage, Pavan was on the stockier side. I wasn't sure if it was his parents who'd come from India, or if it was someone else down the family line. He had little in the way of an accent, so I was pretty sure he'd grown up in Cardinal Lake, though I wasn't an expert and could be mistaken.

"It's all right to admit it if you two are a thing," Edna said, which caused Pavan to titter right along with her.

A wave of nausea ran through me, though it had nothing to do with Leon, who, as I said before, *was* on the attractive side. "Really," I said. "I've been at Snoot's and Leon's been..." I waved a hand vaguely in the air. "Wherever he's been."

"You weren't together?" Edna asked. She sounded disappointed.

"Nope, sorry."

"That's too bad," Pavan said with his own disappointed sigh. "He's sweet on you, you know, Ash. You might want to jump on that before the feeling fades."

"Jump on it, indeed." Edna snickered, which set Pavan to laughing.

"Yeah, yeah," I said, wishing my head would stop spinning. "Laugh it up. When I start thinking straight again, I'm going to have a witty comeback for the both of you."

"I can't wait," Pavan said, still chucking. "I best get back to Seo-Jun." His wife. "She's likely wondering where I've gotten off to. I'll talk to you tomorrow, Edna." He glanced at me and winked. "You too, Ash. *If* you can make it out of bed, that is."

I would have stuck my tongue out at him, but I wasn't sure I could manage it without throwing up, so I just glared. I was quickly running out of steam. All I wanted now was to go inside and fall into bed. The shower could wait until tomorrow.

As soon as Pavan was gone I took a step toward my own door, but paused. "Hey, Edna?"

She was halfway to closing her own door. She leaned back into the hallway, white eyebrows raised in question.

"Did you see Leon leave last night?"

"No. Why do you ask?"

Why had I? Good-looking or not, I had no interest in my neighbor. What he did in his own free time was his own business.

"I'm not sure," I said, and then shrugged. "Just curious, I guess. Good night Edna."

She hesitated a moment and then said, "Good night, Ash," before closing her door.

I entered my apartment and immediately scooped up Luna, who'd come to the door to greet me. I absently locked the door and headed for the bedroom, mind a million miles away.

Perhaps it was my muddled mind at work, but I couldn't stop wondering about Leon.

Where had he gone last night?

Why was he injured this evening?

Who was the man he was talking to in the lobby?

And because my mind wanted to make connections, could it all somehow have something to do with Grady Richards's death?

Chapter 4

Regret is a powerful thing.

I regretted letting Sierra talk me into going on the blind date with Grady Richards. I regretted not doing more to calm Edward down when he'd approached me at Market Inn after having a few too many. I regretted not asking Grady more about himself while we were on the actual date. I regretted not keeping better tabs on him when he got up to go to the restroom.

But most of all, I regretted going to Snoot's with my friends.

The morning hit me like a sledgehammer. My alarm, which was set to play one of my favorite songs to bring me gracefully into the day, sounded as if someone had turned it up full blast and set it off inside my skull. When I rolled over to silence the noise, I did so with my eyes squeezed tight against a headache that threatened to do me in if it wasn't immediately dealt with.

A shower helped ease some of the pain. So did the two cups of coffee I gulped down afterward. Breakfast consisted of a single piece of unbuttered toast, which went down with the grace of sandpaper and sat in my stomach like a lead weight.

Luna watched me from her perch, paws crossed in front of her, chin resting atop them. After her breakfast, she'd jumped up, as was her custom, though the way her eyes followed me around the room as if she were waiting for me to collapse was new.

"Never again," I told her with a groan. I wasn't normally a heavy drinker, but after the last couple of days, I'd needed the stress relief. But *man*, was I paying for it now.

And I still had classes to run.

I stared at my phone and considered making a round of calls to cancel the entire day. I could have Tyra put up a sign on the door of A Purrfect Pose so anyone I couldn't reach would know I wouldn't be in. She was likely already gathering up the cats, so it wouldn't be too much trouble for her. Inconvenient, yes, but doable. And then, once that was done, I could crawl back into bed and sleep until the very act of breathing no longer hurt.

I was halfway to picking up the phone when I caught myself.

I can do this. I refused to let one night of overindulgence defeat me. I could look at the day as my penance for the mistake, as a reminder of what could happen if I let myself go.

With a reluctance overcome solely by sheer stubbornness, I returned to the bathroom, downed a couple of Tylenol, and then got dressed for what would inevitably be the most uncomfortable session of yoga I'd ever experienced in all my twenty-odd years of life.

My first thought once I was out the door and heading down the stairs of my apartment complex was to climb into my car and drive the short distance to the studio, but I quickly realized that wasn't possible. My car was still sitting at Snoot's where it would remain until Alexi could take me back there later that day. That meant walking the short ten minutes through town, which, right then, felt like I was considering walking the circumference of the planet. The air was dry, but chilly. My heavy jacket had a hood, so I pulled it up over my head, hunched my shoulders, and began the trek, mentally going over my regrets once more and promising myself I'd do better in the future.

As expected, Tyra Potts was already inside A Purrfect Pose when I arrived.

"The cats are here and ready for some yoga," she said before giving me a good looking over. "Wow, Ash, you look like hell."

I removed my jacket and tossed it onto my office chair. "Thanks. It takes practice to look this awful in the morning."

She laughed before clacking her tongue piercing against her teeth. "But no, really. What happened to you?" She took a step back from me. "You're not sick, are you?"

"No. It's just a headache. I'll be fine."

Tyra looked skeptical, but let it slide. "I let myself in since you weren't here when I arrived. Cats are fed, have their toys, and I checked to make sure the litterboxes were clean and filled with fresh litter. Did I miss anything?"

"Nope, I think you've got everything. Thanks, Tyra. I'm sorry I was late." My brow furrowed. Was I? I'd forgotten my Fitbit, so I couldn't check without pulling my phone from my pocket, which I didn't have the energy for. *Today's going to be a blast.*

"You weren't late; I was early." She grinned. "I woke up and decided to get a fast start, just in case something came up. First-day jitters and all."

"Well, thank you again," I said. "I really do appreciate you coming in and helping out, especially on days like this."

"No prob." She headed for the door, but stopped short before leaving. "Oh, I almost forgot. Kiersten wanted me to ask you if you'd be willing to go with her to the Holloway farm between classes tomorrow. She's gearing up to have a heart-to-heart with Harlan about his latest 'donation'"—she made air quotes—"to the shelter."

I groaned. The Holloways had barn cats on their farm that

they refuse to neuter or spay. As soon as a new batch of kittens were born, they'd drop them off at the animal shelter, often without weaning them first, thinking they're doing a good thing for the community, when all they were doing was stressing out an already overpacked shelter.

"Sure, I can do that," I said. "What time?" I only had an hour between most sessions, which likely wouldn't be enough time to get to the farm, have a chat with Harlan, and get back again.

"I think she said she'd like to head that way after two sometime." Tyra made a face. "You might need to ask her to be sure."

"After the two-o'clock session would be great." That meant I'd have a few hours to give her since the next session on Tuesdays didn't start until seven. "I could meet her at the shelter by three. That'd give me time to clean up first."

"Okay, cool. I'll call her when I'm on the way to class to let her know. Catch you later, Ash."

"See ya, Tyra."

She slipped out the back door with a wave. Once she was gone, I found myself staring at the boxes full of shirts I couldn't—or more accurately, *wouldn't*—sell. With a sigh, I mustered enough energy to grab my phone and shoot Mom a text.

Lunch? The Hop? I can be there by 11:30.

While I waited for her reply, I went about finishing up setting up for the morning session, which was thankfully more of a wake-me-up than one that would require heavy exertion on my part. Once that was done, I checked my phone, saw the *I'm very busy, but I suppose I can attend* from Mom, and opted to leave it at that. She was going to be there; that's all I needed to know.

At ten till, a knock on the door startled me from a brief zone-out where my mind had drifted from the yoga to come, to my disaster of a date. I'd been standing in the middle of the room, a hand towel hanging limp from my hand, as I stared at the wall, thinking about Grady and if he'd said anything at all that would tell me who would have wanted to kill him. I didn't know why, but I felt responsible for his death, despite the fact he'd abandoned me. If I'd refused to let him leave the table, would he still be alive today? Or what if I'd followed him? Gone looking for him?

Deep down, I knew berating myself over something I couldn't change was pointless, but I couldn't help it. Someone was dead, and I was one of the last people who'd seen him alive.

I hurried over to the door and was surprised to find Lulu O'Brien waving at me through the glass with a wide grin on her face. Her reddish-brown hair was pulled back and held in place by a headband. It accentuated the gray at her temples. As always, she was wearing her favorite spandex yoga outfit, topped by a slightly too large tee. It would have been ridiculous if it was on anyone other than Lulu, yet somehow, she pulled it off.

George Wilkins was standing behind her.

I unlocked the door and held it open for them. "What are you two doing here?" I asked. "You don't normally attend Mondays."

"I hope it's all right," Lulu said. "I can't make my normal sessions this week, but didn't want to miss out. George came along since I felt weird about coming without someone I knew. I could pay extra if need be." She gave me a worried look. "There'll be room, won't there?"

"You don't need to pay extra," I said, closing the door as they entered. "You've already paid for the classes." Lulu had paid for a year up front, which meant she could attend five classes per week at a discounted price, though most people only showed up for two or three. "And I can make room if we're full up, though Monday mornings tend to be the least attended sessions, so there'll likely be more than enough space for the both of you."

Lulu clapped her hands together. "That's fantastic. I was worried that I might have to miss this week entirely, and who knows what that would do to my discipline. I truly do love coming to yoga with you, Ash, but I can't say that it hasn't been a challenge." She patted her stomach, which was looking flatter ever since she'd started coming to classes with me.

"You've done great," I assured her. "How's the kitten adjusting to life in the O'Brien household?" Lulu had adopted the little gray guy after spending her first handful of yoga classes with him.

"Mombo is doing amazing!" she said. "Cal took to him right away, though he tries to pretend he's too rough and tough for a cat. Every time he thinks I'm not looking, I find them snuggling together on the couch." She laughed. "It's done wonders for our relationship, having a pet again."

"That's good to hear." Though *Mombo*? I was afraid to ask.

"Well, we should let you get set up," Lulu said. "And I suppose George and I should claim our floor space before the floodgates open!" She patted the rolled-up yoga mat under her arm before looking to George. "Usual spots?"

He shrugged, not looking up, and the two of them moved to place their mats. I watched them with a frown. George seemed almost sullen as he unrolled his yoga mat in his favorite spot near the cat room window. Every few moments, he'd glance at me out of the corner of his eye, and then quickly look away. Something was bothering him and I had a pretty good idea what it might be.

Before I could talk to him about it, however, the usual Monday morning group started filtering in. Not only was the Monday group the smallest of my sessions, it was also the oldest when it came to the average age, with Josie Mohr being the youngest at a fit fifty-seven.

By the time everyone had arrived and the cats had been picked out and let loose, my headache was just a dull throb behind my eyes. I felt as if I could get through the day, as long as I didn't overexert myself. I took my place at the front of the room and then gave everyone a moment to get acquainted with their chosen feline. Let's just say that a lot of happy meows and baby talk filled the room for the next five minutes before I clapped my hands together and got everyone started with a few easy stretches.

"Okay, now let's move on to the half-moon pose." I shot a side-eyed look at George, who almost always corrected me whenever I didn't use the Sanskrit version of a pose name.

He flowed into the pose, eyes distant, mouth firmly shut. When we changed up to the downward dog a few moments later, he likewise remained silent and didn't so much as glance at me as he settled into position.

Unease caused me to make a few mistakes as we continued through the class. George never corrected me, never attempted to cover for my goof-ups. Lulu was her normal boisterous, chatty self, which made George's odd behavior stand out that much more. It made me worried that it was more than Edward's actions at dinner that had George acting so strange.

He couldn't possibly have had anything to do with Grady's death, could he?

"Ouch!" Tasha Poyer straightened suddenly and then laughed as her friend Angie Rich removed a clingy kitten from Tasha's back. I was glad to note there didn't seem to be any blood, just a shirt with a thread pulled lose from the tiny kitten claws. Tasha checked her shirt, and then proceeded to mock discipline the kitten, which involved a lot of finger-waggling and chewing of fingertips.

Class continued. George flat-out refused to acknowledge me or anything I said. I think Lulu noticed because she started watching him nearly as much as I was, though she didn't call him out on his silence.

When we finished up, I couldn't bring myself to let him leave without checking in with him.

"George?" I said as we finished our cooldown. "Can I talk to you a moment?" I nodded toward the office door down the hall.

He grimaced, but nodded. While everyone else rolled up their mats and returned their kitties to the cat room, George and I retreated to the office. Once inside, I closed the door and then turned to him.

"Is everything okay?" I asked. "You didn't seem like yourself today."

He ran a hand through what remained of his hair. "Sorry about that. I've got a lot on my mind." He looked away when he said it, telling me that whatever it was that was bothering him, it had something to do with me.

I rested a hand on his shoulder and squeezed. "Is this because of what happened the other night at dinner?"

The way his teeth clamped shut and how he swallowed, I knew I'd hit the mark. *As if it could be anything else.*

"George," I kept my voice soothing, despite how my heart was pounding in my chest as if it were trying to escape. "I'm not angry about what Edward said to me. He thought he was doing the right thing. You shouldn't hold it against him, though I understand it was embarrassing."

George closed his eyes, took a deep breath, and blew it out through his nose. "The police showed up at my place yesterday. They were looking for Edward."

"Did they—" My voice caught and I had to clear my throat before I could go on. "Did they say why?"

"Not at first. They asked me where I was on Saturday night, where I went afterward. Standard stuff, really. Then they started asking about Edward. Asked me if I knew where he'd gone, and if he knew that guy you were eating with."

I took a deep, calming breath that did little to ease my mind. "Did he?"

George paced away, throwing his hands into the air, and for a moment, I thought I'd crossed some sort of line and he was angry with me. When he spoke, I realized the anger was targeted at his cousin instead. "Hell if I know. I wasn't happy with how he'd acted when I ran into you, but that's Edward. He doesn't think before he acts. It's not like this is new behavior for him."

"So why exactly did the police want to talk to you about Edward?" I asked. I could see them asking him about Grady, but that was only if they'd known George was there. . . .

And then it hit me. Who was the one who'd opened her big mouth and brought up the confrontation at my table, naming names? Me, of course. How else would the police have known that George and Edward had a run-in with a guy who was murdered later that night? I could add *that* to my ever-growing list of regrets.

George ran a hand over his face. I noted it trembled. "They think he might have had something to do with that man's death." He paused, seemed to realize that I might not have heard about Grady. "I didn't mean to—"

"I've already talked to the police about it," I said, cutting him off.

George breathed a sigh of relief before going on. "This whole thing is a mess. The police chief was asking me questions about you, too, as if there's a world where you could hurt anyone, let alone commit murder. I'm not sure he believes it, but it rankled me that he'd even consider it." He shook his head. "But Edward . . . He's been in trouble before. Assault. Stupid stuff. Never killed anyone, but he isn't afraid to throw a punch or two if he thinks it will get him what he wants."

"George," I said, my nerves growing, "What happened that night after you left?"

He took a moment to compose himself before he answered. "After Edward's outburst, we left, as you know. As soon as we were outside, I laid into him a little. I know what he was trying to do, but it didn't sit right with me that he yelled at your date like that. He embarrassed me and I know it had to have embarrassed you. I told him as much when we got to the car, which only upset him. He refused to get in and instead stormed off and left me standing there, holding the keys with no idea where he thought he was going. It was too far to walk home."

I went cold. "Edward didn't leave with you?"

"No, and I have no idea where he went after we parted. I waited for about ten minutes, but he never came back, so I left. I know I should have stayed, should have gone looking for him. I didn't, and the next thing I know, the police show up at my door and start asking me all these questions about him, but I don't know anything. They treated me like I was a criminal, or at least, guilty of harboring one. As soon as they left my place, I called Edward to tell him to go downtown and to sort this whole mess out before it got out of hand, but he didn't answer."

That didn't sound good at all. "Have you talked to him since?"

"I wish." George huffed and then sagged. "I don't know what I'm going to do. Edward's not a bad person, but he was drunk. You saw him. He's family, but that doesn't mean I condone violence. If he did something . . ." His grimace told me exactly how he felt about that possibility.

I hated to, but I had to ask it. "Do you think he might have hurt Grady?"

"No. Maybe. I don't know." George paced away, fists bunching and releasing over and over again. "I would have said no before, but now that he seems to be avoiding not just me, but the police, I have to wonder."

I tried to imagine it. Edward yells at Grady, threatens to find him and hurt him if he hurts me—which Grady later does by abandoning me with the check—and then Edward leaves Market Inn with George. Outside, they argue and Edward storms off on his own.

And then what?

Did he come back into Market Inn without me noticing? Could he have followed Grady to the bathroom, then forced him to leave with him? Or could he have waited outside, caught Grady sneaking out, and then followed him home?

But if so, why kill him? Leaving me with the check was a crappy thing for Grady to do, but not something that warranted his murder.

"I'm sure Edward has a good explanation as to why he's not answering his phone," I said. "Maybe he lost his cell or realized he went too far that night and is too embarrassed to call you back."

George sighed. "I wish I could believe that, Ash, I really do."

He left a few minutes later, clearly distraught. Lulu tried to talk to him on the way out, but George merely tucked his mat under his arm and walked away.

Once they were gone, I began to ready the studio for the next session, but my mind was a million miles away. Someone had killed Grady Richards. They'd done so after he'd walked out on me. The only person I knew who'd shown anger at how Grady had treated me was Edward Wilkins, who was now missing and refusing to answer calls.

Yes, it was a leap to think that he'd followed Grady home and killed him over a bad date with a woman Edward didn't even know, but it wasn't outside the realm of possibility. People did stupid, impulsive things all the time, especially after having too much to drink. Could that be what happened here?

Until I knew more about who Grady Richards really was, or where Edward had gone Saturday night after he'd parted from George, I had no choice but to consider Edward Wilkins as a suspect for murder.

CHAPTER 5

The second yoga class of the day went smoothly, and by the time we were done, I was feeling much better than I had when the day had started. The headache was a distant memory—mostly—so as I finished cleaning up the studio in preparation for the post-lunch session, I found myself whistling under my breath. Sure, I was still concerned about what happened to Grady, but at that point, there wasn't much I could do about it.

The Hop was only a short hop, skip, and a jump (har-har) away from A Purrfect Pose, so I wasn't in a rush. Mom would likely beat me there as she always did when we had lunch together, no matter what time I left. I was okay with that. I kind of wanted to make her wait as punishment for the shirts, but not for *too* long because I didn't want to deal with the fallout from that on top of everything else.

Once the floor was swept and the cats settled into place with a lunch of their own, I cleaned the litter boxes. That done, I grabbed my purse, as well as the trash bags containing the used litter, and headed for the back door to dump it before going to lunch with my mom.

"I'll see you guys in less than two hours!" I called, which

earned me a couple of farewell meows, before I opened the back door and stepped out into the alley . . .

And face-first into a bucket's-worth of flying water.

The sudden chill caused me to gasp and drop the trash bag full of litter. Water dripped from my face, drenched my clothes, and when I spat out the little bit that had gotten into my mouth, I found my lips to be covered with tufts of fur.

"I . . . ugh!" I wiped my face and blindly took a step sideways, which turned out to be the wrong thing to do. I ended up kicking the bag of litter, and because nothing can ever go right, I managed to tear a hole in it. The litter instantly spilled out over my shoes, mixing with the water, turning it into a gray, pasty mess.

J. Allen stood frozen outside Bark and Style, a bucket in his hand. Short, with white hair that he kept combed to near perfection, Jordan Leslie had quickly become my rival, despite our businesses having nothing in common, other than working with animals. His mouth was pulled in a perfect O and his eyes were wide and full of guilt. His Pomeranian, Ginger, was nowhere in sight.

"Ash," he said in his high-pitched, whiny voice. He quickly deposited the bucket just inside the door of his dog grooming studio. "I didn't expect you to come out of there like that."

"You didn't expect me?" I spat more fur and water. "It's *my* studio!"

"I suppose I mean I didn't expect you to come sneaking out the back like a common criminal." He made a disapproving sound that made me want to smack him. "They make front doors for a reason."

"I was taking out the trash."

He glanced at the ruined bag and grimaced. "I see that. You really should clean that up before someone steps in it."

I sputtered, at a complete loss as what to say. I was wet and cold and so angry, I was starting to see red.

"I'd best get back inside," J. Allen said. "I have an impatient couple of customers who are waiting for their post-grooming treats."

He started to step back, but I refused to let him off that easily.

"No, I don't think so." I stepped over the pile of litter, and put myself just inside his doorway before he could close the door. "You threw dirty water at my door."

He looked down at my shoes with an expression of pure disgust. "Yes, well, I had to do something with the water, now didn't I? I couldn't just leave it sitting around where it could grow stagnant and start stinking up my place of business."

It might be petty, but I shook off some of the quickly congealing gunk on my shoes, splattering it onto his floor. "This isn't the first time you've done this," I said, remembering the puddle I'd stepped in yesterday. "And it's not like you don't have drains for the water. Use them!"

He took a step back, still eyeing my shoes. "I do, but they are currently clogged. The plumber can't get here until tomorrow, and since I have a perfectly good alley out here, I figured I could dump the used water where it wouldn't get in the way. There's no harm in that."

"No harm?" I gestured toward my drenched torso.

"Bad timing is all." And then, with no remorse at all, he said, "Sorry about that."

"You could have dumped it outside *your* door. Or off to the side where it wouldn't get either of our doorways wet." Some of the heat was fading from my tone. And with the anger retreating, the cold was quickly taking its place. I hugged myself as I started to shiver.

"It's not like I didn't spill some on my own doorstep." He glanced down at a few stray drops nearby that had likely come from my shoes. "You aren't the only one who has had to deal with this unfortunate circumstance."

I closed my eyes, took a deep breath, and stepped back. "Please, Mr. Leslie, do not dump your hairy water outside my studio. I'm asking nicely." And in the back of my mind, I added, *Because if you don't stop, I'm going to start dumping wet litter outside* your *door.*

Jordan heaved a put-upon sigh. Somewhere inside, a dog barked. "I'll be there in a moment, Susie-Q." He turned back to me. "All right, I'll do what I can. It might make things extraordinarily difficult on me to accommodate you and your demands, but I'll find a way to manage. Happy?"

Not really, but I nodded.

"Good. I suppose I'll see you around, Ash." He closed the door, already making cooing sounds toward the dogs.

I huffed and then turned back to the mess outside my studio. I had half a mind to leave it just to spite Jordan, but that would mean I would have to step over it, as would Tyra when she showed up later to retrieve the cats.

"I should have made him do this," I muttered as I went back inside A Purrfect Pose to retrieve cleaning supplies.

It took a good fifteen minutes to clean up the mess as best as I could. It wasn't an easy task and made me wish I had some sort of power washer on hand so I could just blast it away instead of trying to scoop it up. I got most of the fur, but the rest was simply too wet and runny to deal with. I'd have to get it when it dried out.

Thoroughly frozen through, and smelling of dirty dog water, I speed-walked my way home to change. I was glad to note that neither Edna nor Pavan were in the hallway as I unlocked my door. I didn't want to have to explain my disheveled state to them, especially since I still had to go to . . .

My eyes widened and as soon as I was through the door, I tossed my purse aside and grabbed my phone and dialed.

It rang once and then went straight to voicemail.

Oh no. That's not good.

A quick look at the time told me I was only ten minutes late for the lunch date with Mom. Ten minutes was nothing, yet I knew, just *knew*, she was going to take it like I'd stood her up just to spite her.

"No, no, no. Come on."

I tried her again, and was once more immediately shunted to voicemail. A third try resulted in the same thing, so I reverted to a text instead.

I'm sorry I'm late. Got hung up at the studio. I'll explain when I get there. Give me fifteen minutes!

Fifteen minutes without my car would be pushing it, but if I ran, I could manage it.

I tossed my phone aside and sprinted into the bedroom, shedding clothing as I went. Luna watched me rush from the room, and then, thinking it some sort of game, she shot after me, nearly tripping me as she pawed at the back of my legs as I ran to my dresser to grab a change of clothes. I carried them to the bathroom with me, with Luna still following in my wake, and took the quickest shower known to man, before hurrying back out into the living room and to my phone, where a response awaited me.

Don't bother.

I groaned and all but collapsed onto my couch. Luna hopped up, butted her head against my elbow, and then leaned her entire body against me, purring away.

My fingers hovered over the screen as I vainly tried to come up with something I could say that would make Mom understand why I'd been late. I could tell her about J. Allen and his dirty dog-fur water, how she wouldn't have wanted to be seen in public with me drenched like that, which was true, but she wouldn't accept it as a reason for not showing up on time. She'd want to know why I hadn't texted *before* I was late, to which I had no good answer other than, "I forgot."

I flopped back with a groan. Mom would focus solely on the fact I was late, ignoring the rest of whatever I said. Never mind that I very nearly drowned and froze to death outside my own studio—an exaggeration, yes, but at the time, it didn't feel like it. Never mind that I did text her as soon as I remembered our lunch date, and promised to be there soon, well before we would have left if I'd shown up on time.

No, she'd simply say I should have called her before she'd left Branson Designs so that she wouldn't have wasted her time waiting for me. She'd tell me that I didn't respect her or her valuable time, and that it shows I can't handle a business of my own, so why don't I come on back and work for her again. And when I said "no," she'd sniff, say something flippant, and leave me feeling like I was the world's biggest disappointment.

With a sigh, I tossed my phone aside without bothering to respond. She wouldn't read it anyway.

A crash sounded in the silence that followed.

Luna shot from the couch like a bullet, vanishing before I could track her movements. The crash was followed by a series of thumps, and then a larger *crack*.

I found myself standing, though I had no recollection of leaping to my feet. My heart was pounding in my ears, and for a moment, I was positive someone was in my apartment with me, though how I'd missed them during my frantic run through the bedroom and shower, I had no idea.

I stood there and listened, and was soon cognizant of another sound. A faint grunting noise and a dragging, like someone moving something heavy across carpet. I followed the sound to my bedroom, and quickly realized that the noise was coming from the other side of the wall.

Leon?

While the apartment complex I lived in was relatively nice, the shared walls weren't as thick or soundproofed as they should be. Leon was the ideal neighbor in that he didn't have pets, lived alone, and wasn't into loud music or watching TV at max volume. Normally, I never heard much more than the occasional thump from his side of the wall.

At least, not until today.

My mind instantly flashed back to him leaving his apartment, wearing all black, in the middle of the night, on the same night in which someone was murdered. Then, the next evening, I find him injured and talking to a stranger in the lobby of the apartment complex in a way that I was finding more and more suspicious the more I thought about it.

No, there's no possible way Leon could have been involved in Grady's death.

But Edna *had* said he'd been acting strange as of late. Pavan thought Leon had a thing for me. Then there were his injuries, the late-night excursions, and now these strange noises at a time when he'd normally be at work.

I returned to the living room and picked up my phone from where I'd tossed it onto the couch. I could always call Olivia and let her know what was happening. She was police. She'd know what to do.

And if Leon was just rearranging his living room?

You're just being paranoid, Ash. Calling the police over a few loud noises was the mark of someone who needed a serious vacation.

"Okay. All right." I took a deep breath to calm my nerves. Luna peeked out from my bedroom, but didn't come back into the living room quite yet. Her back was bristled and her stub of a tail looked like a fluffy black bunny tail.

Some semblance of sense returned and I considered walking

away—or more accurately, sitting down and doing nothing—but what if something *was* going on next door? It didn't need to be Leon hiding a body or destroying evidence or whatever it was I thought he might be doing. Someone could have broken in. Or perhaps an antique cabinet collapsed and Leon was cleaning it up and in need of help.

A good neighbor wouldn't ignore the sounds. They'd at least check to make sure everything was okay, that Leon hadn't fallen and hurt himself. It was the neighborly thing to do.

Phone still gripped in my hand, I moved to the door, and then, after listening for any further noises, of which there were none, I stepped out into the hall. Edna, who'd normally appear at the slightest of sounds, wasn't waiting for me, which I hope meant there was nothing to worry about, that this sort of thing happened all the time when I wasn't around.

Leon's door was closed. I considered what to do, and then opted for the reasonable thing and knocked. If it was Leon, he would answer and could explain the noises I'd heard. If it was a thief, they'd either try to escape or would fall silent. If that happened, I could call the police and let them deal with it.

Footsteps approached. I held my breath, anticipating the door opening, but only silence followed.

"Leon?" I called, knocking again. "It's Ash Branson from next door. Is everything okay in there?"

A chain lock rattled. It was followed by the door's lock, and then the door swung open to reveal a sweaty Leon Fitzgerald. His hair was a mess and he looked as if he hadn't slept for a week. He was holding his injured hand close to his body, as if he feared I might reach out and grab it.

"Ash?" he said, glancing down the hall toward Edna's closed door. "What are you doing home? I thought you had classes today."

"I do. It's my lunch break." I tried to look past him, but

Leon was standing in a way that took up the entire doorway. "I heard a crash. Since you are usually at work at this time, I was worried it might be a thief."

Leon wiped an arm across his brow, leaving a faint dirty trail. "I took the day off. I figured I could do some cleaning and ended up knocking something over. It's nothing."

It didn't sound like nothing. Leon was injecting false cheer into his voice. There was a tremble there, a nervousness that had *me* glancing over my shoulder to make sure no one was sneaking up on me.

"Do you need help?" I asked. "I have a little more time before I need to get back to A Purrfect Pose, so if you need me to help you with anything—"

"No, that won't be necessary, Ash. I made the mess, so I should clean it up." Leon shifted and I noted a hammer propped up against the wall beside him before he settled back into place.

My phone buzzed in my hand, causing me to jump. A quick glance showed me it was a text from Alexi. It could wait.

"It wouldn't be any trouble," I said. I had no idea why I felt a desperate need to see what was happening in his apartment. I wasn't normally this nosy, but with everything that had happened recently, I was feeling rather paranoid. "I've been known to break a glass or two and it always makes me shaky. I hate picking up broken glass."

"Thankfully, it's just wood. There's not much to clean up."

As much as I wanted to press him about it, I was getting nowhere. And besides, I had another question that had been bothering me.

"Who was that guy you were talking to in the lobby last night? I've never seen him around here before and was curious—"

Inside Leon's apartment, a phone rang. His entire body

went tense and I swear he stopped breathing for a full two rings before he stepped back. "I should answer that. I'll see you around, Ash."

Before I could say anything more, he closed the door.

That was . . . strange.

Edna was right: Leon was acting weird. The late-night jaunts. The injury. The nervousness now. Something was up. And while it might not have anything to do with Grady Richards and his murder, I did find the timing rather conspicuous.

I returned to my apartment, mind churning over the possibilities. Yes, I knew I was jumping to conclusions, but I desperately wanted to know what was going on with Leon, just so I could exclude him from suspicion. My wild assumptions weren't helping anyone, and my own mental well-being was included in that.

Mindlessly, I tossed a piece of bread into the toaster. It wasn't much of a lunch, but it was *something*. That done, I checked Alexi's text.

What did you do? Mom has got that cold, dead expression on her face that says she's liable to kill someone. And since she'd left to have lunch with you, I have a sinking feeling you're the reason why she's acting this way.

I winced. It figures that Mom would take her frustrations with me out on the rest of the family. I didn't even want to think about how many times over the years Alexi had suffered the consequences of my actions.

I waited until the toast had popped and I'd buttered it before shooting her a response. *I may have had something come up and forgot to tell her about it until after I was already late.*

The response was immediate. *You didn't!*

Oh, but I had. *I didn't mean to,* I sent as I left my apartment. *I'll be by later to try to talk to her. Soften her up for me?*

I'll try. You owe me big-time.

Thanks. I'll make it up to you. I promise.

I dropped my phone into my purse and put Leon Fitzgerald's strange behavior and my inevitable confrontation with Mom out of my mind as I headed back to A Purrfect Pose, and my afternoon yoga class.

And hey, at least the day couldn't get any worse, right?

Chapter 6

"See you later, Ash!" Clementine Lewis skipped her way out the door with a wave. A new student at Cardinal Lake University—and here at A Purrfect Pose—she still had that youthful exuberance of a teenager, and often applied it to her yoga. She was constantly in motion, to the point that she struggled with poses because it meant she had to stop shaking her leg or swinging her arms long enough to hold them. With her dangling, jingling bracelets and necklaces, she was a favorite of the cats.

Clementine was the last to leave after the post-lunch session. As soon as she was gone, I closed and locked the front door, and went about cleaning up and cooling off. I don't know why, but I'd made the session far more vigorous than usual. I hadn't done it on purpose, yet by the time we were halfway through, my legs were screaming and half the class looked ready to collapse. I'd managed to slow down during the last ten minutes, but by then, most of us were already dead on our feet.

A chorus of meows followed me as I grabbed the kitties their lunch. And by followed, I mean I was swarmed by furry little bodies that wound around my feet and ankles and threatened to trip me with every step.

"All right, all right," I said with a laugh. "It's coming."

Once the cats were fed, I was able to slip out the kitty room door with only a few curious eyes following me. I went to the small bathroom, rinsed off my face, and after giving myself a good examination in the mirror, decided I was as presentable as I was going to get.

"Here goes nothing," I muttered at my reflection. Then, with nothing to do but get on with it, I left the bathroom, grabbed one of the branded shirts, and left A Purrfect Pose.

It was time to face the dragon.

The cold air sent a jolt through me as I stepped outside. I hurried down the street to the crosswalk, shoulders hunched against the chill. The square was busy with cars zipping by carelessly, their drivers ignoring the YIELD signs as if they assumed that it was the other guy who needed to stop. That meant there was an inordinate amount of honking, and quite a lot of screaming out windows as I scurried across the street at a break in the traffic caused by a pair of cars that had to slam on their brakes lest they crash into one another.

The fountain has got to go, I thought as I made it safely to the other side of the street and to the door of Branson Designs. While there were surprisingly few accidents at the square, they'd been known to happen, and were often spectacular when they did. The speed limit was posted at fifteen, but only one in ten cars ever seemed to go anything less than thirty.

Or maybe it just felt that way when I was dodging incoming car-missiles.

The showroom of Branson Designs wasn't flashy. Shirts hung on the walls, purses and masks sat on shelves in between or on tables by the windows. A big book full of popular designs sat on the front counter where my cousin Juniper sat, looking bored. A couple of customers were browsing, though most of the business was done over the phone or online since the catalog of designs could be found on the website. Only those who wanted something custom-made needed to come in.

As soon as Juniper saw me, her gaze shot to the back door which led to the offices and meeting rooms where a large chunk of the Branson family were theoretically hard at work. She stood, setting her phone aside as I approached the counter.

"What are you doing here, Ash?" she asked before I could say anything. A year younger than me, Juniper and I were something of kindred spirits when it came to how we felt about the family business. I gave her a year, maybe two, before she flew the coop. "Do you realize how pissed Aunt Cecilia is with you right now?"

"I'm sure she is," I said. "But!" I held up the shirt. "See this?"

Juniper scanned the shirt from top to bottom, then winced. "Ouch. I take it that wasn't your idea."

"No, it wasn't. I need to talk to Mom."

Juniper dropped back into her chair. "I'm supposed to tell you that you can't go back there under any circumstances."

"A command from Mom?" Of course she would ban me from the offices over a missed lunch.

Juniper shook her head, surprising me. "Not exactly. This came from *my* lovely mother, not yours."

Same difference, I thought, not unkindly. Claudia Branson was just like her sister, Cecilia, though she was far more bitter about her place within the family hierarchy. Claudia had always assumed that she was her parents' favorite and would inherit Branson Designs when they retired. Instead, it went to the eldest, Cecilia, which, for about two horrid weeks, had caused major strife between the siblings, which also included Uncle Cliffton, who'd decided not to take any sides, but happily contributed to the drama, nonetheless.

The family, thanks to intervention from my grandparents, were able to set aside their differences and all three of the

Branson siblings now worked together under one roof, though it wasn't always harmonious behind closed doors.

"I get that I don't work here anymore, but I'm still family," I said, balling up the shirt. "I just need to talk to Mom for a minute and then I'll go. I'm not here to cause any trouble."

Juniper picked up her phone and shrugged. "Go right ahead. If anyone asks, I'll tell them you must have come in while I was in the bathroom." She tapped her screen. "Good luck."

"Thanks, Juniper. You're the best."

"I know."

I made for the back door, which had a large EMPLOYEES ONLY sign hanging on it. Somewhere back there, Alexi was at work and I hoped she'd had the chance to soften Mom up for me like she'd promised. Even on a good day, Cecilia Branson could be a bear to deal with, so I wasn't looking forward to this little chat in the slightest.

I pushed through the door and was thankful to see that no one was blocking my way like the last time I'd tried to come back here. Nearly every door was closed, which meant Cecilia had dropped the hammer on everyone and they were keeping to themselves to avoid her wrath. The one open door I did see led to a meeting room, which was unoccupied, so I felt relatively safe as I hurried down the hall to the farthest—and biggest—office of them all.

"I don't care how it makes you feel. I need you to do your job." Anger seethed from Cecilia's voice, which came from the other side of the closed door. "I need as much as you can give me, and I need it now." A pause. "Yes, it's time critical." Another pause, this one longer. "That seems reasonable. Do it." The heavy sigh that followed told me the conversation had ended.

I waited at the door for a heartbeat before realizing she must have been on a call, not talking to someone face-to-face. So when the door didn't open on its own, I decided to forgo knocking, and pushed my way inside Cecilia Branson's office. She was seated at her desk, head lowered as she massaged her temples. Her cell phone sat on the middle of her desk, face-down, next to a closed file folder labeled JUSTICE stuffed with so many papers, it looked close to bursting.

"What?" she demanded without looking up.

"Mom," I said, closing the door behind me. Her head snapped up, just as I unfurled the shirt for her to see, figuring it would serve as explanation enough as to why I'd barged in on her in the middle of the workday.

She eyed the shirt a moment, expression never shifting away from annoyed, before she met my eye. "What are you doing back here, Ashley? You don't belong on this side of the door. I'm sure you saw the 'employees only' sign."

I gritted my teeth and tapped a foot as I gently shook the shirt, drawing her attention back to it.

Cecilia sighed, sat back in her chair. "What about it?"

"This!" I pointed at the "A Branson Designs company" branding.

Mom picked up her phone, glanced at the screen, before returning it to her desk. "I don't see the problem."

"You don't see—" I sputtered. "I didn't ask you to put that on there."

"No, you didn't." *But you should have,* was implied.

"A Purrfect Pose isn't a part of your company. It's mine."

"Are you a Branson?" Asked with a straight face and in a perfectly reasonable tone, as if she were asking the time of day.

I knew I shouldn't have answered, that it was a trap of some kind, but did so anyway. "Yes, but—"

"Then your company is under the umbrella of the Branson family of businesses." Cecilia sighed and stood. "Honestly, Ashley, you should thank me. It means I'm accepting your rebellion to some degree. Of course, after you stood me up at lunch, I'm beginning to regret that decision."

"I tried to call you," I said, doing my best to keep the frustration out of my voice. I'd known going in that this wasn't going to be easy, yet I found myself flustered already. "I know I was late, but something happened and I couldn't get there right away. You wouldn't have *wanted* me there."

Mom wasn't moved. "Respect is important in this family. And you could respect my time by appearing when you are supposed to and by not barging into my office when I'm extremely busy. So, if you would . . ." She motioned for the door.

My Branson stubbornness welled up and I almost held my ground. I wanted the shirts reprinted without the branding. I wanted Mom to do it without complaint. In fact, I wanted her to apologize for assuming I'd be happy with it and for not taking my call when I was trying to tell her I'd be late.

But the fight was already lost. Mom's heels were dug in and nothing I could do or say would move her. Maybe in a day or two, things would change, but here, now, I was wasting my time.

I balled the shirt up, and then, even though I knew it would be taken as spiteful and disrespectful, I tossed it onto one of the chairs by Cecilia's desk. "I can't sell these," I said, before turning and walking out of the office.

I wanted to scream, to punch a wall, but I somehow managed to keep my composure all the way out of Branson Designs. Juniper, for her part, gave me a sympathetic look on my way out, which was more than I'd get from anyone else there, other than Alexi and her husband, Evan. Once outside, I stopped and took a couple of deep, calming breaths. Mom could be difficult. I knew that. Everyone knew that.

And yet, every time she did something like this, it was like a punch to the gut. I understood that she cared about me in her own way. Her parents, my grandparents, were just like her, so her stubbornness and frustrating ego was something of a family trait, passed down through the generations, though it had somehow missed Cecilia's children, much to her annoyance.

The door opened behind me. I turned, almost positive it would be Mom coming out to yell at me some more, but was glad to see it was one of the few people I could talk to about Mom and not feel like it would get back to her.

"Hey, Ash," Alexi said, rubbing her hands together as she came to a stop beside me. "I saw you storm out of there from my office. I take it your chat with Mom didn't go well."

I sighed. "It went just like I expected it would."

She put an arm around me and hugged me to her side. "I'm sorry about that. I tried."

"It's not on you. I should have known barging in on her like that would only make her wall me off that much more."

"She'll get over it." She released me and blew into her hands. She hadn't grabbed her jacket on the way out and was clearly suffering for it. "How about we get together tonight after your evening class? Snoot's. We can plan on how to deal with Mom over a few drinks."

"That sounds great." I paused. "Though, not too many drinks. After last night . . ."

Alexi laughed. "I'll pick you up and make sure you're good to drive home. We still need to retrieve your car as it is."

With the date made, I let Alexi get back inside where it was warm and then I made my way back to A Purrfect Pose. Once there, I stared at the boxes of shirts. For a moment, I considered giving in for this round and just selling them. It might help ease the tension between me and Mom, though if I let it slide now, there was a good chance I'd never be rid of the branding.

I turned away with a shake of my head. No, best to just leave them. If I couldn't get Mom to see things my way, then perhaps it was time I found someone else to make the shirts. It'd be more expensive, and I doubted they'd be of as high quality, but at least they'd be *mine*.

It was just after three, which meant I had a few hours to kill before the seven p.m. class. I checked on the cats to make sure everything was in order, and then packed up and walked home, figuring I could decompress there easier with Luna at my side than at my studio where a look at the building past the fountain would make me angry all over again.

The apartment complex was quiet when I entered. It felt empty without Edna and Pavan standing outside Edna's door, chatting. Leon's apartment was quiet as well, and I wondered if he'd left after our earlier conversation.

Luna was waiting for me by her food dish when I entered. Her entire backside wobbled back and forth as she wagged her stub of a tail. I briefly wondered if the tail was genetic, or if it had happened after she was born. It was something I could ask Kiersten at the shelter when I saw her, though she might not know either since the cats often came to her well after their birth.

Once Luna was fed, I plopped down onto the couch with a huff. I was both mentally and physically exhausted. Mom. Leon.

Grady.

I picked up my phone and did a quick search on him since I knew nothing about the guy. There were dozens of Grady Richardses out there, but none from Cardinal Lake as far as I could tell. There was one who lived in a nearby town, but his profile was set to private, and the picture showed a man who looked nothing like the guy I'd had dinner with, so that one was a miss as well.

Figures.

I tossed my phone aside and closed my eyes. Almost immediately, Luna hopped up onto my lap and curled up for a nap.

I might as well join her.

I rested a hand atop her back and was asleep in seconds.

I felt recharged by the time I was back at A Purrfect Pose for the evening class. The nap had done more than rejuvenate my body, it reset my mind. I felt as if I could deal with Mom, with the fallout of Grady's death. I just had to take everything one step at a time and not allow myself to become overwhelmed or let my mind to start jumping to conclusions about the people around me.

You know, people like Leon Fitzgerald.

My renewed energy seemed infectious. A pure white cat with one green eye and one blue one took one look at me and started zooming around the room to the point he was very nearly running along the walls. This, of course, bled into the other cats, so that by the time the first students arrived, the cats were all chasing each other around and rolling around like the kittens most of them were.

The door opened and the first of the evening students started filtering in. Unlike the morning session, the Monday night class consisted mostly of college students, almost all of them female. They came in laughing in groups of two or three, talking about how classes had gone that day. They barely paid me any mind as they went straight for the cats.

I stood back, out of the way. The cats were having a ball, and the kids were having fun. With how some of them were acting, I was hoping that adoptions would follow. Yes, I would miss the kitties when they were gone, but there was nothing like finding them a good solid forever home.

A man cleared his throat, drawing my attention. He was clean-shaven, hair close cropped. About thirty-five or so.

And was awfully familiar.

"I'd like to take part in a class," he said, glancing past me toward the room full of college girls. His face flushed and he took a step back as if reconsidering.

"Just the one?" I asked, desperately trying to place him. When he just stared at me blankly, I added, "Let me show you the options."

"Ash!" Maya Stevenson called from across the room. There was panic in her voice, but with Maya, there always was.

"One sec, Maya." I flashed the newcomer a smile. "Sorry about that . . . I didn't catch your name?"

There was a beat where it appeared as if I'd caught the man by surprise with the question. He stared at me, mouth hanging open, seemingly at a loss for words. He took another step back. "I shouldn't have come. This was a mistake."

"Are you sure? If you just want to pay for a single class and see if you like it, that's okay. I don't need any information if it doesn't make you comfortable." A flash. A man walking through a door and being led past me. I snapped my fingers. "You were at Market Inn the other night."

Something akin to panic flashed across the man's face. "I—"

"Ash. I think this little guy has a hairball and is about to explode!" Maya called, her voice rising in pitch.

I turned to find half the class standing around a ginger kitten with three white paws and one orange one backing up, head and neck extended as if, indeed, he had a hairball.

"One sec," I told the man before hurrying to the back to grab a roll of paper towels and a spray bottle of cleaner, just in case. By the time I returned to the front, the orange guy was rolling around with two larger cats, nary a hairball in sight.

"He's okay now," Maya said. "False alarm."

"I see that." I turned to the doorway, but the man was gone.

"He took off." This from Maya's friend Callie Webster. "As soon as your back was turned, the dude practically sprinted out the door."

"I think he was afraid the cat might actually spew," Maya said, making a face.

He was afraid of something, all right.

Whether it had to do with me recognizing him, or because of the cats and college-aged girls, I wasn't sure. But with how he'd acted, I was leaning toward the former.

I called the group to order and we started in on our stretches before moving on to more difficult poses.

"All right, let's try the crow pose again."

There was a collective groan as everyone dropped to the floor to attempt the pose. We'd worked on it last week and I was determined to get it to work with this younger crowd before moving on to the more demanding crane.

As I lifted my knees, I found myself glancing toward the door. I know I'd promised myself I'd stop jumping to conclusions, yet I couldn't help it. What were the chances that a guy would show up at Market Inn during my fateful date with a soon-to-be murder victim, and then later, have that same guy show up at my yoga class?

Okay, sure, it was within the realm of possibility since Cardinal Lake wasn't that big of a town, but to have that guy run away at the first sign of being recognized? *That* couldn't be a coincidence.

I wobbled and forced myself to focus on yoga. I made a few minor mistakes, but no one appeared to notice, not with the cats still flying around like furry acrobats. I decided to end class with a basic plank since I'd already abused them enough.

"And . . ." I held the final pose for an extra couple of seconds, arms trembling only slightly. ". . . we're done." I eased my legs back to the floor and sat up on my haunches. There was a general groan of released tension as wobbly legs and shaky arms came to rest. "Take a minute with the cats if you'd like, and then please return them to their rooms." I paused, smiled. "Unless you found one you'd like to take home. The applications are waiting."

I wiped my face with a towel I kept up front, and then carried it to the back. There was the usual post-class chatter amongst the girls, but unfortunately, nobody asked for an application, though I did notice how Maya and Callie fawned over the ginger kitty. It was only a matter of time before he captured their hearts for good.

As students began filtering out, I began cleaning up. Tyra would be there at any moment for the cats and I wanted to be ready to leave for Snoot's the second she was gone. I was anxious to talk to Alexi about the strange guy who'd showed up and get her thoughts on him.

I'd just rolled up my mat when my phone rang. It was sitting on the floor, next to the portable speaker I used for light music during class. A glance at the screen and dread washed through me.

Hunter.

I picked up the phone, steeled myself for what was to come, and answered with a pleading, "Hunter. Please tell me everything is okay."

"Hey, Sis," Hunter said, sounding sheepish and a whole lot nervous. "Can we talk?"

A glib "We *are* talking" was on the tip of my tongue, but I thought better of it. Hunter didn't sound like he was in the mood for jokes. "What about?"

"I . . . It's personal."

Great. With Hunter, that could mean anything.

I sighed and made a snap decision. "Alexi and I are meeting

at Snoot's once I'm done cleaning up here. If you want, you could always join us."

There was a long pause before, "Sure, okay. I'll see you there."

Before I could say anything more, Hunter had clicked off.

"Fantastic," I said, setting my phone aside. As if my own troubles weren't bad enough, now something was up with Hunter.

But he was family. If that meant putting my own issues aside to help him out, I'd do it.

Chapter 7

Snoot's wasn't as busy on a Monday night as it was on the weekend so Hunter was easy to spot in the still somewhat sizable crowd. He'd found a table near the far wall and was seated, head in his hands, looking all the world like a man whose entire existence was in peril.

"I guess that answers our question," Alexi said. On the drive over, we'd discussed Hunter and why he might have called. With him, it could be anything from problems with his relationship with Lita to trouble with the law. We'd both settled on issues with Lita as the most likely scenario since the baby was due at any moment, and from first looks, it appeared as if we were right.

"It might be something else," I said.

Alexi snorted. "Right. With Hunter, you know it's going to be worst case, and this whole baby thing is definitely a worst-case scenario for him."

"I don't know; he seemed pretty excited about it to me." And, I supposed, terrified as any dad-to-be would be, especially when the mom's father just so happened to be the chief of police.

"I'm sure he is," Alexi said as we started toward the table.

"But as soon as it comes out that he's the daddy . . ." She made a face that echoed my own thoughts about Chief Higgins.

Hunter sensed our approach and looked up just as we reached the table. "I was starting to wonder if you two had decided to ditch me." It came out at a near whine.

"Don't give us that, *Reginald*. We're early." Alexi lifted her nose in the air and sounded so much like Mom, I cringed.

"Oh, I'm sorry, *Alexandra*." Hunter likewise put on Mom-adjacent airs. "I wouldn't want you to rush yourselves while I'm having a life crisis."

I stood by and remained silent lest one of them decided to bring my middle name, Cordelia, into the conversation. Let's just say none of us were thrilled with Mom's contributions to our names, hence why Hunter went by his middle name and Alexi had shortened her first. I'm just glad Dad won out when naming me and I got a halfway decent first name.

Alexi and I sat and a waiter immediately materialized. I knew Benji from the numerous times he'd served me, yet I'd never gotten his last name. "What can I get ya?" he said, eyeing a group of college kids two tables over. They appeared to be on the verge of being kicked out due to their overly rambunctious gyrations and too loud voices.

We put in drink orders, with me opting for a Sprite/raspberry lemonade combo that was better tasting than it sounded. It was often spiked with alcohol, but I opted out since I was still reeling from last night's overconsumption. Hunter and Alexi had no reservations, which made me only slightly jealous.

"So," Alexi said, folding her arms on the table and leaning forward the moment Benji was gone. "What's going on, Hunter?"

Hunter, being Hunter, avoided the question. "I haven't eaten today. I'm a little strapped for cash and if I don't eat, I'm not sure if I'll last much longer." He looked to me hopefully.

"I'm buying," Alexi said, drawing his attention back to her. "Please tell me you're not in trouble, Hunter."

"I'm not in trouble." He looked away when he said it. "Let me eat first and then I'll tell you everything."

Alexi and I shared a worried look. Then, with a resigned sigh, she changed the subject.

"I talked to Mom after you left earlier," she said, turning her focus on me.

"Uh-oh. How'd that go?"

"I got the usual lecture about failing as a mentor to my siblings and yada-yada." She rolled her eyes. "She wants me to sit you down and have a long talk with you about responsibility to not just yourself, but the family."

"I'm not giving up the studio."

"Actually, I think she's finally starting to believe that. From what I'm able to figure, she pulled that little stunt with the shirts because it's the only way she felt as if she could keep you under her wing. She thought she was protecting you in her usual roundabout way."

"What shirts?" Hunter asked.

"Long story," I said before turning back to Alexi. "She should have asked me first. I doubt I would have let her brand her name all over my products, but I might have been willing to advertise for her or something. It's not like I don't care about Branson Designs or the family. I just don't want to work there."

"Hey," Alexi said, raising her hands. "You don't have to tell me that. I get it."

Our drinks arrived then, causing us to fall silent while Benji passed them out and then took our food orders. It was the typical extra-greasy bar fare, which I was completely okay with. In fact, I don't think I could have survived if I'd been forced to eat something healthy. Right then, I wanted comfort food.

Before Benji could retreat to the back to put in our orders, one of the college kids tipped over backward, taking his chair— and nearly the entire table—with him. There was a loud crash that caused the entire bar to fall silent, other than a round of loud guffaws from the guy's buddies.

"All right, that's it! Out!" Benji marched over to them. The entirety of Snoot's watched as he wrangled the college kids and all but shoved them out the door. As soon as the door swung closed, everyone went back to their conversations as if nothing had happened.

"I guess Dad and Kara are on the outs," Alexi said.

"What?" I gaped at her. "I thought they were doing fine?"

She shrugged. "I haven't talked to either of them directly, but it's the rumor going around the office. Mom's not normally one to gossip, and I heard her talking to Uncle Cliffton about it, so there's got to be some truth to the rumor."

"It's true," Hunter said. "Dad's in the dumps about it."

"You knew?" I glanced between them. "Both of you? Why haven't I heard anything about it until now?"

Hunter grunted. "Because you're their favorite and they wouldn't want to upset you."

"And you have more of a history with Kara than the two of us," Alexi added.

She wasn't wrong. Kara Mullins was once my best friend. In high school, we were near inseparable. Then, somehow, someway, she ended up falling for my dad after he and Mom had separated, and the next thing I knew, Kara was no longer a Mullins, but a Daniels, and had become my stepmom. *Our* stepmother, actually. None of us would ever call her that.

"Yeah, but Hunter had the hots for Kara!" I pointed out.

Hunter pulled a face. "Like five years ago. It's just weird now."

"Tell me about it," Alexi said. "Imagine being in my shoes and watching the trainwreck unfold from the outside. I thought the two of you were going to pack up and move to England to escape the whole thing."

"Trust me," I said, "I thought about it." Though, now, things were better between all of us. I was trying to reconnect with

Kara, one painful step at a time. And Dad... Well, he was Dad. We've always had a strange relationship, but in this family, who didn't?

Our food arrived a short time later. Hunter immediately started to gorge himself like he hadn't eaten for a week. Both Alexi and I watched him as he downed his burger in a couple of honking huge bites and started in on his fries. He paused halfway, gave us each a "what are you looking at?" look, and then dove right back in.

We gave him until he was most of the way through his fries before Alexi said, "Okay, Hunter. Spill."

He mopped up the remains of his ketchup with a soggy fry and shoved it into his mouth. He took his grand old time chewing before he answered with, "It's about Lita."

"Well, duh," I said. "We kind of figured that."

Hunter frowned, picked up another limp fry, and wagged it at me. "Do you want me to say this or not?"

I mimed zipping my lips and motioned for him to go on.

Hunter dropped the unappealing fry and then pushed his plate away. "She's talking about moving to Maine."

My heart did one of those surprised thumps that left me briefly breathless before I managed to ask, "Permanently?"

He shrugged. "She's got family there, I guess. And while things between us are cool and all, I don't think it's going to work out." He looked at me, then to Alexi, almost pleadingly. "It's not my fault."

"We didn't think it was," Alexi said. I nodded my agreement.

"It sucks," Hunter said. "I thought about trying the long-distance thing, but neither of us would want to do that. Better to just... not."

"I take it that means you're not going with her?" I asked, selfishly relieved.

Hunter closed his eyes briefly before sighing in a way that

was close to heartbreaking. "I'd never survive if I left Cardinal Lake. Besides, I don't know anyone in Maine, and it's not like I have job prospects lined up here, let alone there, so how would I even get there? And if I somehow managed to land a job there, what then? Mom would cut me off and if things fell apart, I'd be completely out of luck, trapped in a place I know nothing about, without you two to help me out."

I doubted Mom would go as far as cutting him off, but I understood his point. Cecilia Branson would *not* be thrilled if one of her children were to up and leave town without her blessing. She might not turn her back on him, but she *would* make him regret leaving her every second of every day until he came back.

You know, kind of like how she treats me and my studio.

"I know I probably don't have to ask, but why exactly is Lita leaving town?" Alexi asked.

"What do you think? Her dad." Hunter nearly spat it. "I think he found out about us."

Alexi winced. "Has he confronted you about it?"

I almost answered for him. If Chief Higgins had confronted Hunter about getting his daughter pregnant, Hunter wouldn't be sitting here right now. I imagined we'd be sitting with him in a hospital room, surrounded by beeping machines.

Exaggeration? Maybe. But it was hard to imagine things *not* going badly when the time came for Hunter to go face-to-face with Dan Higgins about Lita and the baby.

"Not yet, he hasn't," he said, sagging. "But I think he's been having me followed."

"Followed?" I asked. "Like, someone's been watching you wherever you go?"

The look Hunter gave me was of the "no-duh" variety. "That's what 'having me followed' means, Ash."

I stuck my tongue out at him. He returned the favor. Anyone watching would have thought we were teenagers who had yet to grow up, not adults in our twenties who had yet to grow up.

"All right, children," Alexi said, "let's get back to the point."

Hunter sighed and leaned back into his seat. "It sucks. I thought things were going great and then, the next thing I know, I'm seeing the same dude wherever I go. He's not doing anything suspicious or taking notes or anything like that. He's just . . . there."

Alexi's brow drew together and she frowned. "Are you sure it's Chief Higgins who sent him?"

"It's not like I asked the guy," Hunter said. "I mean, who else would it be?"

Something in Alexi's expression had me sitting up straighter. "What?" I asked her.

"I'm not sure." She considered her beer, but didn't take a drink. "The last time Fiona and I went out, I'm pretty sure someone was watching us." Fiona was her best friend and near-constant evening companion when Alexi wasn't at home with Evan and the kids. "He didn't do anything more than sit there, but I'm almost positive he was keeping an eye on us."

I stared at her, mouth hanging open. There was no way. . . .

"You too?" Hunter asked me.

"I think so." I thought back to the guy I'd seen at Market Inn and then at A Purrfect Pose. "I've only seen him twice. Talked to him once."

"You *talked* to him?" Alexi was incredulous.

"He came to my studio and said he wanted to sign up for a class. He acted strange and when I turned my back on him for a few seconds, he vanished."

"What did he look like?" Alexi asked.

I shrugged. "Like a man?"

She glowered at me. "This isn't an old *Mad TV* skit."

"Doesn't that go, 'He look-a—'" Hunter cut off and raised his hands in surrender when both Alexi and I glared at him.

"Come on, Ash," Alexi pressed. "What did your guy look like?"

"I think he was in his thirties?" It came out sounding indecisive. "Short hair. Normal. He didn't really stand out."

"Sounds like my guy," Hunter said. Alexi nodded.

"It could be a coincidence," I said. "This *is* a smallish town."

"All three of us seeing the same guy watching us is a coincidence?" Alexi said. "Really, Ash?"

My heart was thumping hard in my chest. No, it couldn't be a coincidence. Nor could the fact that this guy showed up in our lives right about the time my blind date is murdered, and right when Lita decides to up and move to Maine. Was something going wrong in Alexi's life as well? Was there someone trying to destroy our family, one sibling at a time?

"You know," I said, abruptly standing. "I think I might have a drink after all."

I made my way to the bar, head on a swivel. If the guy had been following each of us in turn, could he be here now, hiding amongst the crowd, since all three of us were together? I didn't see him, but that didn't mean he wasn't there. He could be outside, waiting in the parking lot. Or perhaps he had an accomplice, someone none of us had spotted as of yet.

I put in my beer order and leaned against the counter. Relief washed through me when I looked over and saw someone I knew, someone who was most definitely *not* following me.

Even though Drew Hinton and I had broken up years ago, we were still on good terms. He was a friend, in fact. A good one. And right then, a friend was exactly what I needed.

"Hey, Drew," I said, scooting down the bar to join him. "Where's Ginny?"

He jerked in surprise and then grinned as he wrapped me in a hug that I'd needed far more than I cared to admit. "Ash! She's waiting at our table." He pointed as he released me.

Drew's girlfriend, Ginny Riese, was glaring daggers at me from their table across the room. She'd had her back to me, which was why I hadn't noticed her when I was scanning the crowd on my way to the bar, but she must have sensed my presence because she was turned in her seat now. Even though I had no desire to get back with Drew, Ginny swore up and down that I did. That little hug of greeting Drew had given me would only reinforce her delusion, and I knew I'd end up paying for it somewhere down the line.

"I'm here with Hunter and Alexi," I said, motioning to our table, which was opposite of where Ginny and Drew were sitting. "Siblings' night out."

"Sounds fun." Drew's and Ginny's beers arrived. He scooped them up. "I wish I could stay and chat, but Ginny's waiting. We should get together for lunch sometime soon. Or maybe coffee?"

"I'm off Wednesday," I said, thinking that a coffee with Drew sounded like the perfect way to relax.

"Wednesday would be perfect. Ginny's got an appointment at eleven. How about we meet at Shakes around then? We could grab a coffee and catch up while we wait for her."

"I'd love that."

"Then it's a date." He winked and then carried the beer back to his table. Ginny immediately started in on him, likely grilling him about what we'd talked about. She wouldn't be happy about the coffee date, but she'd get over it.

My beer arrived a moment later. As I picked it up, I considered going over to Ginny and Drew's table to let her know that I was delighted that the two of them were happy and to assure her that the upcoming coffee date was just two friends getting together, nothing more, but I nixed the idea before it could fully form. Best let Drew handle it on his own. I'd only make it worse.

I was about to turn away and return to Alexi and Hunter when another face I recognized crossed my field of view.

He'd just come in and was still wearing his coat. He crossed the room to a table occupied by two women and another man. He said something to them, laughed, and then he tossed some money onto the table before he turned and headed back for the door.

I blinked and rubbed my eyes, not quite sure I believed what I was seeing.

But sure enough, he was still there. The man strode right past me, close enough that I could have reached out and grabbed hold of him—which, looking back, I probably should have done, even if it meant dropping my beer. As it was, the man walked for the door, alive and well, and seemingly without a care in the world.

And that man was Grady Richards.

I didn't think. I returned the beer to the bar without looking and ran toward the door Grady had just exited. My heart was pounding and there was a strange humming in my head that made me feel disconnected from my own body.

I hit the door at a sprint. Cold air slammed into me the moment I was outside, took my breath away. I shivered as I scoured the lit-up parking lot. I immediately saw Grady walking away from the lot, toward a nearby residential area opposite the lake. His hands were shoved into his pockets and the hood of his coat was pulled up against the cold wind coming off the lake so I couldn't see his face, but I was positive it was him.

I started running, desperately trying to make sense of what was happening. How could Grady be alive? How could Chief Higgins have made such a massive mistake by declaring Grady dead when he was *right there*?

His stride was brisk, but not so fast that I didn't think I'd catch him. I would have reached him too if it wasn't for a chance glance over his shoulder when I was still a couple of yards away.

Fear flashed across his features the moment Grady saw me. He took one stumbling step forward, eyes widening, before he turned and started running away.

"Grady! Wait!" I shouted. "I just want to talk."

Not surprisingly, he didn't listen.

I could have let him go, but at that point, I was determined. I refused to be outrun by a dead man, living or not. I'd just spent most of the day doing yoga, but I pushed myself for all I was worth despite the burn in my legs, and was soon catching up to him.

Grady glanced back as we reached the residential district. He saw me nearing and put on a burst of speed, but it was short-lived, and I was soon a hair's breadth from reaching him. I gritted my teeth and lunged, snagging the back of his coat with my hand.

Grady yelped as we both lost our balance and went down. I angled my body so that I didn't hit the sidewalk, but the ground was cold and felt just as hard as concrete as I landed on my hands and knees, panting. Grady wasn't so lucky as he went down on his rump hard enough that his teeth clacked together.

"You," I gasped, barely able to breathe. "Alive." I licked my lips and tried again. "You should be dead!"

Grady's expression changed from frightened to terrified. He pushed himself away from me and started to rise. I reached out and grabbed his coat again. His fear gave him enough strength that when he stood, he pulled *both* of us to our feet.

"Let go!" he shouted, batting at my hands.

"Not until you tell me why you're not dead."

He grabbed my thumb and tried to pull it back, but his gloves were too thick and refused to allow him the grip he needed. "Help!" he shouted. "Somebody help me!"

"What's going on?" An outside light snapped out and a woman stepped outside a nearby house. "Hey, you. Stop that! Let that man go!"

I released Grady out of reflex. He didn't hesitate. Before I could grab him again—or explain to the woman what was happening—Grady started running. He leapt over a nearby hedge, and before I could blink, he vanished into a darkened yard, and into the night.

Chapter 8

"There's no way it's possible, Ash," Sierra said. "You must have been seeing things. Or maybe you made a mistake. How much did you have to drink?"

"Nothing." I shot a warning look toward the kitty room where Tyra was busy settling the cats in for the Tuesday morning yoga session. I lowered my voice, hoping Sierra would do the same. "I was completely sober. I laid hands on the guy, so it wasn't a ghost. I'm telling you: Grady Richards is alive and was at Snoot's."

Sierra frowned as she carried a small, portable speaker to the front of the room and set it next to my mat. "I don't get it. How could Grady be there when he's dead?"

"You tell me."

I'd spent the entire night going over it in my head to no avail. How could Chief Higgins have made such a huge mistake? Even if Grady had somehow faked his death, that wouldn't account for the body in his apartment. I suppose he could have stuck his ID into the dead guy's pocket and the police just figured the case was closed and didn't bother to check him any further. It was a stretch—and shoddy policework if true—but it was within the realm of possibility.

But if he'd faked his death, did that mean *Grady* was the murderer? And if he was pretending to be dead, why would he risk going to Snoot's where people would see him and possibly recognize him? It didn't make sense.

"Did you talk to the people he was with?" Sierra asked. "Maybe they know what's going on."

I shook my head. "When I got back to Snoot's, they were already gone. I can't even remember what they looked like to be honest. I was too focused on Grady."

"I still can't believe it. Something else *has* to be going on," Sierra said. "Like, maybe Hunter slipped something into your drink as a joke and you hallucinated the whole episode."

I gave her a flat look.

"What? You know how he can be. He could have spiked your whatever-you-had and it messed with your head. It didn't even have to be drugs. It could have been, I don't know, really potent vodka or something."

"I know what I saw, Sierra. Grady's alive."

The kitty room door opened, causing both Sierra and me to snap upright.

"Everything's set up and ready to go," Tyra said as she exited the room. "I've got to get to class, but I'll be back tonight to pick the kitties up."

"Great. I'll see you then." I flashed her a too wide smile that showed far too many teeth. Beside me, Sierra did the same.

Tyra sighed and rolled her eyes in that way that teenagers did. "You know, that room's not soundproofed. I could hear everything the two of you said. It's no big deal; I'm not twelve."

I winced. "Sorry. I just didn't want to drag you into my problems. It's not that I believed you couldn't handle it."

"But still, maybe keep this between us?" Sierra said. "I wouldn't go talking to your parents about dead people walking around town. They might think you're experimenting with drugs and blame Ash for it."

I glared at her, to which Sierra merely shrugged.

"I don't think you have to worry about that," Tyra said. "They'd probably go hunting for zombies long before they'd ever believe I'm into drugs."

"Just don't go talking about it," I said. "At least not yet. We're not sure what's really going on and we wouldn't want to get you into trouble. Sierra's probably right; there's a good chance I made a mistake and this will all blow over in a day or two." Though I doubted it.

"Don't worry about me. I won't say anything." She started to turn away, then paused. "And don't forget about later."

I stared at her blankly.

"The Holloway farm? With Kiersten?"

"Oh! Right." Crap. I'd completely forgotten about it with everything that had been going on. "I'll be there."

"She wants you to meet her at the shelter. She'll drive from there," Tyra said. "Don't forget that you said you'd be there at around three."

"Got it."

Tyra gave me a worried look before she grabbed her things and was out the door. Classes started in fifteen minutes, which meant the first of my students would arrive at any moment. I needed to get my head on straight before then.

"I'm off tonight," Sierra said. "We should get together and talk about this whole Grady being alive or dead thing after you're done here."

"Two nights off in a row?" I asked. Sierra worked at Snoot's and rarely had more than a day off at a time. "How'd you manage that?"

"Pulled a couple of doubles last week," she said. "Had one day where I handled breakfast *and* came in later for my normal shift. One of the other girls was sick, so I took it on so I could have an easy week this week. Good thing I did, considering all of . . ." She waved a hand vaguely in the air. ". . . *this*."

"Lucky you."

"Yeah, well . . ." She shrugged. "Tonight. My place. I'll order pizza and we can talk about it. Cool?"

"Cool." Why did I feel *uncool* saying that?

Sierra shot me a thumbs-up. "I kinda feel like I got you into this mess."

"Only kinda?"

"Okay, I definitely got you into this. But in my defense, you weren't exactly setting the world on fire with your love life. You needed a nudge."

Too bad that nudge shoved me straight off the cliff and into a big ole pile of you-know-what. "I'll see you tonight."

A face appeared at the glass door, signaling the arrival of my first student of the day. Sierra mouthed, "Good luck," before slipping out the back.

"Thanks," I muttered, because, man, was I ever going to need it.

I plastered on my best "everything is fine" smile and went about welcoming everyone as they arrived for yoga. The cats were especially rambunctious, so as soon as they were released, they began zooming around the studio like their tails were on fire. They quickly became the center of attention, which meant barely anyone was paying me any mind. I allowed my smile to slip and moved to the front of the class, eyes lingering on the door.

Come on, George. I'd hoped he and Lulu would be back this morning, but they had yet to show. No, I didn't think George had anything to do with the murder or whatever it was that had really happened at Grady's apartment, but I hoped he'd seen *something* that night that might explain how a man found dead one evening was showing up at Snoot's, alive and well, the next.

Of course, George wasn't the only one I was watching for.

The family stalker had yet to make an appearance and I hadn't seen him at Snoot's when I was with Alexi and Hunter, but that didn't mean he wasn't out there somewhere. It was possible we were all jumping at shadows and he *wasn't* watching us, but considering we'd all seen him, I found it unlikely.

"Uh, Ash?"

It took me a moment to realize someone had spoken. "I'm sorry. What was that?"

Addison Teige was watching me with a concerned expression on her face. Actually, the whole class was.

"You were, like, just standing there."

Nods went around the room. Even the cats appeared worried about my mental state.

"I . . ." I gave myself a shake. "It's been a long couple of days. I spaced out a bit there. Where were we?"

It took some doing, but we got class back on track—or, more accurately, *started*. I hoped that the routine of yoga would help ease my mind, but it didn't. Neither did the hijinks of the cats. Every time someone walked by outside, I found myself watching the door, hoping that it would be George. Or my stalker. Or even Grady, come to explain what in the world was going on.

But it never was.

By the time class was over, I was a mess. Yoga was supposed to be relaxing, yet I was even more stressed now than I was when we'd started. Even when I carried a white ball of fluff with a bright pink nose back to the kitty room, I couldn't stop thinking about Grady. If I didn't get to the bottom of this soon, I was going to drive myself crazy.

Once everyone was gone, I went about cleaning up and mentally prepping myself for the next session. I considered cancelling the rest of the day because, quite frankly, my heart wasn't in it. If someone got hurt because I wasn't paying attention and they overextended, I'd never forgive myself.

If only I had a partner. I could ask them to run the class for me whenever I didn't feel up for it. They could even run classes on days and times when I wasn't there. The studio was a hit, so having more classes throughout the week wouldn't be a bad thing. In fact, adding two or three other instructors might be ideal. It would take a lot of pressure off me and make it easier for those with busy schedules to find a time that worked for them.

I decided not to cancel and went ahead with class, despite not being in the right headspace for it. I went through the motions, keeping the poses to simple, risk-free stretches, and made it through class without too much trouble.

Still, my mind had been elsewhere, and it showed.

"You okay, Ash?" one of the Tuesday regulars, Dylan Cole, asked once we were done.

"Yeah, I'm fine. Just distracted."

He didn't look as if he believed me, but he let it go. "A few of us are going to The Hop for lunch in case you want to join us. Should be fun." Behind him, both Brittany Hamp and Sissy Tom were waiting with another girl, Arianna Hall, who'd only started coming to classes last week. She was tentative to the point of being shy, but looked as if she'd found a place where she belonged.

Lunch at The Hop was tempting, but I said, "I think I'm going to stay here and get some work done." My stomach was in knots and I didn't think I could eat much more than a granola bar without being sick.

"You sure? We'd love to have you." Dylan glanced back at the girls, who all nodded in agreement.

"I'm sure. Maybe next time."

After a slight hesitation, Dylan and the others left, leaving me alone in the quiet of A Purrfect Pose. It didn't take long before I regretted not going, but I didn't chase after them. I kept thinking that if someone *was* watching me, I didn't want anyone else to become a target. Why a stalker would go after my yoga students, I had no idea. I wasn't even sure there *was* a stalker, yet the thought that there could be had me worried.

Get it together, Ash. If I kept going like this, Mom would end up getting her wish and I'd be sitting back behind the desk at Branson Designs within the month.

I went into my office and retrieved one of the granola bars I kept in my desk for times when I didn't want to leave the studio for lunch. After munching on it, I went about cleaning the cats' litter boxes even though they appeared as if they hadn't been used, but was something to do. That done, I set the mostly empty bag aside, filled the food dishes and changed the water, all while weaving through the flood of fuzzy bodies intent on tripping me with every step.

"There you go," I said, returning a fresh water bowl to the floor. "Cold and clean." An orange cat with a crooked tail immediately shoved his paw into the water and licked it off. He repeated the process another dozen times. "No wonder there's always fur and grit in there," I told him, and then left him to it.

I pulled on my coat and then picked up the bagged litter and carried it to the back door so I could dump it into the trash out back before going for a walk around the green to clear my head. I still had to get through the post-lunch yoga class before I was to meet Kiersten at the shelter. Then, all I'd have is the evening class to get through, and then I could meet with Sierra for pizza and we could hopefully come up with a solution to this whole Grady mess.

"I'll be back soon!" I called over my shoulder as I opened the door and took a step outside.

Someone put a hand on my shoulder.

I screamed and reacted on pure instinct. I swung the only thing I had on hand as I recoiled backward, hitting the man squarely on the face with a partially filled bag of kitty litter.

"I'm so sorry," I said, handing over a clump of damp paper towels. "You caught me by surprise."

Edward Wilkins sullenly took the proffered paper towel. "You didn't have to hit me with . . . *that*." He made a disgusted face and scrubbed at his cheek.

I felt bad, but at least the bag of litter hadn't exploded all over him. It *had* broken, so some had spilled out, but he wasn't covered in it. That had to count for something, right?

"It was mostly clean," I said, earning myself a glare from Edward. "It's been a stressful couple of days, as I'm sure you are aware."

He sighed and nodded as he finished wiping off his face before ruffling his hair to make sure nothing was in it. He tossed the paper towels into the trash can by the bathroom door, looked at himself once in the small bathroom mirror, and then stepped out into the hall where I was standing.

"I've heard all about it," he said. "It's why I'm here, actually."

That knot in my stomach tightened. "You know something about Grady's murder." Or whatever it was that really happened.

"No." Edward frowned as he continued to pat himself down in a way that was almost obsessive. I suppose if someone had smacked me with a bag of kitty litter, clean or not, I'd act the same way. "But I thought it best if I came down here and explained myself, just in case you or the police get some funny ideas about me."

I crossed my arms and took on something of a defensive stance. "Please do. The police *are* looking for you, you know? And George was worried."

"I know." And he didn't sound too concerned by it either. "I . . ." He scowled over my shoulder. "This isn't easy. I'm not quite sure where to start."

"Let me start then," I said, heat rising in my voice. I'm not sure if it was the stress of the last few days or if something else had gotten into me, but I found myself growing angrier by the second. And Edward, being right there, seemed like a perfect target for that anger. "You went out to eat with George at the same restaurant in which I was due to have a blind date with Grady Richards. You had too much to drink, got belligerent—"

"I wouldn't go that far."

"—And then you interrogated me about a date I knew nothing about before you turned on him when he finally did show up. Once you had your say, you left, got into it with George outside, and then you wandered off. He goes home, leaving you to your own devices. Am I right so far?"

Edward opened his mouth to object to something I'd said, but snapped it closed again without voicing it. He shrugged and nodded at the same time, which I took to mean that I was close enough for whatever I'd gotten wrong to not matter.

"Then, after everything blows up, you vanish. The police want to ask you questions. George tries to call you. But instead of answering them and sorting things out, you avoid them."

"I wasn't avoiding anyone."

"Then what were you doing?" I crossed my arms, but the anger had already dissipated.

Edward took a moment to gather his thoughts before he spoke. "I admit; I drank too much that night. It was stupid of me, yes, but it happens."

Considering my night out with my friends, I could relate. "Where did you go after dinner with George? Why didn't you call him back when he was trying to reach you?"

"Honestly? I don't know." When I narrowed my eyes at

him, he amended it to, "I mean, I don't know why I didn't call him back. I suppose I was scared." He cringed on the last word, like it physically hurt him to admit it. "I caught wind that the cops were looking for me and was worried that they thought I'd done something wrong when I didn't, and they'd, I don't know, frame me for a crime or something."

"The police here don't frame people."

"I'm sure they don't," he snapped. "But I wasn't thinking. I heard about the murder. I know how it had to look after I'd confronted the guy so publicly. And, as I'm sure you've heard by now, I've had my issues in the past. It wouldn't be hard for the police to put two and two together, though, this time, it sure as heck don't equal four."

Edward paced away from me, hands balled into fists. He looked like he wanted to punch someone and was glad he had better control of his emotions than he'd had the other night.

"I get it," I said. "You were scared they'd pin the crime on you because you stood up to Grady and have a history of getting into trouble."

He walked back over with a nod. "I panicked. I decided to take a few days off and get out of town to let things cool down. I get that it wasn't the smartest thing to do, that it makes it look like I was hiding from something, but I wasn't. I knew that if the police came sniffing around, I'd say something I'd regret, and the next thing I'd know, I'd be sitting in a jail cell, framed for that guy's murder."

"You need to talk to the police," I said.

He pinched the bridge of his nose. "I can't. It won't work. It's why I came to you. I figured that since I stood up for you at Market Inn, you could do the same for me."

"You want me to defend you?"

He scowled. "No, not defend. But you could talk to the police for me. Tell them my story so that they'll stop looking at me like a suspect. I can't be seen in public or I just *know* they'll arrest me for something I didn't do. It's why I came to your back door instead of the front. Too many people watching."

I wondered if he was talking figuratively, or if he'd actually seen someone—someone like my stalker—watching A Purrfect Pose. I decided not to press and instead, searched his face, looking for some sort of deception. I understood that he was scared, that he was afraid that his past would cause the police to overlook evidence and blame him for the murder—Grady's or whoever it was that they'd actually found.

But how he thought that sneaking around Cardinal Lake, hiding from his family, from the police, and asking what was pretty much a stranger for help, would make anyone think him innocent, I had no idea.

"What happened that night, Edward?" I asked.

He ran a hand over his mouth, didn't respond.

"If you want me to help you," I said, "I need to know exactly what happened. Where did you go after you got into the fight with George?"

"It wasn't a fight." At my glare, he sagged. "Okay, fine. Like you said, I got belligerent. George called me out on it. I don't like it when my mistakes are pointed out to me, so I told him off and stomped off like a child. Happy?"

No, I wasn't, but I motioned for him to go on.

"But I didn't wander off, as you put it. I hung around." Before I could say anything, he raised a hand. "It was stupid, I know. I had no real plan in mind. I wasn't sure why I'd stuck around, to be honest. To cool off, I suppose. I paced around the block a little, then came back to the lot, thinking maybe George would come back for me, but he didn't. So, I called someone to pick me up, but I had to wait on them."

"You waited at the Market Inn?"

He nodded. "I didn't want to stand around in the parking

lot, so I went around the side of the building, out of sight, figuring that I'd caused enough problems for everyone for one night. Out of sight, out of mind, and all that."

Understandable. "Were you still there when Grady left?"

His face clouded over. "I was. I didn't realize it was him at first. The side door opened and someone stepped outside. I figured it was an employee coming out to smoke or toss the garbage. I could hear kitchen sounds, so I assumed the door led directly into the kitchen itself, meaning it was likely a server or cook. But it wasn't."

"It was Grady?"

Another nod. "He didn't see me, which I guess was a blessing in disguise." He chewed over that for a moment before he said, "If he'd been alone, I might have gone over and clocked him one to blow off some steam. I was still feeling pretty rank, so it would have felt good, but I'm smarter than that."

"Wait." My heart was thumping in my ears. "Grady wasn't alone?"

"No, there were two of them. Your date came out first. He was laughing and mucking it up with the other guy, who seemed none too happy about it. I couldn't hear exactly what was being said, though I'm pretty sure your date mentioned something about giving you a discount."

A discount? "Did you see who he was talking to?" I asked, though I was pretty sure I already knew.

"Yeah." Edward rubbed his hands together as if he were cold. "Your waiter. He's the guy who helped that date of yours sneak away."

CHAPTER 9

Kiersten Vanhouser was waiting for me outside the Cardinal Lake animal shelter just before three. I'd promised her I'd be there, and so I was, though I had to admit, I wasn't in the mood to deal with Harlan Holloway, who could be cantankerous at times. After Edward had left A Purrfect Pose, I'd struggled to focus, and had probably the worst yoga session I'd ever had. Not that I was doing a great job of keeping my mind on task before, but after what he'd told me about Alan the waiter, I was in an even worse state of mind.

Could *Alan* have been the corpse that was found in the apartment? It would explain how Grady was still walking around town days after his supposed murder, but how could the police have confused the two men? They looked nothing alike. And I was pretty sure someone would have reported Alan the waiter missing by now, though, I supposed it was possible that someone had and I hadn't heard about it yet. It wasn't like the police were rushing over to tell me about their progress in the case.

Kiersten waited for me to get out of my car and walk over to her. She looked grim when she asked, "Are you ready for this?"

"Not in the slightest."

She chuckled and motioned toward her SUV, which had a bumper and back window covered with animal rights stickers. "Harlan is going to act the innocent victim. He'll try to be sweet, try to act like I have no idea what I'm talking about. Even though I doubt he'll be combative, I'll do all the talking, just in case he goes on the offensive. I mostly need you there for moral support."

"Gotcha. What about his wife?"

"Enis? What about her?"

"Would talking to her help?" I knew Harlan Holloway was bullish about letting his cats breed willy-nilly, but I'd never heard anything about what Enis or their five kids thought about the situation.

Kiersten didn't answer until we were in her SUV and she'd pulled out onto the road. "No, talking to Enis won't help. She believes spaying and neutering is cruel. Last time I talked to her about it, she demanded to know if I would do the same thing to my kids, if I had them. Never mind the fact that if you let the animals breed out of control like this, they end up homeless and starving. They're not like people who can take care of themselves."

Cats *could* take care of themselves to some degree, but I knew what she meant. "Well, you could make a case that some people shouldn't breed."

She glanced at me out of the corner of her eye and chuckled. "True. But that's beside the point here. The entire family seems hell-bent on making sure cats in Cardinal Lake outnumber humans ten to one. Now, if you think you could handle having another nine or so pets . . ."

"No thanks. One is enough for me."

"Didn't think so."

The Holloway farm was on the outskirts of Cardinal Lake,

down a long stretch of too narrow roads bordered by wild fields and small forests. We passed other farmhouses, many of which were abandoned and left rotting on land that had become overgrown with weeds and wildflowers. It made me wonder why someone didn't come along and rebuild. It was pretty out here. Peaceful.

A glint of sunlight on metal reflecting in my side mirror caught my attention. A car was behind us, but it was far enough away, I couldn't make out much more than the glint. So far, it was the only sign of life I'd seen since we'd left civilization.

Eventually, Kiersten pulled into a long, sloping gravel driveway that was more pothole than road. We jounced our way to the front of the Holloway house, which, despite being built sometime over a century ago, appeared well-tended and surprisingly modern for a farmhouse. I could see the barns out back, along with seemingly endless fields spotted with idle machinery. The animals must have been tucked away in their barns because, while I could smell them, I couldn't see them.

Nix that. Almost as soon as I thought it, two cats zipped from under the porch at warp speed, ears pinned back, tails poofed. I didn't know if our arrival had spooked them, or if something else had gotten into them.

"Must be Mama and Papa," I said.

"Let's hope they were chasing mice under there."

Kiersten climbed out of her SUV as the front door opened and Harlan Holloway stepped outside, arms crossed, a ratty orange ballcap on his head.

Harlan was in his mid-sixties, but looked younger. He was built like a man used to working physical labor. He had a slight paunch and his shoulders hunched as if his back were bothering him, but his arms were muscular and exposed by sleeves rolled up to those bunched shoulders, despite the chill on the air. He had a pleasant enough smile on his face, but I could tell he wasn't amused by our presence.

"Well now, what can I do for you, Ms. Vanhouser?" he asked, though his tone said he knew exactly why we were there. "I didn't expect company or else I would have cleaned up first."

Kiersten sighed. "We need to talk about the cats, Harlan. Can we go inside to talk?"

"The calicos are perfectly fine." He spread his booted feet, planting himself on the porch, blocking off entrance to his house. "You didn't need to come all the way out here about this. You know my stance on the situation."

"I do," Kiersten said. "And I think I did need to stop by, Harlan. We really do have to talk about this."

A silver car passed by as I got out of the SUV. I'd kind of hoped it might be one of the Holloway kids since I could already see that talking to Harlan wasn't going to work. Maybe someone younger would be less stuck in their ways and would listen to reason.

Harlan said something I missed as I moved to stand behind Kiersten. Whatever it was, it set her off.

"I don't have room for them, Harlan! The shelter is overstuffed as it is. The more cats you bring to us, the worse it gets. Please, get them spayed at least. If something happens and you need more barn cats, the shelter can provide more for you, free of charge. I'll even make sure they're up on all their vaccines and have a clean bill of health before personally dropping them off here."

The briefest flicker of compassion flashed across Harlan's face before vanishing. "Enis won't have it, so neither will I," he said, not unkindly. "And seriously, Kiersten, you can't tell me that people don't want kittens. They snatch those suckers up like kids getting offered sweets for free."

"No, Harlan, they don't." But there was no more oomph to Kiersten's complaints. She already knew she'd lost and no amount of pleading would change his mind. "Some kittens go fast, sure, but not all of them. And what do you think that means for the older cats? They get passed over for all these kittens you keep bringing to us. They need homes too."

"I feel for you," Harlan said, "I really do. But I'm sorry, I can't help you. Things are the way they are for a reason."

And that reason seemed to be Enis.

I stepped forward, drawing Harlan's eye. "What if you could do something else that would reduce the number of kittens, but wouldn't require you to have them spayed or neutered?"

Harlan's brow furrowed as he looked me up and down. "Ms. Branson, right?"

I cringed inwardly. Mom was Ms. Branson, never me. But right then, I was willing to roll with it. "That's right. Ash." I took a deep breath and pressed on. "You could give away, let's say, all the female cats. Give them to friends or family or whatever. Or, if no one you know has room, you could take them to the shelter."

Kiersten winced at that, but didn't interrupt.

"You could keep all the males. You wouldn't have to spay or neuter them, but you'd be significantly reducing the stress on the shelter. Fewer cats would go hungry and more of them would have happy families. You wouldn't have litter after litter to worry about either. And then, like Kiersten said, you could go to her if you need more cats."

Harlan studied me for a long moment before his arms dropped to his side. "You know what? I'll talk to Enis. Might be that it's a good idea, though I'd wager she'll be apt to want to keep the girls around more than the boys. She's partial to them since she never did get that daughter she wanted." He chuckled.

"Either way would work," Kiersten said, sounding relieved. "Just let me know what she says and what I can do to help."

Harlan rubbed at his chin, nodded. "I can't promise anything, mind you," he said. "But I'll ask."

"That's all I'm asking."

A few minutes later, Kiersten and I were back in her SUV, heading toward the shelter.

"Thanks for that," she said. "I know it's not a perfect solution, that his cats aren't the only ones around here, but it might help."

"I got the impression it's not Harlan who's making the decisions about the cats," I said. "Maybe if they stop having kittens around here, Enis will see reason and they'll finally do the right thing."

"We can hope. I might have to bring you with me whenever I need to talk to someone about their pets, Ash." Kiersten grimaced. "You wouldn't believe some of the things I've had to deal with."

Honestly, I didn't think I wanted to know.

I looked out my window, figuring I could watch nature fly by, when I noted another glint in my side mirror. I leaned forward with a frown. A car was back there, though I couldn't tell if it was the same one as before.

Somehow, I thought it might be.

Kiersten picked up on my sudden spike of anxiety. "Ash? What's wrong?"

"It might be nothing," I said, squinting, but it was just too far to make anything out clearly. "There's a car back there."

Kiersten adjusted her rearview mirror to get a better look. "Okay? There is. So?"

How to explain? Kiersten didn't follow the news, so she probably hadn't heard about Grady's—or whoever it really was—murder. And my presumed stalker was just that: presumed.

"Ash?" she pressed. "What's going on? Please tell me you haven't done something that has the FBI tailing you."

"The FBI?" I asked, shooting her a side-eye glance before turning my attention back to the car behind us. I was pretty sure it was silver, but it could also be a light blue or gray. "Did you see a badge or dash lights or something?" Did the FBI even use dash lights?

She laughed. "No, but with you, I never know what to expect."

"You're thinking of Hunter."

"Oh yeah. I get the two of you confused sometimes." She sobered. "What is it then?"

"Like I said, it might be nothing." Silver. It was definitely a silver car. "I think someone is following me."

Her head whipped my way, then back again as she stared hard into the rearview. "And that's them?" She frowned. "Why would someone be following you?"

"Honestly? I don't know. And I might be wrong." I quickly explained about my blind date, how he had left me with the bill, and then was seemingly murdered and later resurrected. I left out a whole heap of information for brevity. "I saw a guy at Market Inn who later showed up at A Purrfect Pose for a class. Then, later, when Hunter said he thought someone was watching him . . ."

"It made you think of your guy."

"Exactly."

"And you think that's your stalker back there?"

"I don't know. It could be. A car was behind us when we were on the way to Harlan's. Now there's one behind us again. Could be a coincidence."

Kiersten was silent as she thought about it. We were nearly out of Farmland, USA, and back to Cardinal Lake proper when she slowed. I noted the car behind us did as well. If ever I doubted whether they were following us, I had my answer right there.

"Do you want me to stop?" she asked.

"What?" My heart skipped a beat. "Why would you do that?"

"If we stop, they'd only have a couple of choices and it would tell us a lot about their intentions."

"And those choices would be?"

"They could stop and sit back there until we made up our minds on what to do next. They could drive on past and pretend they weren't tailing us. Or they could turn around and run."

"You're missing an option."

Kiersten glanced at me long enough to raise her eyebrows in question.

"They could approach us and kill us. What if it's the murderer and they think I know something?"

"There's two of us."

"And we're unarmed." Kiersten had slowed further and I noted the car was a tiny bit closer, but had likewise slowed. "Keep going. Let's see if they follow us all the way to the shelter."

For a moment, I feared Kiersten wasn't going to listen and would stop the SUV so she could confront our tail.

And then, much to my immense relief, she pressed on the gas and sped up.

Behind us, the car retreated until it vanished from sight.

Could I have been wrong? I watched the side mirror all the way back into town. The car never reappeared. We'd passed multiple turnoffs, all of which led into no-man's-land where there were a few homes speckled in the countryside, and that's about it. The car could have slowed when we did because we were on a country road. There could be deer and other wildlife. You see someone slow down in front of you out in the middle of nowhere, it made sense to slow down yourself, just in case.

Kiersten pulled into the shelter lot. I kept my eye on the road, but the silver car was gone.

"Let me know what Harlan decides," I said, climbing out of her car. "And if you need me to talk to Enis for you . . ."

"I'll call you first thing." Kiersten rounded the car and gave me a hug. "Be safe, Ash. If you learn something about this stalker of yours, let me know, all right?"

"I will." I returned the hug and then stepped back. "I'm sure I'm overreacting."

Kiersten didn't look convinced as she returned to the shelter. I wasn't convinced either. Someone *had* been following me. I just needed to find out why.

I stood at the plate glass window facing the street inside A Purrfect Pose, studying the building past the fountain. I had an hour before the final class of the night, which would be followed by pizza with Sierra. The silver car hadn't appeared again, nor had the guy I thought might be following me. And while Grady Richards might be alive, someone *had* been murdered.

I was so desperate to worry about anything else, I was considering heading across the street to talk to Mom about the shirts again. It would be frustrating, but I could handle that. Life-or-death situations? No thank you.

But while I could deal with Mom, did I really want to ruin the rest of my day by arguing with her?

No. No, I didn't.

So, instead, I called Dad.

"Ash?" He sounded surprised, and somewhat confused, by my call. After his split with Mom and subsequent relationship with my childhood best friend, I didn't contact him as much as I probably should have. Yes, I still loved him, but boy was it hard to talk to him without thinking about Kara. And yeah, Kara and I were working out our differences, but it was a process. A *slow* process that might take years before it was finally resolved, but we were trying.

"Hi, Dad." A quick internal debate on how to go about what I wanted to ask before I dove right in with, "What's going on between you and Kara?"

He sighed heavily into the phone. "Have you talked to your mother?"

"About you? No."

He grunted. "Well, that's a shock. You know how she likes to gloat." A pause. "No, that's not fair. Cecilia's been understanding from the start, as much as it pains me to say it."

"What happened?" I asked. I couldn't keep the impatience out of my voice.

"Nothing's really *happened*," he said. "It's just . . ." I imagined him wheeling his hand in the air as he thought about it. "I'm old."

I couldn't help it, I grinned. "As dirt."

"Very funny," he said, though there was a smile in his voice. "You'll get here someday."

"Not for a very, very, *very* long time."

"Yeah, yeah." He sighed. "It's silly, and I didn't even realize what was happening until it was too late."

A strange sort of fear gripped me then. Could I truly be worried that my dad and Kara might break up? "Dad? What's going on?"

"I . . . It's . . ." He made a frustrated sound. "Kara wanted us to go to a concert together. Not only had I never heard of the band, I couldn't imagine myself going to a place that would be packed with people a quarter my age. I told her I wasn't interested, thinking she could just go with some friends. Little did I know that this was a sort of bucket list thing for her. She took it as me not caring about her, like I was, I don't know, ignoring her needs by not wanting to go."

It only took me a half a second to realize what band he was talking about. "She wanted to see Imagine Dragons, didn't she?" Kara had listened to almost nothing *but* since I'd known her.

"That's them," he said. "I might have put my foot in my mouth and said something about music these days not being as good as it was in my day. It was a joke, but I think I hit a nerve."

I closed my eyes as my anxiety ebbed. This was something they could get past. "Did she find someone to go with?" I asked, thinking that if not, it might be a good way for us to reconnect. I wasn't as big of an Imagine Dragons fan as Kara, but I didn't *dislike* them either. I was indifferent at best.

"I think so?" It came out as a question. "Honestly? I don't know. She hasn't talked to me about it since."

And she probably wouldn't until the concert was over. Then she'd tell Dad about how amazing it was and make him regret not going. It was the Kara way.

"If she found someone, she'll get over it and you two will be back to normal in no time," I said. "But if she ends up missing the concert because you refused to go with her, then she might never forgive you. She's been wanting to see them since she was in high school."

"I know that *now*. I wish someone would have said something to me before I all but belittled the band because I'm an old fart with no idea about hip new music."

I could have pointed out that Imagine Dragons wasn't exactly new, but Dad wouldn't know that. He'd stopped listening to anything "new" once he'd hit his twenties.

"I'd say you aren't *that* old, but I promised I'd never lie to you."

"Ha-ha." Deadpan. It was followed by a pause and a more sober, "There's something's up with you, Ash, isn't there? I can hear it in your voice."

Was there ever? But did I really want to tell Dad about my murdered blind date who wasn't actually murdered? About how he'd left me with the check? About my stalker? If that was even what he was?

Not in the slightest.

"It's Mom," I said instead.

"Oh boy. What'd she do now?"

I turned away from the window, not wanting to look at Branson Designs while talking about it. "I have these shirts. . . ." I went on to explain how Mom branded them and then tried to make me feel guilty for not being happy about it. "I don't understand her half the time."

"I'm not sure anyone ever will," he said. "But that's not it. There's something else going on."

"I'm just really busy." I bit my lower lip at the white lie. "There's nothing to worry about."

Dad was quiet for a long time. I think he was hoping I'd break down and tell him all about whatever was bugging me, but I held my ground. Dad and I were just beginning to repair our relationship. I didn't want to drag him into the mess of my life, even if he would do everything in his power to help me.

Besides, I wasn't even sure what was really going on.

"Okay," he said. "If you need me for anything . . ."

"I'll call. I promise."

"Good." He sighed. "I suppose I should go buy some flowers and chocolates."

"I'm not sure bribing Kara is going to work this time."

Dad chuckled. "Probably not, but it can't hurt."

"Tell me how it goes?"

"I will. Be careful, Ash. I'll see you soon, all right?"

"See you soon." I clicked off and then held my phone close to my chest. It wasn't quite a hug from Dad, but right then, it was close enough.

Chapter 10

A tiger-striped mammoth waddled its way over to me, sniffed my fingers, and then promptly began licking them.

"No, Herman," Sierra said from across the room where she was making a trio of rum and Cokes. "No human food."

"I'm kind of worried he thinks humans *are* food, not just what we're eating," Aaron said. He was lounging on the couch, one leg thrown over the armrest. His hair was out if its usual ponytail, leaving it to cascade across his shoulders like fine silk. No wonder Henna spent so much time petting his head; his hair looked so soft and inviting, I itched to reach out and touch it myself.

"He's been known to nibble, so I'd be careful, Ash." Sierra scooped up all three glasses and carried them to the coffee table in the middle of the room. "If you give him a nudge, he'll roll away."

I showed Herman my empty hands, which did indeed smell like pizza, and then shrugged. "All gone."

The super-chonk of a cat eyed me a moment longer, and then waddled over to Aaron to beg.

After the evening yoga class, I'd waited for Tyra to pick up the cats before I headed straight over to Sierra's apartment.

Aaron was already there, having stopped by since Henna was at work and he didn't know what to do with himself when she wasn't around. Every so often, he'd pick up his phone and would send her a quick text, often a simple—and likely perverted—emoji. I swear, the two of them were inseparable, even when they were apart.

"All right, Ash," Sierra said, sitting down in the chair across from me. "Lay it on us."

Aaron perked up. "She's doing what now?"

Sierra rolled her eyes at him. "You be quiet. I'm tallying up swat moments and reporting them to Henna. You're going to be battered and bruised by the end of the night if you keep it up."

Aaron smirked. "Sounds kinda fun, actually."

Sierra made a gagging sound before turning her attention back to me. "You said you saw Grady? Like, in the flesh, full-on face and all? Not just a glimpse in a dark room or something?"

I picked up my rum and Coke and took a sip. A grimace and I set it back down. Sierra, despite working at a bar, didn't seem to understand that it was rum *and* Coke. Not just rum and more rum.

"He was at Snoot's," I said. "I looked right at him and then followed him outside."

"Did you talk to him?" Aaron asked.

I made a seesaw gesture with my hand. "More like I yelled at him. When he saw me following him, he took off running. Why would he do that?"

"Because you were following him?" Aaron said, which caused Sierra to hold up a pair of fingers, as if indicating a new tally of Henna-smacks against him.

She dropped her hand and turned to me. "I hate to admit it, but dingbat here is right. He looks back and sees you coming at him, so why wouldn't he run? He abandoned you a few nights back, so maybe he thought you were out for revenge."

"Or maybe you saw someone else that looked like him," Aaron said. "Like a doppelganger or something?"

"A brother, perhaps," Sierra said. "He might not have known why you were chasing after him all hot and bothered."

Aaron opened his mouth, likely to say something smart-alecky, but snapped it closed again with a grin when Sierra shot him a warning glare.

"No, I'm almost positive it was him," I said, though now that it was a day later, I was beginning to wonder. No, I hadn't been drinking, but what if Grady did indeed have a brother who looked identical to him? Or, as Aaron said, a doppelganger. I'd only spent something like a half an hour with Grady, so it wasn't like I had his features and mannerisms memorized.

"This is like one of those crime shows I watched with Bri," Aaron said. Brianna was a big fan of crime shows, especially the foreign kind. "Girl meets guy, goes out and has a great night with him. Guy ends up dead. The next day, the girl is being stalked by said dead guy."

"How did it end?" Sierra asked.

Aaron took a drink and shrugged. "No clue. It was in German."

Herman, having given up on begging for food, jumped a half-inch off the ground in an ill-fated attempt to get up onto the couch next to Aaron. He dug his claws into the cushion, and pulled himself up with much kicking and wheeling of back feet. Aaron helped pull him up, and then Herman walked in a circle and fell over onto his side for a nap.

"You really should put him on a diet," I said, watching the cat with mild concern. "That's not healthy."

"Trust me, I have," Sierra said. "No matter what I do, he

seems to get rounder with every passing day. I swear he's got a secret stash of treats hidden around the house somewhere."

"More like an entire cow," Aaron said, stroking Herman, who began to purr. He sounded like a lawnmower.

"I really don't know what to think about this whole thing," I said, turning my focus back on my own concerns. "I've gotten to the point where I'm positive someone is following me and I don't know if he's involved in the murder or is just a big fan of yoga. I'm constantly looking over my shoulder, paranoid that someone is going to leap out at me at any moment. How could Grady have been murdered, yet still be walking around Cardinal Lake?" I pointed at Aaron when he opened his mouth. "And don't say 'zombie.'"

He snapped his mouth closed again.

"Maybe we're right and he had a brother," Sierra said. "And if it's a twin, it would explain the similarities between them, and why you thought you were chasing after Grady."

"I suppose it's possible," I said, though I wasn't feeling it. "It's just . . ." I scowled at my rum and Coke without taking a drink. "I caught up to him. I *spoke* to him. He was freaked out, sure, but that could have been because I'd caught him and he was afraid I was angry about dinner. But I'm positive it was the same guy. Not a twin. Not a doppelganger. The same guy."

"Maybe Grady wasn't the one who was murdered, but his brother was," Aaron said.

Sierra perked up at that. "It *would* explain a lot. Maybe someone killed this brother guy, thinking it was Grady. The police assume it was Grady since it was his place, but he'd been out on a date with you, so the killer got the brother instead."

"Yeah, but why would Grady show up at Snoot's days after his brother's murder, acting like nothing is wrong? And why wouldn't anyone be looking for the brother if he's the one who's dead? It doesn't make sense."

"Unless this Grady guy was the one who killed him and stole his identity," Aaron said.

I considered it. It *would* make sense, but I didn't find it logical. Sure, that sort of thing might work in the movies, but in real life? Someone would miss the brother, would be able to tell the difference between the two men, be it a family member or close friend. You couldn't just up and steal an identity like that, especially in a place like Cardinal Lake.

"This would be a whole lot easier if Grady had a social media profile," I grumbled. "Then I could, I don't know, look for pictures of him with family or something. Maybe then we'd know if he had a brother or not."

Sierra's brow furrowed. "You couldn't find him online?" She picked up her phone. "I swear I remember him talking about posting about Snoot's at some point."

"Not that I could find," I said, swirling the ice in my drink. "I found quite a few Grady Richardses, but none of them were *my* Grady." I frowned. "Not that he was mine. You know what I mean."

Aaron put his leg down as he sat forward. "Do you think someone could have deleted his social media profiles after killing him?"

"It's possible, I suppose," I said. "But that means they had access to it, which also makes it sound like it could be family."

"Which makes the whole brother-swap thing more likely," Aaron said, clearly warming up to the idea. "He wouldn't want there to be evidence lying around that he's not who he said he was."

"Found him," Sierra said. "I don't know if someone had deleted the profile when you went looking for it, but it's back now."

"What?" I stood and rounded the coffee table. Sierra offered me her phone. I took it and looked down at the profile on the screen. "That's not Grady." I handed the phone back. "That's another guy from out of town."

"What are you talking about?" Sierra asked. "This is Grady Richards, the guy I talked to at Snoot's."

Quite suddenly, I was finding it harder to breathe. "No, that's not Grady. It can't be." Because if it was . . .

"Ash, I'm telling you, this is Grady Richards." Realization seemed to smack her upside the head and her eyes widened. "Wait. You didn't go on a date with this guy?" She showed me her phone again, but I didn't need to see the profile picture to know the answer.

"No." I swallowed a lump the size of Herman that had formed in my throat. "I've never seen that man before in my life." Other than when I looked for Grady online and found that very same profile and dismissed it because it looked nothing like the man I'd had dinner with at Market Inn.

"So if that's Grady Richards . . ." Aaron said, nodding toward the phone.

Sierra finished his thought for him. "Who did you go out on a date with on Saturday night?"

It felt like my entire world had been turned upside down. The debate on who the real Grady Richards was didn't last long. Sierra had met the guy, had talked to him for weeks. He was right there in the photo. I was the one who'd met a stranger, a man who'd pretended to be Grady, but was someone else entirely.

Of course, that created a whole slew of new questions. How did this strange man know about my date with Grady? Did he have something to with Grady's death? Was that why he'd run when he saw me? Could he think that I know more than I do?

Was I in danger?

It was the last question that had Sierra and me pulling on our coats with plans to head to the police station to tell Chief

Dan Higgins about what we'd discovered. Aaron was due to meet Henna after her shift at work, so he didn't come with us, though he wished us luck.

As Sierra drove me to the Cardinal Lake police station, I mentally replayed every moment over the last few days, looking for clues I might have missed. Did the stranger say something over dinner that might tell me who he really was? What about the guy I thought was stalking me? Could he be involved?

No matter how hard I tried to come up with answers, I was at a loss. The only thing I felt somewhat sure of was that the man I'd had dinner with *had* to have had something to do with the real Grady's death. Nothing else made sense.

When we pulled into the police station lot, Officer Olivia Chase was just heading to her car after her shift. Her hair was down and she'd unbuttoned the top button of her uniform. She looked exhausted, but as soon as she saw us, she came over.

"What's going on, Ash?" she asked, looking me up and down. "Please tell me you haven't come across another body. I don't want to say you look like you've seen a ghost, but you're pale enough that you've got me worried here."

I shook my head. "No new bodies."

"But we need to talk to Chief Higgins right away," Sierra said. "We've discovered something that relates to his murder investigation."

Olivia frowned. "You weren't trying to solve his case on your own, now were you?"

"We were talking amongst ourselves when we realized something," I said. "Please, Olivia. It's important."

Olivia studied Sierra's face and then mine. Whatever she saw in my expression was enough for her because she turned to the station doors and led the way inside.

"Wait here," she said. "Dan's not going to be happy about

this since we're both off duty, but I'm sure he'll see you. Just give me a minute."

"Thank you, Olivia," I said. "I really do appreciate it."

She nodded once and then vanished down a hallway that I presumed led to Chief Higgins's office.

Sierra wound her arm through mine and clutched my hand the moment we were alone. I was trembling ever so slightly and couldn't seem to stop. I kept coming back to the thought that I might have gone on a date with a murderer. Higgins had said Grady was found next to an open planner. My name had been written on it, which would explain how the killer—if that's who I'd eaten dinner with—would have known my name. Chances were also good that he'd interrogated Grady, learned that Sierra had set us up together. Or maybe my stalker told him. I simply didn't know for sure, and *wouldn't* know until he was caught.

"You'll be okay," Sierra assured me. "I won't let anything happen to you."

I smiled at her and leaned my head against her shoulder. For as dire as things felt at that moment, I believed her.

Olivia returned a short time later, looking grim. She motioned for Sierra and me to follow her, which we did. She took us into the same small, stale room I'd talked to Higgins in a few days prior. Somehow, it felt far more claustrophobic now than it had before.

"He said he'll be right in. As expected, he's not happy." Olivia paused at the door, lowered her voice. "I'll wait outside in case you want to talk about it once you're done here, all right?"

I nodded and thanked her before she closed the door.

"Do you want me to do the talking?" Sierra asked. "I'm the one who knew the real Grady."

I thought about it, but shook my head. "No, I'd better do it. He'll want to know more about this other guy." Not that I knew anything. No wonder he'd been so vague when he'd talked about himself over dinner. "I can't believe I didn't put it together sooner."

"Why would you?" Sierra asked. "You were on a blind date. It was me who should have realized something was off when you said Grady was late and that he left you with the check. I never would have set you up with someone who would do a thing like that."

A knock at the door had us both falling silent. A moment later, Chief Higgins entered the room. His face was drawn, eyes heavy. He sat down as if his legs had been cut out from beneath him and placed his hands flat on the table between us.

"Officer Chase said you wanted to talk to me about the murder investigation," he said. "Please tell me you haven't been snooping."

"I haven't been snooping," I promised, with a silent "much." "But we *have* been talking about it."

Higgins grunted before gesturing for me to go on.

I glanced at Sierra, who gave me a subtle, reassuring nod, before I said, "I didn't go on a date with Grady Richards."

A scowl flashed across Higgins's face. "What are you talking about? Did you lie to me?"

"No, I didn't lie." I took a deep breath and then explained it as best I could, as fully as I could. I mentioned the guy I was thinking of as my stalker, told him about my running into this fake Grady at Snoot's. Higgins listened, teeth grinding, but he didn't interrupt.

When I finished, he heaved a sigh that seemed to deflate him. "So, you have no idea who you had dinner with?"

"None."

"But you think he might have killed Mr. Richards?"

I almost nodded, but caught myself. "Honestly? I have no clue. He didn't *seem* like a man who'd just killed someone when we ate. He was a little weird, sure, but the whole situation was strange. It was a blind date." As if that explained everything.

Higgins rubbed at his eyes, and then his temples. "Okay, describe your date to me again."

I did, but my description sounded about as generic as you could get. There were probably a hundred other guys who fit the description in Cardinal Lake alone. Probably double that.

"He talked to some people at Snoot's," I said. "Perhaps one of them could tell you more about him. Or, if he's a regular, maybe someone who works there knows him."

"I don't," Sierra said when Chief Higgins's eyes landed on her. "Well, I suppose I might, but I can't be sure until I see him."

Higgins drummed his fingers on the table. I could only imagine what was going through his head and none of it was good. All I seemed to be doing was making his job harder. First I told him I'd gone on a date with Grady Richards. Now I was telling him it was another guy, and that there might be a third guy involved, if my stalker was connected to it, which he might not be.

Eventually he stood with a tired groan. "Thank you for the information, Ash. Ms. Wahl. I appreciate you coming down here to let me know about this. I'll look into it."

"What if this imposter is the killer?" Sierra asked. "Shouldn't you have someone keep an eye on Ash? Make sure she's safe?"

"Describe the man you believe might be watching you," he asked me. Higgins listened, then said, "If we see anyone matching that description, you'll be the first to know. And Ash, if you see someone or something that doesn't seem right, call me or Officer Chase immediately. Don't play the hero when we're right here."

"I won't." I paused. "I mean, I won't play the hero. I *will* call."

"Good." Higgins crossed the room and opened the door.

Sierra and I stepped out into the hall and he followed us. "Good night, you two. Please be safe out there."

"Thank you." For as frustrating as Higgins's vendetta against my brother could be, he was a good cop and I knew he'd do his job.

Chief Higgins retreated to his office as Sierra and I left the police station. True to her word, Olivia was waiting for us just outside, blowing into her cupped hands.

"Everything taken care of?" she asked.

"It is." I considered telling her about it, but I was tired and just wanted to go home. "Thanks, Olivia. I'll call you soon and fill you in, okay?"

She studied me a long moment and then nodded. "You'd better. Evan would kill me if something were to happen to you and I could have prevented it."

"I'll keep her safe," Sierra said, flinging an arm around my shoulder. "Even if I have to move in with her to keep an eye on her."

With how I was feeling, that probably wasn't a bad idea, though I'd never admit it. Right then, the sentiment was enough.

We said our good nights and I collapsed into Sierra's car with a groan. I was both mentally and physically exhausted.

"We should do something about this," she said, climbing in behind the wheel. "Find out who this guy is and confront him."

"You want to confront a killer?"

"We don't know that he killed Grady," she said. "But I see your point." She tapped a finger on the steering wheel. "What if we just ask around about him? We could go to Snoot's, maybe the restaurant you ate at, see if someone knows something. We don't have to talk to this guy, but if we learn something, we could take it to the police and put an end to this whole mess before it gets out of hand."

I considered it, but right then, all I wanted to do was sleep.

"I'll think about it." I leaned back in my seat and closed my eyes.

Sierra didn't press. She started the car and was soon driving back to her apartment, leaving me to wallow in my own thoughts.

For as much as I wanted to put this whole murder investigation behind me, I knew it wouldn't be as easy as closing my eyes and wishing it away. I was going to have to do something.

I just hoped that something didn't end up causing the killer to decide to come after me next.

CHAPTER 11

I tapped my phone into my palm as Luna lounged on her perch by the window. She was keeping a close eye on me as I paced the room, as if she could feel my tension. They say that things are always clearer in the morning after a good night's sleep, yet I was as confused as ever. Maybe it was because I didn't sleep all that much, which kind of voided the whole "good night's sleep" part of the equation. Or maybe my confusion was due to the fact that I didn't have all the information and was running on sheer guesswork and paranoia.

Whatever the reason, I was desperate to talk to someone who could help, which was why I was considering calling Olivia Chase. She was a police officer, yet she was also family. She might know something about Grady's murder that Chief Higgins wouldn't—or couldn't—tell me. And, as family, she might be willing to go out of her way to find out something Higgins was keeping close to his chest, something that might tell me what he was thinking when it came to the murder.

But doing that might get her into trouble and cost Olivia her job. Was my ease of mind worth that?

Pocketing my phone, I decided it could wait. Besides, I was due at Shakes in less than an hour to meet with Drew. No, he wouldn't know anything about Grady, my family's possible stalker, or the mystery man who'd pretended to be Grady during our date. But he knew me better than almost anyone. If anyone could keep me from falling in the deep end, it would be Drew Hinton.

A tiny meow drew my attention to Luna, who was still on her perch. She cocked her head to the side, almost as if asking, "What's wrong?"

"I'm okay," I told her, stroking her head and back. "Maybe we can watch a movie together later. Popcorn and cat treats. Then perhaps a good romp around the apartment with a feather toy. Sound good?"

She stretched her paws out and laid her chin atop them. I took that as a yes.

That decided, I grabbed my purse and coat and headed for the door. I was going to be early, but I figured I could grab a table and get started on my coffee. I'd had a cup with breakfast and was already jonesing for another. I had a feeling I was going to need it to get through the rest of the day.

I stepped out into the hallway, mind a million miles away. A pounding next door caused me to jerk to an abrupt halt, but it wasn't Leon breaking something inside his apartment this time. It was the man with the bowling-ball build and too short arms that Leon had talked to in the lobby the other night.

"Hey, Leon? You there?" He pounded on the door. "It's Jake. We should talk before tomorrow night."

I closed and locked my door. When I turned toward the stairs, the man—Jake—was staring at me like he expected me to say something.

"He's not here," I said, giving in to the pressure. "He left for work early this morning." I noticed because, as I said before, I hadn't slept all that well and had been standing by the window with my morning coffee when he'd crossed the courtyard.

Jake frowned at the door before turning back to me. "Ah,

well. I suppose I'll have to catch him later tonight. You're Ash, right?"

I had a moment where my paranoia caused me to panic, thinking that this guy must have had something to do with Grady's death because how else would he know my name? Then I remembered that Leon had addressed me by name when I'd seen him in the lobby with Jake.

I took a breath and managed a smile I hoped didn't look too unhinged. "I am. I'm Leon's neighbor."

"I see that." He glanced at my door, eyes lingering on the 201, as if memorizing it. "You know Leon well?"

"Not really. Our schedules don't align much. Usually we just pass each other in the hall on our way in or out. We don't get to talk for more than a few words here or there."

Jake made a sound I couldn't quite interpret. "That's too bad. You look—" He cut himself off, raised both his hands, palms facing me. "Not my place to say, not my place."

A faint snort came from the other side of Edna's door, telling me she was listening to our conversation and that Jake's comment had struck her as funny.

"You're Leon's friend?" I asked, ignoring her. "I saw you two together, and since you have plans tonight?" My voice rose at the last, making it a question.

"Tomorrow. Not tonight."

"I see." I eased toward the stairs and motioned toward them as I did.

Jake, catching the hint, started walking with me. He spoke as we started downward. "Name's Jake Palmer. Leon and me are acquaintances. I'm not sure you could call us friends, but close enough, I suppose. We haunt the same places, have aligning interests. He's been known to scratch my back and I've done the same for him a time or two."

What does that even mean? I thought back to Leon and his limp and bandaged hand, at how Jake kept telling him that everything was taken care of, that Leon shouldn't do anything rash. I tried really hard not to make connections between Leon's injuries and Grady's death, but right then, with how my life was going, it was near impossible not to.

"What is it you two do together?" I asked, suddenly aware of how tight a space the stairwell could be, and how easy it would be for Jake to give me a shove and send me tumbling down the stairs. I picked up the pace.

"This and that." He chuckled. "You know how it is?"

No, I didn't, and at that point, I didn't want to ask.

Thankfully, we reached the lobby and I had an excuse to extract myself from the conversation. It was sunny outside, but cold. The light coming in through the glass door wasn't quite warm, yet I appreciated it anyway.

"I should get going," I said, jerking a thumb toward the door. "I'm meeting a friend. He's expecting me and if I don't show up soon, he might come looking for me."

Jake nodded, as if he completely understood. "Good luck with that." He rubbed at his chin, took a step toward me. "Leon hasn't talked to you about me at all? About what we do?"

I inched closer to the door. "Not a thing. Like I said, we don't really get to talk all that much."

That seemed to appease him. "All right then." He punctuated it with a clap that reverberated in the small lobby. "Maybe I'll see you around, Ash. Stay safe out there."

"Thank you. You too." I turned and hurried outside. Jake remained standing in the lobby, for which I was grateful. If he'd followed me outside, I might have screamed.

Calm down, Ash, I thought as I headed for my car. *Not everyone has something to do with Grady's murder.* But with the way I could feel Jake's eyes lingering on me as I walked away, it was hard not to imagine him murdering Grady in some odd sense of loyalty to Leon.

I didn't relax until I was safely ensconced in my car. I took a moment to make sure there were no silver cars parked nearby, and then I drove to Shakes, trying to regain some semblance of control. I knew I was losing it, that everything that was happening had me jumping to wild conclusions. Before long, I was going to start to suspect Edna and Pavan of killing Grady, just because they thought Leon had the hots for me and they wanted to pave the way for him to score a date.

The more I thought about it, the more I realized I was being stupid. Jake had no reason to kill Grady, especially for Leon, a guy he called a mere acquaintance. The most likely suspect was the guy who'd showed up for dinner in Grady's place, a guy who was, for all intents and purposes, a stranger to me.

Feeling calmer, I parked in the lot at Shakes and headed inside. The coffee shop was small and snug, with tables a smidge too close to one another for them to be private. They didn't sell food at Shakes, just coffee and coffee-related drinks. A pastry shop was located next door if you needed a bite to eat with your coffee, and they shared an outdoor seating area with Shakes, making it convenient to do just that. There were a few brave souls seated in the cold even now, hands wrapped around their steaming coffees as they chatted.

I, not being a masochist, spotted an empty table inside and draped my coat over a chair to claim it before heading to the counter to order. I opted for the Shakes specialty, the Quake, which was a triple-shot espresso with a squirt of vanilla. It was made to be extra potent and was sold in only one size: small. Anything more would probably be fatal.

My coffee arrived after only a short wait. I took a sip and immediately felt my heart rate increase. If anything would make up for my lack of sleep, a jolt of Shakes's best would.

I was headed back to my table when the door opened and Kara Daniels entered.

Conflicting emotions shot through me as our eyes met. There

was the instant jolt of an old friendship, along with the feeling of betrayal because of her falling for my dad. Everything from happiness to anger to frustration swirled through me in the span of a heartbeat. Joy, with a heathy dose of concern, won out and I found myself smiling as I approached her.

"Kara! It's good to see you. Is Dad here?"

"Ash!" She gave me a hug that had all those emotions zipping through me yet again. The whirlwind was enough to make me queasy. "Wayne's at home." Her gaze flickered to the counter and I could see the longing that passed over her face. Kara had always loved her coffee, possibly more than she loved anything.

"I'm over here." I nodded toward my table. "I'll let you order."

"Thanks. I'm dying for a latte."

Kara hurried to the counter and ordered, while I sat down, facing her. She didn't *seem* upset, but the Kara I knew was good at hiding her emotions. When she smiled at the cashier, her entire face lit up beneath the beanie she was wearing. She got her latte, dropped the change into the tip jar, and then walked over to join me.

"I can't stay long," she said, perching at the edge of her chair.

"That's all right. I'm meeting Drew in a few minutes."

Kara's eyes widened. "Drew? You two . . . ?"

"No. He's still with Ginny."

Kara actually appeared disappointed. As far as I knew, she and Ginny got along, but since Kara and I hadn't hung out since she'd started dating—and then, later, married—my dad, their relationship could have changed since then.

"You and Drew were always good together," she said. "I was surprised when you two broke up."

"We're still friends." I wasn't sure what else to say. I could tell her that I sometimes regretted breaking up with him, but that would make it sound like I wanted to get back together with Drew, which I didn't. It was complicated, which was, of course, a cop-out, but it is what it is. "I heard that you and Dad were having some trouble?"

Kara took a long drink from her cup before answering. "I don't know. It's just . . ." She fought for a word, seemed lost, so I helped her out.

"You wanted him to see Imagine Dragons with you."

She nodded, then made a face. "Stupid, isn't it? He doesn't listen to them, so why subject him to their music? I didn't mean to get mad, but I guess I kind of did." She sighed. "For the first time, I really felt our age difference." A pause. "That's not true. I've felt it before, but this time, it hit me differently. We don't like the same things. We grew up in different eras. You know what I mean?"

I did. And it was one of the things that had confused me the most when the two of them started dating. I mean, how does a girl who loved Imagine Dragons, who slept over at my place, watching corny movies until dawn, end up with my dad of all people? Who cares that he's kind and gentle and had spent much of his life putting up with Cecilia Branson and deserved to be happy. He was my *dad*!

"He didn't mean to upset you," I said.

"I know." Kara looked down at her latte, as if she might find answers there. "I know I overreacted, but it's as if it all hit me at once. All the differences. All the little things that I ignored before, things that aren't and never were important, suddenly made me start wondering if I'd made a mistake, that I'd leapt into a situation I didn't quite understand. I still love him, don't get me wrong, but are we right for each other? Truly?"

I had no answers for her, and was saved from having to come up with one when her watch beeped.

"Crap." She abruptly stood. "I'm sorry, Ash, but I've really got to go. I didn't mean to get all sappy on you."

"It's perfectly fine," I said, and I meant it. "Go. Let's talk soon, all right?"

Kara flashed me a smile, and then leaned down and gave me one of those one-armed hugs that were as awkward as they looked. "Of course. I'll call you." Her watched beeped again. She tapped it, gave me an exaggerated eye roll, and then she hurried out of Shakes, just as Drew waltzed through the door.

I waved, catching his eye. He shot me a thumbs-up, pointed to the counter, and then headed there to order. I watched him with a faint sense of regret. If I hadn't broken up with him, I wouldn't have gone on the blind date with Grady, which meant I wouldn't have been in this mess. Grady still might be dead, but at least I'd have nothing to do with it.

Or so I hoped.

The regret vanished almost as quickly as it had appeared. I'd done the right thing when I'd upended my entire life. I couldn't let one bad week make me regret the most important decision I'd ever made, the one that had finally allowed Ashley Cordelia Branson to just be *Ash*.

Drew was handed his coffee. He thanked the woman behind the counter, who watched him all the way over to where I sat before she turned away, fanning herself off. Drew always had that effect on women, which used to make me a little jealous. Now it was just cute. He sat down with a smile, oblivious to what was happening behind him.

"Hey, Ash," he said, taking a sip from his coffee and sighing in contentment. "I really needed this. It's chilly out there." He eyed me a moment and the smile faded. "Okay, what's wrong?"

"Is it that obvious?"

"You're glowering at your coffee like it turned into vodka and milk."

I made a face.

"Yeah, just like that." Drew leaned forward. "Tell me what's up."

I took a deep breath, thought about giving him some line about it being nothing and that I was overreacting, but when I opened my mouth, the whole thing just sort of spilled out. I told him about my blind date, how he'd up and left me with the check, and then how he later turned up dead, but not really, because someone else had pretended to be him during the date, all while my real date was being murdered in his own apartment. The whole thing took almost twenty minutes to get through, and when I finished, I felt both hollow and exhausted.

"Wow," Drew said as I wound down. "That's . . . a lot."

"Tell me about it. And when you add to it that I think someone has been following me—"

"Wait. What?" Drew sat up and looked around Shakes like he expected my stalker to be sitting there, watching us.

"He's not here now," I said. "And I might be imagining it, though I don't think I am because both Alexi and Hunter thought they were being followed too. Hunter thought it was Chief Higgins—"

"He thinks the *police chief* is following him?"

"Not him personally, no, but . . ." I frowned. "I don't think it's the police, not with Alexi and me having the same thing happening to us."

"Then who?"

I considered it, then shrugged. "No idea. Maybe the murderer is following me because he's afraid I know something."

Drew was shaking his head even before I'd finished the thought. "That doesn't make sense."

"What do you mean?"

"Why would you know something? You said your date didn't show? That it was some other guy who showed up?"

"Yeah. He pretended to be Grady."

"So, why follow you now? What could you possibly know?"

I opened my mouth, closed it again.

"Granted, you did go on the date, and you could identify the guy who was there, but if he isn't the killer, then what does the killer have to worry about?"

"What if my date *is* the killer?" I asked. "Maybe he's the one having me followed." Though, if that was the case, why had the guy I was thinking of as my stalker shown up at Market Inn during the date? Things weren't adding up and Drew could see it as clearly as I could.

"It's probably not related," he said. "I'm not saying it's not happening, but perhaps you're looking for connections where there aren't any. Maybe this guy you're seeing is there for some other reason. Maybe he's not following you at all."

I buried my head in my hands. "I feel like I'm going crazy," I said. "I was looking at my neighbor's friend like he might be a killer, and all he did was knock on a door and talk to me."

"Come here." Drew stood and rounded the table. I instinctively stood and let him wrap me in a hug that was as warm and comforting as I remembered from when we were dating. "Everything's going to work out."

"I know." My voice came out muffled.

"If you need me to help you in any way, just say the word."

I released him, stepped back. "Ginny won't like it."

He chuckled. "No, she won't, but she'll get over it. She understands that we're just friends, but can't help feeling jealous when we're together. She's working on it."

I had a brief flash of Ginny sitting in a therapy circle, telling everyone about how much she hated me and almost laughed. "I'll call you if I need you."

"Good." Drew picked up his coffee, checked his watch. "I need to pick Ginny up from her appointment. Be careful, Ash. And, like I said, call me the moment you need anything, okay?"

"I will," I promised him.

Drew started to walk away, paused. "I'm thinking you might want to find out more about this guy who showed up and pretended to be your date. If anyone seems suspicious enough to be a part of this whole thing, it's that guy." And then he was gone.

I sagged back into my chair and blew out a breath. Drew was right: fake Grady was a better suspect than Leon, Jake, and my maybe stalker. The guy had run from me for a reason, and it *had* to be about more than just him leaving me with the check, didn't it?

But was I truly ready to take Sierra up on her offer to go running around town, looking into a guy who might be a killer? Even if we didn't confront him directly, even if we took everything we learned to the police, the mere act of talking to people he knew might be enough to set him off. Was I willing to risk putting my friends in harm's way, just to find a killer?

Chapter 12

"Ash!" Pavan called from where he was standing with Edna outside her apartment door. "Ash! Come over here a moment."

I carried my two bags of cat supplies over to them. "What's going on?" I asked, setting the bags down, figuring that, with the two of them, I could be out there a while. Right then, a little bit of light local gossip might be just what I needed to improve my state of mind.

"It's Seo-Jun's birthday tomorrow." Pavan's entire face beamed when he said his wife's name. "She's going to be..." He trailed off with a grin. "Well, I suppose I shouldn't go around telling everyone *that* without her leave."

"A woman's age should never be revealed unless she is the one to say it," Edna said with a sharp nod. "Or maybe I'm just old-fashioned."

"You?" Pavan placed a hand over his heart. "Never, dear Edna. You shall be forever young."

"Tell that to my knees. And my back." She stretched her arms upward, which caused her entire body to sound off like popcorn. "My *everything*." She settled back to lean against the doorframe. "Don't worry, the both of you will get here someday."

Pavan patted her on the shoulder before turning back to me. "Seo-Jun wants a quiet birthday at home, which I, being the most amazing husband in the world, will provide for her. She doesn't want to deal with crowds of people, even if it's just a small group of friends. She likes her solitude, and I will give it to her, though I do feel slightly sad about it since I do love to show her off."

It was obvious Pavan was still madly in love with his wife. I wasn't sure how long they'd been together, but if I were to guess, I'd say it had to have been most of their lives. I couldn't imagine them apart, nor could I think of a more perfect match.

Well, unless you counted Aaron and Henna, which I absolutely did.

"Are you going to pamper her with bubble baths and chocolates?" I asked.

"Of course. But that is a typical day for us." He chuckled and then removed a long, thin black box from his back pocket. "But, since it's her birthday, I decided to get her something special." He handed the box over and motioned for me to open it.

Carefully, I did. Inside, surrounded by a black velvet material, was a necklace. The chain was silver in color, though I wasn't sure if it was made of the metal, or if it was of something else, like platinum. Not being a heavy jewelry wearer, I didn't know my metals all that well. Hanging from the chain was a purple gem that took my breath away.

"It's amethyst," Pavan explained. "It's the national gemstone of Korea. Seo-Jun has a necklace similar to this one that once belonged to her grandmother, but she never wears it because she's afraid of breaking it, or worse, losing it. This one, while not identical, is close enough that they could have been made by the same jeweler. Seo-Jun often brings out her grandmother's necklace whenever she's thinking of home and simply holds it in her hands. I'm hoping that, with this one, she can take home with her wherever she goes."

I blinked back a sudden tear. Jewelry was a popular choice of gift for women, but I didn't think that too many men put as much thought into the gift as Pavan had done for his wife.

"That's . . ." I sniffed, handed the box back lest I drop it.

"It's lovely," Edna finished for me.

I nodded my agreement.

Pavan looked at the necklace a long moment, a wistful smile on his face, and then closed the box before shoving it into his back pocket. "I'll tell you how it goes," he said. "I should get back upstairs before she realizes I snuck out while she took her afternoon nap."

"You do that," Edna said. "And tell Seo-Jun happy birthday for me."

"From me, too," I added.

"Of course, of course." Pavan headed for the stairs. "Don't expect to see me until Friday. I'm hoping to give her a *very* happy birthday." He winked, and then, with a chuckle, he was gone.

Edna and I watched him go.

"I don't know about you, but a nap sounds fantastic right about now," Edna said.

I picked up my bags with a yawn. "You're telling me."

Edna laughed. "You get some rest, Ash. You look as if you've been run ragged these last few days, though with that face of yours, you can pull it off." She patted my cheek. "If I don't get my beauty sleep, I'm liable to scare children." She leaned toward me. "Good thing there are hardly any children around here these days. Perhaps you could change that sometime in the near future?"

I gaped at her, which only caused her to laugh as she stepped inside her apartment and closed her door.

It took me a moment to recover from her comment, joke as it may be, before I carried Luna's fresh new toys and treats over to my apartment door. Jiggling things around, I fished out my keys and then paused to listen. No sounds were coming from Leon's apartment. Was he home? Still at work? It was still the early afternoon, so I assumed he was, but with how things had been going lately, I couldn't help but wonder.

Unlocking my door, I slipped inside my apartment and set the plastic bags on the table. The rattle of the bags had Luna's head popping up on her perch by the window. She stood and stretched, eyes never leaving the bags. She hopped down and immediately began winding her way around my ankles, meowing and purring up a storm.

"Hold on, hold on," I said with a laugh. "You have to give me a minute."

Luna already had a box full of cat toys, but whenever I felt down in the dumps, buying her new ones made me feel better. Sure, she'd play with these ones for an hour or so over the next couple of days, would lose the rattle balls under the sofa and chairs, would lick the catnip right out of her pickle-shaped catnip toy, and then would promptly forget about all of them in favor of the milk ring or some stray thread fallen from one of my older sweaters. But that was okay. With cats, it's expected for them to be fickle.

Playtime helped keep my mood from drifting back into paranoia. I only thought about Grady once, my presumed stalker twice, and they were fleeting thoughts. I had her jumping and doing near flips in the air, so much so that I was worried my downstairs neighbor might complain to our landlord, Ian.

Once Luna was panting from chasing her new feather toy around the living room, I lay down on the couch and closed my eyes. Without hesitation, she hopped up onto my stomach and curled up with a rapid series of purrs that soon leveled out and stopped as she started her catnap. Me? It took longer, but I was soon drifting off, mind finally at ease after a week of near-constant worry.

I was just about out when there was a pounding on my door. This wasn't a simple knock, but a full-fisted thump that sounded like whoever was out there was trying to knock the door off its hinges. Luna's head shot up, eyes wide, and then she leapt off me and sprinted down the hallway, toward the bedroom, to hide.

I sat up, mildly confused. My heart was hammering and my head was swimming from being jerked out of being oh so close to sleep.

There was a brief respite from the pounding as I tried to knock the cobwebs loose from my brain before it came again, harder this time. A name flashed through my head in that brief silence, one that seemed like the most likely culprit to my rude awakening.

Ginny.

This wouldn't be the first time she'd beat on my door after I'd spent time with Drew. I could sign a legally binding document proclaiming that I had no interest in dating Drew ever again, that she could keep him for all eternity, and she would insist that it was all some sort of ploy so that I could win him back.

I rubbed at my temples and considered lying back down to wait her out, but nothing would be gained by ignoring her. I stood and called out, "I'll be right there!" as I crossed the room to the door, smoothing down my hair as I went. The pounding didn't cease. In fact, it only seemed to grow more demanding at the sound of my voice.

This is going to be fun.

With a sigh, I unlocked my door and opened it, already talking. "Ginny, I—"

I never got to finish.

A blond woman who most definitely wasn't Ginny Riese lunged toward me the instant the door opened. A hand came down—open, thankfully—and struck me upside the head. I staggered back in surprise, hands going up to ward off further blows.

"You killed him! I know it's all because of you!" the woman cried. Her face was red, eyes puffy, as she followed me into my apartment, still swinging openhanded slaps at my face and head with every word. "It's. All. Your. Fault!"

I couldn't respond other than to cover my head with my arms as I backpedaled toward my couch. The woman continued to sob and shout as she swung at me. The blows hurt, but they weren't as forceful as they could be.

"It's not fair!" she wailed. "I did everything I could to make us happy and then *you*"—that was accompanied by an even harder slap—"came along and ruined everything!"

I took another step back and tripped over my own two feet. I fell backward, hitting hard on my keister, which only seemed to urge the woman on that much more. She leapt atop me, straddling me, and then started raining slaps down on me with both hands, one after the other, in a flurry I couldn't begin to intercept. Her purse fell from her shoulder, into the crook of her elbow, which took the force out of most of the blows, but it was still disorienting, especially since I'd never seen this woman before in my life.

"I don't know what—" I managed before a lucky blow caught me behind the ear. My head instantly started ringing, and my teeth just about snapped closed on my tongue. I decided it best not to try to talk until after her fury had subsided.

"Why would you do this to me?" she cried. "Just because I

made mistakes, it doesn't give you the right. It's not fair." Another good solid whack had me seeing stars.

"Ash?" Leon's voice cut through the ringing in my ears. A moment later, the woman was yanked from me, still sobbing, and with little to no resistance, as Leon pulled her from atop me. The woman said something completely incoherent and then buried her face against Leon's chest, heaving great big whooping sobs.

I sat up, shaken, but mostly unharmed. Nothing was broken and I wasn't bleeding, though my head was still ringing from that smack behind the ear. I used my couch to work my way to my feet, eyes never leaving the woman, just in case she broke from Leon's grasp and came at me again.

"It's all right, Kathryn," Leon was saying as he patted her on the back. "I'm here." He glanced at me. "Ash did nothing wrong. She didn't know." And then, again, "She didn't know."

Kathryn sniffed as her sobs began to subside. "Her name was in his planner. How couldn't she have *not* known?"

While I was afraid speaking might set her off again, I couldn't help myself. "You knew Grady Richards?"

Kathryn stiffened at the sound of my voice, but she didn't lunge at me. She swallowed, wiped at her eyes, and attempted to step back from Leon, but he held her tight. "I'm okay now," she told him. "You can let me go."

His brow furrowed as he looked to me. I nodded, so he reluctantly released her.

Kathryn took a deep breath as she ran her fingers through her hair. Her makeup was smeared from her tears. "Of course I knew Grady," she said once she was composed. "He was my husband."

I rocked back on my heels as if she *had* swung at me again. "Your *husband*?" It just wasn't computing in my head. "You're his wife?" Dumb question, I know, but I couldn't help it. I was flabbergasted and caught completely off guard.

Kathryn clenched her teeth, looked as if she wanted to throw herself at me again, before she deflated.

"You didn't know." It came out flat. "Why am I not surprised?" The laugh that followed was humorless. "Five years of my life, and this is what I get for it? I tried to do right by him, I really did, but I guess you can't really know someone. I didn't want to believe it, thought I was being stupid, and . . ." She trailed off, jammed the heels of her hands into her eyes. "This is too much."

"Kathryn . . ." Leon reached for her, but she jerked away before he could touch her.

"No. I . . . I just can't." She spun and without another word, she walked out of my apartment.

I stared after her, trying to piece everything together. Grady was married, lived outside Cardinal Lake, yet he had an apartment here in town, one I suspected his wife didn't know about. He went to Snoot's, talked to Sierra. Thinking him lonely, she sets him up with me, and, despite being married, he agrees.

A secret apartment. A blind date.

Was Grady Richards a serial cheater?

It made sense. Why else would he have an apartment that his wife didn't know about, in a town in which he didn't live? It would also explain how he'd ended up dead. If Kathryn had found out about his extracurricular activities, then she might have killed him in a fit of rage. Or, if he indeed was cheating on his wife with multiple women, perhaps one of them killed him once they realized he wasn't being exclusive to them. Or perhaps it was a disgruntled boyfriend. If Grady had hit on the wrong woman . . .

My gaze moved from my now-empty doorway to Leon.

No, I didn't think he was the disgruntled boyfriend. As far as I knew, Leon was single.

But he *had* called the woman Kathryn, which meant . . .

"You know her," I said, realization dawning.

Leon paled. "No." There was no force to the word.

"Yes, you do. You called her by her name."

Leon closed his eyes. When he swallowed, his Adam's apple bobbed like it was fighting to be free.

He's scared. But of what? That I'd discovered that he knew the wife of a murdered man? That didn't prove anything.

Did it?

"I don't know her," he said. "She . . ." He fought for the right word, seemed to be unable to grasp it. "I have nothing to do with any of this, Ash. You have to believe me."

Any of what? I wondered. The murder? Kathryn coming after me? "You know Grady Richards's wife. Did you know him?" A new thought. "Who is Jake?"

He ran his good hand over his mouth. I noted his other was no longer bandaged, though he still held it close to his body, as if he felt the need to protect it.

"I'm sorry, Ash," he said, taking a step toward the open doorway. "I really didn't think it would spill over on you like this. I should have said something before it went this far."

"Said what? What's going on, Leon?"

He shook his head. "I'm sorry."

And then, before I could stop him, he rushed out of my apartment, and into his own.

The urge to follow him and demand he talk to me was so strong, I took a step toward the door, but I remained in my apartment, still stinging from the flurry of slaps inflicted upon me by Grady's wife—no, his *widow*.

I closed my door with a soft click and leaned my head against the wood to cool the burning of my face. The welts would fade in minutes, but my concerns wouldn't. Leon knew Kathryn. That meant he knew Grady, or at least, knew of him. He lied about it to my face, even though I'd heard him say her name.

I had to know more.

I pushed away from the door and retrieved my phone. A single button press and it was ringing. As soon as I heard the click of it being answered, I was talking.

"Okay," I said. "Let's do this."

Sierra didn't even have to ask what I was talking about. "When do you want to start?"

I glanced down the hall to where Luna was peering at me from the bedroom doorway. She looked half scared out of her mind. I couldn't let that stand.

"How about now?" I asked.

"I'm on the way."

Chapter 13

"How do you want to do this, Ash?" Sierra asked from the front seat of her car. We were idling in the parking lot of Market Inn, and had been for the last ten minutes. When we'd arrived, neither of us had made a move to get out or said a word until now. We'd just sat there, staring at the door, as if we expected our answers to come waltzing out of them on their own.

"We should talk to Alan the waiter," I said. "Edward told me that Alan was the one who let Grady . . ." I scowled. ". . . let whoever it was I had dinner with out the back door. That means he knew him to some capacity because I don't think he would have done it if the imposter was a stranger to him."

"Okay, that sounds great and all, but what if he's not here?"

A perfectly reasonable question, one I hadn't considered. "Then I'll ask someone who might know where we can find him."

Of course, I doubted anyone working at Market Inn would up and tell me Alan's home address without good reason. If nothing else, maybe I could get one of them to call him and ask him if he'd see me. Or at least tell me when he next worked.

"Well," Sierra said, shutting off the engine. "If we're going to do this, we'd best get to it. Sunlight's a-wasting."

We climbed out of her car and started toward the doors of the restaurant. The wind had picked up and I could smell an incoming storm on the air. I huddled deep into my coat and hunched my shoulders against the cold. Sierra shivered next to me and shoved her hands into her jacket. The closer we came to the doors, the closer we moved to one another, and I'm not so sure the wind had anything to do with it.

Market Inn wasn't quite as crowded in the middle of a weekday as it was on the weekend, but it wasn't empty, either. A quick glance through the dining room showed me that over half the tables were full, though neither the imposter, nor my stalker, were amongst them. The only person I could see waiting on tables was a middle-aged woman who looked as if she was working only because she had to.

"What now?" Sierra asked, glancing around. "Do we just walk up to someone and start asking them questions about this waiter of yours? Or do we, I don't know, wait for something to happen?"

I answered her by approaching the hostess, who'd been lingering to the side of the room. She wiped her mouth with her hand as she approached. She was still chewing on something when she said, "I'm sorry about that. Let me find you two a seat."

"Actually, I was wondering if Alan is working tonight?" I asked her. "We'd like to be seated in his section if it's possible. He's an old friend."

The hostess seemed startled at first, and then she smiled. "Of course. Right this way."

"Smooth, Ash," Sierra whispered into my ear as we followed the hostess across the room to an empty table near where I'd had my fateful dinner date. We sat and Sierra immediately started perusing the menu the hostess had handed her.

"What are you doing?" I asked.

"I'm looking for something to eat," she said. "We're in a restaurant. We should blend in." A pause. "Besides, I haven't had dinner yet."

I rolled my eyes, but picked up a menu myself. My stomach was in knots, but, like Sierra, I hadn't eaten. And she was right; it was best to blend in and not appear conspicuous, though why anyone would care about us being there, I had no idea.

It took only a few minutes before Alan arrived, dressed much the same as he was four nights ago. He approached the table with some trepidation.

"Hello, Alan," I said, smiling up at him. "I'd like a Coke."

"I'll take one of those sparkling lemonade things," Sierra said. "The raspberry one."

"And once you're back with our drinks, I'd appreciate it if you took a few minutes to sit with us," I added. "I'd like to talk."

Alan didn't quite pale, but I could see the fear flash across his face when he nodded. "Of course. It'll be just a minute." He glanced around the room once, and then turned and speed-walked to the back.

"Think he'll run?" Sierra asked when he was gone.

"He'd better not." And it wasn't just because I was desperate to talk to him. I was thirsty. "But if he does, it'll tell us something."

"Tell us what, though? That he's worried you might attack him for helping the other guy out? We already know that he did that."

"Do I look like someone who'd attack another person?" I asked. When Sierra grinned, I narrowed my eyes at her. "Answer carefully."

"Of course you wouldn't, Ash." She tried to settle her features, but failed. "I mean, *I* haven't seen you throw down with anyone, so I suppose it's safe to assume you are like the rest of your family and prefer mind games over physical confrontations."

I would have been insulted if it hadn't been true. "Very funny, Sierra. Just you wait." I wagged a finger at her, which only caused her to laugh.

It took Alan less than two minutes to return with our drinks. He handed them over, and then sat, keeping a glass of water for himself. He took a long drink before saying, "I'm taking my break now so we have time to talk. If you're hungry, I can call Greta over." He motioned toward the unhappy waitress I'd noted earlier. "She can put the order in for you."

"Actually," Sierra said, eyes going back to the menu, "I think I'd like—"

"No, we're not here to eat," I said, cutting her off. "You know why we're here."

"I suppose I do." Alan fiddled with his water and then downed the rest of it in one go. "DK."

"DK?" I asked. "Is that the name of the guy I had dinner with Saturday night?"

Alan nodded. "It's what I've always called him."

I shared a look with Sierra. Already and we were getting somewhere.

"Okay," I said. "Tell me about DK."

Alan sighed and tapped his empty glass on the table before answering. "I don't know much, to be honest. He showed up out of the blue that night, looking for a job. I hadn't seen the guy for like five years before then. I hadn't even thought about him for that long, truth be told. He came in and acted like we were friends and that I could pull some strings for him. I mean, we went to a few shows together back when we were kids, but that's about it."

"But you *do* know him," Sierra said.

"*Knew*." Alan stressed the word with a finger jab at the

table. "I didn't even realize he was still living in Cardinal Lake until he showed up here begging for the job. I'd always figured he'd gotten himself into some sort of trouble or was scraping by out there somewhere. DK wasn't the reliable type, if you catch my meaning."

"And yet you let him sneak out the back door and abandon me with the check," I said. "That doesn't sound like something you'd do for a guy you barely knew."

Alan, for his part, appeared ashamed. "I know. But I was—" He shook his head, cut himself off. "No, there's no excuse for what I did. I shouldn't have done it, and for that, I'm sorry. When he sat down with you, I assumed you two knew one another. I didn't realize what was going on until after he'd cornered me in the back. I should have told him to grow a pair and tell you he didn't have the money for dinner."

"But you didn't," Sierra said.

"But I didn't." Alan looked down at his hands. "Call it loyalty to an old acquaintance. Call it stupidity. Whatever. I felt guilty as soon as I did it, which was why I gave you the discount. I probably should have paid for his meal myself, but it's not like I'm rolling in cash working here."

I studied Alan's face and all I saw was shame. "He called himself Grady Richards."

"I know."

"Grady Richards was murdered sometime that night."

Alan nodded, didn't speak.

"Could your friend have had something to do with his murder?"

"He's not my friend." A pause, and then Alan's shoulders sagged. "I wish I could tell you. I don't *think* he would do something like that, but like I said, I hardly know the guy anymore. He came in for a job, which would seem like an odd thing to do if you'd just killed someone, so I'm leaning toward no." He made a face. "It's not much of an endorsement of his character, I know, but he's too self-involved to risk himself like that."

"If he was here for a job, then how did he know Ash was here waiting for Grady?" Sierra asked.

"I couldn't tell you," Alan said. "DK has a way about him. He probably figured it out on his own, overheard you say something and pieced it together. He's not trustworthy and will do anything he thinks might benefit him. It's why we stopped hanging out all those years ago, and it's why I told him we didn't have an opening when, in fact, we do."

"Do you know his full name?" Sierra asked. "I doubt he's just DK."

"Dustin Kingsbury. He's always hated his first name, so we all called him DK. I think he still goes by it, but, like everything about the guy, I couldn't tell you for sure."

Dustin Kingsbury. I tested the name in my head, but it meant nothing to me. "Did DK know Grady?" I asked.

"I have no idea," Alan said. "You have to understand; I don't know DK anymore. He just showed up that night asking for the job. Other than that, we've had no contact for years. And, to be honest, if I never heard from him again, it would be too soon. The guy's been nothing but trouble ever since I've known him."

A few minutes later, we were back in Sierra's car with open to-go containers. No, we didn't have dinner, but we'd each scored a Market Inn dessert specialty—a hot fudge brownie with a caramel drizzle that tasted like heaven. Alan, feeling guilty no doubt, gave them to us free of charge before we'd left.

"Do you believe him?" Sierra asked between gooey bites.

I thought about it briefly, taking time to chew my own bite of brownie, before answering. "I guess I do. He's got no reason to lie."

"That means this DK character is innocent of murder, but is guilty of being a tool?"

I nearly choked on a bite of my brownie when I laughed. "Sounds like."

Sierra took another bite, considered it a moment, and then picked up her phone. She tapped something in, scanned the screen, and then with a nod to herself—and with one final bite of her brownie— she started her car and backed out of the parking space.

"Where are we going?" I asked, shoving my plastic spoon into the container with the remains of my brownie. For as good as it was, it was also rich enough to make me feel queasy after only a couple of bites, especially on a previously empty stomach.

Sierra glanced at me out of the corner of her eye and grinned. "Where else?" She motioned to her phone. "I found him."

"Found who?" I asked as I picked up her phone and took a look at the screen.

I should have guessed.

"Dustin Kingsbury," she said. Sure enough, his name, along with his home address, was still up on Sierra's phone. "You'd be surprised what you can find online these days. I figured we might as well pay the guy a visit, and see what he has to say for himself. What do we have to lose?"

"Are you sure we should be doing this?" I asked. We were sitting outside a small apartment complex not far from Snoot's and the lake. When I'd followed DK that night, he'd apparently been heading home.

"Why not?" Sierra asked. "We should get this DK guy's side of the story. Maybe we'll learn something."

"And what if we're wrong and he *is* a murderer?" I'd thought about it all the way over. Just because he was an opportunist, didn't mean he couldn't also be a killer. Yes, it was unlikely when I really thought about it, but that didn't make it impossible.

"If he is, I'm pretty sure he won't do anything with the both of us here."

"Pretty sure? That's hardly convincing."

Sierra shrugged, seemingly unworried.

"I should call Olivia," I said, removing my phone from my purse. "She'll know what to do and will know how best to handle DK if he turns aggressive."

"Ash"—Sierra put a hand on my wrist, forestalling my call—"think about it. Do you think he's going to talk to us if the police are here? Even if Olivia shows up in her PJs, she's got that policewoman vibe to her. She intimidates *me*."

I sighed, considered my phone a moment longer, and then return it to my purse. "I suppose you're right."

"I know I am. Let's just knock on the door, see if he's home, and then go from there. We'll learn a lot by how he reacts when he sees you."

"Yeah. And when he whips out a gun, we'll know he killed Grady and we can be given posthumous medals for solving the crime."

Sierra grinned. "It'll be something for the grandkids to talk about." A pause. "Though, I suppose we'd need kids first." And with that iota of wisdom, she climbed out of her car.

I groaned as I followed her. The wind was still high and dark clouds had rolled in, making for an ominous sign.

Sierra led the way to DK's door. She pointed at the peephole and then waved for me to stand off to the side so DK wouldn't be able to see me if he looked out of it. He lived on the ground floor of the complex, which had doors exposed to the elements. The only shelter came from the metal grating that led to the upper floors. If it were to rain, we'd end up just as soaked as if we were standing in the parking lot. It wasn't like my complex with a cozy indoor lobby and covered stairwells. Looking up, I noted the rust on the metal braces and was glad I didn't have to walk on them.

Once I was out of sight of the peephole, Sierra knocked on the door, plastering on a wide, friendly smile as she did. I could hear the creak of DK's floor as he—or someone he lived with—approached. There was a pause where I imagined DK peeking through the peephole, and then the door opened.

And there he was, my Grady Richards imposter. He was dressed in a button-up shirt that had once been nice, but repeated wearing had worn it thin around the shoulders. He had on jeans, with no shoes or socks, and was holding a sagging slice of pizza in one hand that had a single bite taken out of it.

"Well, hello there," he said, leaning against the doorframe. His voice was cheerful as he looked Sierra up and down. "What can I do for *you*?"

I shifted my stance, which drew his eye. His smile vanished like smoke, and instant panic washed across his face. There was a moment when it looked like he might try to run, and then his shoulders slumped and he uttered a simple, "Oh. Damn."

"Hi, DK," I said, making sure he understood that I knew his real name. "Mind if we come in for a few minutes?"

He glanced at Sierra, seemed to reassess the situation, and said, "Yeah, sure." He took a bite from his pizza. "There's enough for the two of you if you're hungry."

"I'm starved," Sierra said, leading the way inside. I followed with a roll of my eyes.

DK led the way through a tiny dining room and into a lightly furnished living room. An open pizza box sat on a battered wooden coffee table. Sierra immediately snatched up a slice of pepperoni pizza and took a huge bite. My stomach gave a faint grumble, but I ignored it.

"I suppose you should take a seat," DK said, flopping into a chair, leaving the couch open for Sierra and me. "Can't say I'm surprised to see you show up here after you chased after me like a lunatic the other night."

"You ran," I said, choosing to stand. Sierra opted to sit. It put her closer to the pizza box.

DK surprised me by laughing. "I suppose I did. I thought you were pissed at me about the whole date thing and that you might, I don't know, start wailing on me if I gave you the chance."

"I thought about it," I admitted. "You abandoned me at Market Inn. I get that you were taking advantage of the situation, but that didn't mean you had to bail on me. You could have told me you couldn't pay and I'd have taken care of it."

DK took a bite from his pizza before he tossed the rest of it into the box. "I feel bad about that, I guess."

You guess? I bit my tongue to keep from saying something nasty.

"Why pretend to be my date?" I asked. "Why not just be you?"

A flicker of regret passed over DK's face, then was gone. "I thought you might tell me to buzz off if I revealed I wasn't who you thought I was. You were waiting for someone, and it became clear to me that they weren't going to show. I decided to play a part, see if I could make it a win-win for the both of us."

"And yet, you left me there with the check. I don't call that a win."

"I didn't have money." Spoken with a dismissive shrug. "It's why I was there in the first place. I figured my old pal Alan might do me a favor and help pull me out of a bad situation. I owed a few people some cash and wanted to pay them back. They're not gangsters or anything like that, but you know how it is."

I didn't. "That's why you were at Snoot's that night," I said. "Paying them back."

He nodded. "Alan might not have gotten me a gig, but I

pulled a few other strings and landed myself a job. Paid my friends back, and I thought it was all behind me until you showed up."

A question flittered through the back of my mind. Had DK truly found a job? Or did he rob Grady Richards after killing him?

"Look." DK leaned forward, clasping his hands in front of him. "I'm sorry about leaving you hanging like that. When I sat down, I hadn't thought things through. About halfway through dinner, I realized you might expect me to pick up the check, and since I couldn't, I thought it better for the both of us to avoid the embarrassment."

"You could have just told her," Sierra said. "Ash is pretty gullible."

I shot her a dirty look before turning back to DK. "Grady Richards was murdered that night. How do we know you didn't kill him before taking his place as my date?"

DK's eyes widened. "Wait. You can't think I killed that dude, can you?" He looked from me to Sierra and back. "I was there for a job. I didn't even know the guy."

"But you knew about the date," I pointed out. "You knew Sierra had set it up."

"Yeah, because I overheard you tell that angry dude all about it." DK stood, raised both hands in a warding-off gesture. "I didn't kill anyone. Like I said, I'd never met this Grady guy before. I took advantage of you, and for that, I'm sorry. But I didn't kill anyone. I swear."

A part of me wanted to call him a liar because it would be easy. If DK killed Grady, took his place at dinner, then we had him. I could call Olivia or Chief Higgins, tell them where DK lived, and that would be that.

But for as much as I wished DK was the killer, I didn't believe it. Both his and Alan's stories aligned. And I hadn't seen an ounce of evidence that pointed to DK knowing Grady. He was just a jerk who took advantage of people. Killing them seemed beyond him.

Sierra and I left a short time later, with Sierra sneaking another slice of pizza on the way out. DK was in a near panic that we were going to accuse him of murder and begged us to leave his name out of it if we talked to the police. I could have let him off the hook and told him I believed him when he said he didn't know Grady, but I didn't. Call me petty, but I thought the worry would be a fitting punishment for him lying to me and leaving me with the check that night at Market Inn.

"What next?" Sierra asked once we were back in her car.

I thought about telling her to take me to Snoot's so I could ask around about DK's story there. We could also talk to some people about Grady. He wasn't a regular in the everyday visitor sense, but he had dined there often enough to get to know Sierra. That meant someone else might have talked to him, might have gotten to know the real Grady Richards and might know a reason as to why someone would want to kill him.

Thunder rumbled across the darkening sky, nixing that idea before it could fully form.

"Take me home," I said. "I need to figure out where to go from here." And call Chief Higgins. He wasn't going to be happy that I talked to DK, but at least it would be one more suspect he could axe from his list.

And considering what happened with Kathryn Richards in my apartment, one more he could add to it.

Chapter 14

I admit it: I chickened out.

I fully intended to sit down and call Chief Higgins the moment Sierra dropped me off at home. I went so far as to pick up my phone and look up the number to the police station, but when I hit dial, it wasn't Higgins I called.

It was Olivia.

I knew Chief Higgins would be angry with me and with the way the rain was pouring down outside, I wasn't up for a dressing down, so I took the easy route and told Olivia everything I'd learned since we'd last talked. She wasn't happy with me, but she listened and said she'd tell Higgins for me, and said she'd leave out what she could when it came to *how* I'd come across the information.

She'd made no promises.

When I went to bed that night, I was a mess of worry. Had I done the right thing in talking to Alan and DK? What was Kathryn Richards's plan for me? Was her showing up at my apartment and smacking me around enough for her? Could she have killed her husband after finding out about his cheating ways? And what did Leon have to do with any of it?

When I woke, and as I trudged my way through a morning

still damp from last night's rain, I was still churning over it. The stress was making me sick and I had no idea how to make myself feel any better short of having the police tell me they'd arrested Grady's murderer. Until then, I had a feeling I was going to be a wreck, which didn't bode well for a day packed full of yoga.

Still, I was determined to get through it. When I arrived at A Purrfect Pose to prep for the day, Tyra was already inside with the cats. I could see her moving around through the plate glass window.

But she wasn't the only one there.

George Wilkins stood outside the studio, staring at the tops of his shoes. He was dressed in jeans and a zipped-up heavy coat, which meant he wasn't there for yoga. He didn't look as I neared.

"George?" I asked once I was close enough to see the breath puffing from his mouth. "What are you doing here?"

"Hi, Ash." He scuffed his shoe on the sidewalk and then shoved his hands into his coat pockets, still looking anywhere but at me. "I just wanted to say again that I'm sorry about what happened the other day with Edward and that it will never happen again."

"You didn't need to come all the way down here to tell me that. I had a chance to talk to him." I frowned. "Has he contacted you? Edward stopped by a couple of days ago to explain himself to me and we worked through it."

Much to my relief, George nodded. I was half-afraid Edward was still hiding from his family—and the police. "He did. He told me everything, but that still doesn't make it right."

I rested my hand on George's shoulder. He tensed ever so slightly before relaxing into it. "I don't blame you for any of this," I told him, ducking my head so that he had no choice but to look me in the eye. "You can't control your cousin. I never thought you could."

"Yeah, but I was with him. I should have done more to stop him, said something before he made a scene." He made a frustrated sound. "I hate the fact that he caused you more stress than you deserve. And then when this whole murder thing blew up . . ." He jerked his hands from his pockets to throw them into the air, nearly hitting me as he did.

"I get it." And I did. George has admitted that he doesn't make friends easily, and since he considered me a friend, it had to be hard for him to think Edward might have ruined that friendship, even a little.

"But—"

I cut him off. "Really, George. While I wasn't thrilled about Edward getting angry like he did, his actions ended up being helpful."

George glanced at me askance.

"Because he walked off in a huff that night, he saw my date sneak out the back of Market Inn. He saw who let him out the back door. That led me to find out that my date, who really wasn't supposed to be my date, was an imposter who'd thought he could score a free meal."

George frowned at my less than stellar explanation. "What's that now?"

I told him about DK and Alan, and how it was likely that Grady was already dead long before Edward's drunken rant. "If Edward hadn't been lurking out back at the time, I might never have put it all together and the police would still be looking at the wrong man as their killer." Not that I knew who they suspected. Even Olivia wouldn't tell me something like that.

"Edward really helped you with all that?" George didn't sound convinced.

"He really did."

"Well, I'll be. . . ." George heaved a sigh. "And here I was thinking that Edward had made things worse for you."

"I won't say he made my life any easier," I said. "But he didn't make it harder. I understand what he was trying to do, and while I wasn't thrilled with his methods, I don't blame him for what he did."

George's demeanor changed then. Gone was the tentative, worried man. In its place was the George Wilkins I knew, a man who wasn't confident, but who wasn't afraid to step up and say what was on his mind. He might not realize it, but he and his cousin were a lot alike in that way.

"I guess I should get going," he said. "You've got a lot to do and I shouldn't be interrupting that because I'm feeling bad about myself."

"You aren't staying?" I asked, motioning toward the door. "I'm sure there'll be room for you if you wanted to join us."

"No, I've got a few things I should take care of." And from his tone, I imagined one of them was calling Edward. "I'll see you tomorrow, Ash. Normal time."

"All right, George. I'll see you then."

I unlocked A Purrfect Pose and slipped in through the front door as George walked away. Strangely, while nothing had been resolved during our conversation, I felt better than I had when I'd first arrived. Talking to friends did that, especially since I'd eased George's mind about his cousin. Strange how that works.

"Everything in order?" I asked Tyra, who'd just stepped out of the cat room when I'd entered.

"A to Z."

I took that as a yes. I peeked through the window, into the cat room, and noted that everything was indeed in place and the cats were in various stages of cat: napping, washing, eating, or playing. It made me realize how invaluable Tyra was becoming after only a couple of days on the job. Without her, I likely wouldn't have had a chance to talk to George, which meant he might still be standing out there, feeling like he'd somehow ruined my life.

It would be nice to have that more often.

"You know, I was thinking—" Before I could finish the thought, my phone rang. Glancing at the screen, I noted Kiersten's name. I showed it to Tyra, who made a face I interpreted as "You're in trouble now!" as I answered.

"Hey, Kiersten. Is everything okay?"

"You're not going to believe this, Ash!"

The excitement in Kiersten's voice could mean only one thing. "Harlan is giving up some of his cats?"

"The boys," Kiersten said. "Every single one of them. I'm to pick them up later today."

Tyra pointed toward the back door and waved. I shot her a thumbs-up as I said, "That's fantastic. Do you need me to come with you when you get them?"

Tyra grabbed her things and slipped out the back with one final wink and a wave. I'd have to talk to her about a permanent, more involved position at the studio some other time.

"No, I don't think that'll be necessary. I should be able to handle it. You don't know how much of a relief this is, Ash. I couldn't have done it without you."

I didn't agree, but decided to take the compliment anyway. "Tell me how it goes?"

"I will," Kiersten said. "These cats are going to put some immediate stress on our already full shelter, but long term, this is a huge win."

"Glad I could help."

We clicked off a few minutes later and I went about setting up. The day had just started and so far, things were going great. I'd eased George's mind about his cousin and Harlan had decided to give up his male cats. Now I just needed the police to show up and tell me they've arrested Grady's murderer and have it be someone I didn't know—or care about.

The first class of the day came and went so smoothly, I barely had to think about what I was doing. We flowed from one pose to the next, almost as if we'd rehearsed it. The cats were surprisingly tame, playfully batting dangling braids or rubbing up against trembling legs and arms, disrupting some of the more demanding poses, but no one was zooming around the place like their tails were on fire, which made for a rather sedate session.

The next class didn't go as smoothly as the first, thanks to Mrs. Samuel—a retired high school English teacher, who still preferred everyone call her Mrs. Samuel, rather than use her first name, Edith—having trouble with her knee and falling during the tree pose. She was okay, if not embarrassed, and class went on, with Mrs. Samuel mostly watching from the sidelines, along with a pair of sleepy felines who were content sharing her lap.

I was eating lunch in my office after the second class—yet another granola bar, which was becoming a habit I knew I should break—when my phone pinged with a text from Alexi.

Want to go to The Lounge with me tonight at nine? Have reservations, but Fiona had to bow out and Evan is staying home with the kids.

The Lakeside Lounge, most often referred to as simply The Lounge, wasn't lakeside exactly, but was close enough that the name didn't feel too egregious. It was also one of the most exclusive restaurants in all of Cardinal Lake. It wasn't black tie or anything like that, but reservations usually needed to be made weeks in advance, especially during the evening. You could sometimes sneak a meal in during the late afternoon when they first opened on weekdays, but even that wasn't a guarantee.

Do you even need to ask? I sent back, practically bouncing from my chair. I'd only been to The Lounge once, back when Drew and I were dating in high school. It was a pre-prom dinner where I ended up ordering the cheapest thing on the menu because the prices were about equal to the price of a new car. At least, to my teenaged eyes, they were.

Great. I'll pick you up. See you tonight!

I set my phone aside and then, anticipating the meal I was going to have later, I tossed the remains of my granola bar into the trash.

I was ravenous by the time Alexi and I pulled into the parking lot of The Lakeside Lounge. A large swimming pool sat behind the restaurant with tables situated around it where the highest-paying guests could go for a dip while waiting for their dinner to arrive. A trio of lifeguards were often on duty, though they weren't present now since the pool was drained and the tables empty due to the seasonally colder weather.

Bright lights lit up the front of the building where diners were headed inside, most dressed far more nicely than me in my jeans and sweater. Alexi, of course, looked like a million bucks, as she always did when she went out. If there was one thing Alexi got from our mother that I didn't, it was a taste for luxury.

"I can't believe Fiona didn't want to come to this," I said, mouth already watering.

"She didn't *not* want to," Alexi said. "Family drama kept her away."

"I can understand that." Though I'm not so sure I would have let anything keep me from coming to The Lounge if I'd had reservations. "We are the definition of family drama."

"More than anyone will ever know." Alexi grinned. "Do you have room for an appetizer?"

"I skipped lunch, so yeah. And I have room for dessert. And my meal. Maybe two of them."

She laughed. "Then let's have at it."

We got out of her car and made for the front doors. Even with reservations, we had to wait for the line to progress so we could get in. Alexi was wearing an elegant dress underneath her long black coat that left her legs exposed. I eased up closer to her to share our body heat so neither of us froze before appetizers could be served.

"Have you heard anything about . . . ?" She waved vaguely into the air. "Did they ever figure out what happened to that date of yours?"

I groaned. This wasn't the sort of pre-dinner talk I'd been hoping for, but I supposed it was inevitable. "I've learned a lot since we last spoke. When we sit down, I'll tell you everything. You're probably not going to believe half of it."

"Sounds juicy." She rubbed her hands together. "Can't wait."

The crowd outside the doors moved at a glacial pace. Between those of us trying to get in, and those who were leaving—many of whom were drunk or well on their way to it and wanted to stop and chat with every living soul they passed—it felt like an eternity before we neared the doors.

My stomach was grumbling so much from the smells wafting from The Lounge that I was contemplating the merits of fishing around in my purse for something to snack on, when Alexi bumped me with her elbow.

"Hey, Ash." Her voice sounded strange, causing my head to jerk up in alarm. "You see that guy over there?"

She didn't make an overt gesture or do much more than move her head slightly to her right. She didn't need to. As soon as I looked up, I saw him. Clean-shaved. Close-cropped hair.

My stalker.

"I see him." Even though there was no way he could have heard me from as far away as we were, I whispered it.

The man was trying to pretend he wasn't watching us, but it was kind of obvious considering he was standing off to the side of the parking lot, shoulders hunched in his coat, shooting us glances every few moments. He wasn't smoking. Wasn't doing anything but lurking, which made him stand out more than if he'd jumped in line behind us.

We shuffled forward a step, putting us next through the doors.

"That's the guy who's been watching me," Alexi said.

A flash of both excitement and worry shot through me. "Me too." If I'd ever questioned it before, I now knew for sure that this guy was stalking me. *Us.* "What do you want to do?"

Someone grumbled for us to move, but neither Alexi nor I paid them any mind.

The man jerked suddenly alert. He fumbled his phone from his front pocket and checked the screen. A frown, and then he looked over at us, seemed to realize we were watching him, and then spun on his heel and started walking back into the parking lot, away from The Lakeside Lounge and my waiting dinner.

"Let's go," Alexi said, stepping away from the door.

I didn't argue, but my stomach did. It let out a loud grumble of protest as we power-walked behind the retreating figure. He wasn't running, but he was making quick time as he tapped something into his phone. Once he was done with that, he pocketed it, and then climbed into a silver Subaru parked a few spots down from Alexi's car.

"What are we going to do?" I asked, and then had to scramble as Alexi got into her car and started the engine. "Are we following *him* now?"

"Why not?" she said, watching the rearview mirror. "He's been doing it to us."

Another complaint from my stomach, but I kept my mouth shut as Alexi put the car in reverse and backed out. Our stalker was already at the exit and was turning right. By the time Alexi reached the road, he was nothing but quickly retreating taillights.

I opened my mouth to tell her that we should just go back and eat, but she gunned the engine, jerking the wheel so hard, I think I left the entire contents of my lungs behind, as she shot around the corner, around a rusty SUV, and was soon trailing a few cars back from the silver Subaru.

"What are we going to do when he stops?" I asked when I could breathe again.

Alexi was silent a long moment before saying, "I suppose it depends on where he goes."

It didn't take long for us to find out.

We weren't there yet, but both Alexi and I knew exactly where our stalker was taking us within ten minutes of us leaving The Lounge. The landscape had become familiar to the point where I knew every turn in the road, every tree at the side of it. We passed houses where I'd gone trick-or-treating as a kid. Places where Alexi and I would go when we needed to get out of the house lest we say something that would get us grounded for life.

"You have got to be kidding me," Alexi muttered as the Subaru pulled into Mom's driveway. Our mutual stalker popped out of his car and rushed toward the door, never looking behind him. Alexi drove past as he entered the house, and then she turned around in the next driveway over before she finally parked beside him. She turned off the engine and we just sat there, staring at the front door.

"What now?" I asked. I was torn between wanting to rush inside and throw a hissy fit and just walking away. On one hand, I wanted to know why Mom had someone following her kids around—her *adult* kids. On the other hand, did I really? It was Mom; Cecilia Branson. This was exactly the sort of thing she would do, and, as usual, it would be solely for *her* benefit.

Alexi appeared to be fighting the same battle as she stared at the house. Unlike me, she worked at Branson Designs. If she got on Mom's bad side, she'd have to put up with her barbs all day, whereas I only had to deal with her every now and again.

"I can go in alone," I said, though I really didn't want to.

"No." Alexi opened her car door. "Let's get this over with."

We didn't bother knocking. We walked in on Cecilia sitting at her dining room table. The man who'd been watching us was standing across from her with a chastised look on his face I'm sure I'd worn a million times before when confronted with Mom's wrath.

Mom, when she saw us, didn't so much as bat an eye.

"Why?" It was Alexi who spoke. One word was all that was needed. Everyone knew exactly what she was asking.

Mom sighed and spun her mug of half-drank coffee on the table. "Alexandra Lee. Ashley Cordelia. Good evening to the both of you."

"Don't Alexandra Lee me," Alexi said, planting her hands on her hips. "Why was *he* following us?" She flung a hand toward the man.

Our stalker, for his part, flinched. He didn't look dangerous standing in my mom's dining room. He looked embarrassed. Scared, even.

Figuring that Alexi had things in hand, I slipped past the man and into the kitchen. I opened the fridge, found a leftover goat cheese and tomato baguette, and took it out with only a mild grimace. I didn't like goat cheese, but beggars couldn't be choosers.

"What on earth are you doing, Ashley?" Mom said, watching me.

I took a bite, chewed. "I haven't eaten."

"Don't change the subject," Alexi said. If anyone could get away with talking to Mom like that, it was her firstborn. "You had me worried about my safety! Not just me, but Ash too. And Hunter thought Chief Higgins was after him. He just about fled the state to get away from him."

Another dramatic sigh and then a dainty sip from her coffee before Mom spoke. "I needed to make sure none of you were into anything that might cause me trouble, *Reginald* included."

"Trouble?" Alexi was near to shouting now. "We might cause *you* trouble? What do you think you've been doing to us?"

"I didn't mean—" the man started, but was cut off by a dismissive wave of Mom's hand.

"Don't talk." She turned her steely gaze on Alexi. "I did not intend to cause anyone distress, but I needed to know what was going on in my children's lives. Reginald, much to my surprise, was the easiest to vet, while the two of you . . ." Her sigh was miffed. "I did what I had to do."

"I don't understand," Alexi said as I moved to stand next to her, still munching on the baguette, despite my distaste for the goat cheese. "Why would you have us followed? Why do you need to know what we're doing in our *private* lives?"

Mom tapped a nail on her mug, eyed it a long moment, and then met Alexi's eye. "Because I'm running for mayor."

I choked. Not just a little cough in surprise, but a full-on, suck-in-a-breath-full-of-bread-and-tomato-and-disgusting-cheese cough, and promptly get it lodged in my throat so that all I could manage was a tiny little half-gagged hack. I dropped the baguette and made distressed, choking sounds as I leaned against the nearest chair so I wouldn't fall.

My stalker, a man whose name I still had yet to learn, rushed over to where I was beginning to see stars, and wrapped his arms around me and squeezed. The clump of food instantly popped free.

"Really, Ashley," Mom said, disgust in her voice. "On my clean floor?"

"Sorry I nearly died," I said before turning to the man. "Thank you."

"It's the least I could do," he said before stepping back.

"Mayor?" Alexi demanded once I was no longer dying. "Of Cardinal Lake? Why is this the first I'm hearing of it?"

"It hasn't been announced yet," she said, as if that's a suitable enough reason as to why she wouldn't tell her family about her plans. "As soon as it is, the entire family is going to be placed under the microscope. You know that. It's why I had Solomon keep an eye on the three of you."

Solomon, I assumed, was the guy standing there, looking like he wanted to be anywhere else in the world but in Cecilia Branson's dining room. I didn't blame him; I didn't want to be there either.

Still, her confession brought a new host of questions to my mind. This guy, Solomon the Stalker, had been following me, watching me to make sure that I didn't ruin Mom's plans. I go on a blind date, but the guy never shows, someone else does. And . . . ? That's what I couldn't figure out, so I blurted the first question that came to mind.

"Did you have Solomon kill Grady?"

"What?" Mom rolled her eyes. "Please, Ashley. Why would I have him do such a thing?"

Because Grady was cheating on his wife? Because if he cheated on his wife with me, it put me and the family in a bad light?

Of course, if I'd really thought about it, wouldn't Mom being connected to a murderer be far worse than me being someone's side piece?

"What's going to happen with Branson Designs?" Alexi asked. "If you're the mayor of Cardinal Lake, you can't run a business."

Mom folded her hands on the table in front of her. "I was thinking you would take over the day-to-day operations until my terms are complete, Alexandra." Terms. Plural. Leave it to Cecilia Branson to assume she would be not just be elected, but more than once. "With assistance from Claudia, of course."

Alexi's mouth slowly unhinged until she was gaping.

"Not you too," Mom said with a displeased sigh. "I swear the two of you make everything overly dramatic. It would only be a temporary position, but one that would last years. Once I decided it was time to step down, I'd reassume my place at the head of the company. It'll all be in the contract."

"The contract?" Alexi asked, still so dumbfounded, she'd resorted to asking Ash-quality questions.

"Yes, the contract. Solomon will be drawing it up shortly."

I glanced at Solomon the Stalker. Was he Solomon the Lawyer as well?

"Here's the deal," Mom said, putting on a businesslike tone. "Alexandra will take over Branson Designs in my absence. Reginald will . . . well, he'll do his own thing as he always does. I've made sure that this new child of his will be taken care of, even if his mother leaves the state as she has indicated she might. I won't have a grandchild of mine go in need."

My brain immediately questioned whether Mom was the reason Lita was thinking of moving to Maine, but smartly decided not to ask. "And what about me?" I asked instead.

"I suppose I'll honor your wishes and remove the Branson Designs branding from your shirts, Ashley." She said it like she was giving up her house and fortune to me. "I would appreciate it if you at least advertised where you got them from, but I assume, like Reginald, you'll do as you please."

A ringing endorsement it was not, but I'd take it. "Thank you."

Mom nodded, sipped at her coffee. "Now, if there isn't anything else, Mr. Justice and I have much left to discuss."

Mr. Justice—Solomon—bowed his head, face reddening at the mention of his name. How I ever thought this man could be a killer, I'll never know. The guy, despite following me, had been timid from the start.

Dismissed, Alexi and I left. Alexi moved as if in a dream, stunned by the revelation that she might soon be running an entire company, albeit temporarily. We all figured that she would take over Branson Designs eventually—likely when Mom passed away because I could never see her retire—but to have it happen so soon, must have been a shock.

"Claudia isn't going to be happy," I said, climbing into the car next to her.

"Neither will Uncle Cliffton." Alexi leaned back into her seat and closed her eyes. "I'm not sure if I am either. She never even asked me if this was something I wanted!"

Which was a Cecilia Branson thing to do if ever there was one. "You'll do great, Alexi," I said. "And I bet Juniper and the others will be thrilled not to have Mom breathing down their necks so much."

Alexi groaned, but nodded. "You're probably right." She glanced at her watch, frowned. "We missed our reservations. I can still take us out somewhere if you want to grab a bite to eat."

I shook my head and rubbed at my throat, which was still a little sore. "I think I'm done with food for the day. I just want to go home."

Alexi didn't press the point. She backed out of Mom's driveway, and with one last lingering look toward the door, she drove me home as requested.

Chapter 15

You'd think that with everything happening, sleep would have been difficult, but that night, I slept, as they say, like a baby. There were no strange sounds coming from next door, and there were no late-night excursions from Leon. I'd lain in bed, listening to his TV through my bedroom wall, and when it clicked off, nothing but silence followed. I'd drifted off soon after and didn't wake until my alarm went off the following morning.

Feeling refreshed, I zipped through my morning routine and was practically skipping as I stepped out into the hall, apple in hand. Pavan and Edna were already up and chatting with one another outside her door. Pavan was still in his pajamas, and was holding a mug of steaming coffee that looked suspiciously like one of Edna's mugs. Edna's hands were empty.

"Ash!" Pavan said, eyes lighting up. "How are you doing this fine Friday morning?"

"Hi, Pavan. Edna. I'm doing pretty good, all things considered. I take it your gift to Seo-Jun went well?"

"It went fantastically!" Coffee sloshed from Pavan's mug as he gestured, barely missing his hand. I don't think he even noticed. "She was ecstatic. Thrilled. And, shall I add, quite appreciative?"

"They just finished celebrating," Edna said with a nudge to Pavan's ribs with her elbow.

He grinned, though I noted the flush running up his neck. "We had a rather pleasant day. I cooked all three meals for her, each one of her favorites, and let her choose how else to spend our time. She, of course, chose to stay inside and read, which I was more than willing to allow her."

Edna snorted, and then steadied her face when Pavan glanced at her.

"It sounds nice," I said. "I'm glad you had fun."

Edna opened her mouth, likely to say something that should never cross an older lady's lips, but Pavan cut her off. "We did, we did. Perhaps you can stop by sometime soon, Ash. We'd love to have you over for dinner."

"I'd like that," I said. The last time I'd tried to have dinner with the Patel family, I'd only made it inside the door before I had to leave to check on A Purrfect Pose when the alarm system went off. "But for now, I should run." I tapped my Fitbit for emphasis.

"Go, go." Pavan shooed me away, spilling more coffee as he did. Edna used a slipper to mop it up. "I wouldn't want to keep you. Besides, I want to wake Seo-Jun up with breakfast in bed. Just because her birthday was yesterday, it doesn't mean I should stop treating her like she's my everything."

"Have a good day, Ash," Edna said, resting a hand on Pavan's shoulder. "We should catch up sometime and talk." Her gaze flickered to Leon's door and, for a brief instant, the worries that I might be living next to a killer—or someone connected to one—resurfaced.

"We should," I told her before I waved and was on my way.

Since A Purrfect Pose was only a short hike, and since I was feeling pretty good, I decided to brave the chilly morning and walk. My nose instantly started running and my cheeks burned as I puffed my way down the sidewalk. The weather report had said it was going to be warmer today than it had been over the last few days, but the temperature had yet to start to rise.

When A Purrfect Pose came into view a few minutes later, I noticed two people were standing outside the front door. My gut tightened when I realized that I knew them both, and that their presence together couldn't mean anything good for me or my studio.

Olivia Chase was standing with her arms crossed, in full uniform, a grim expression on her face as she talked to Jordan Allen Leslie, who was gesturing wildly, despite the fact he was holding his dog, Ginger, under one arm. The dog, for her part, was enjoying the ride, tongue lolling out of her mouth as she panted in time with J. Allen's rant.

I could hear him long before either of them saw me coming.

"You don't understand," J. Allen wailed in his high-pitched, piping whine of a voice. "Each day that this place remains next to mine is another day of lost revenue. I've seen it with my own eyes! People come by with their pups and take one look at the cats next door, and move on. They know the *smell* of them will upset their babies. And you should go into the alley and have a sniff! It reeks of used litter. I can't even open my back door to take out the trash lest I send my customers into a frenzy from the scent of it."

"Mr. Leslie—" Olivia began, but J. Allen rolled right over her.

"All I'm asking is that you cite her. Do it a few times and she'll move her business somewhere that won't disrupt my own, I'm sure of it. Why can't she move her studio out next to the animal shelter where the cats come from anyway? I'm sure her family would help her out and pay for the building of a brand-new studio where the cats could yowl all night without anyone having to listen to it. She'd be close to the college where she could recruit more customers at her leisure. You know how those kids are. They love yoga. It would be a perfect fit!"

Olivia started to say something else—probably pointing out that she herself was part of my family and that Cecilia Branson would in no way help me open a new studio—when she spotted me. She shifted subtly, which was enough to draw J. Allen's eye.

"I can't do it anymore, Ash!" he shouted, pointing Ginger at me like she was a weapon. A single bark was the only shot fired. "You have people coming in and out at all hours of the morning. The cats are loud and they *smell*. Do you know how long it took me to get the reek out of my back room after you made that mess the other day?"

"When *I* made the mess?" I asked, coming to a stop next to them, arms crossed, mirroring Olivia's own stance. "You mean when you threw dirty dog water at my back door, just as I came walking out of it?"

"Well, that's not exactly what happened."

"It isn't?" I asked, an expression of mock surprise on my face. "Why, I distinctly recall getting a face-full of filthy water. And, if my memory serves me correctly, you were the one carrying the bucket."

J. Allen sputtered, shot a nervous look at Olivia, who merely asked, "Well?"

"It . . . I . . ." He narrowed his eyes. "Don't try to turn this back on me, Ash. You know as well as I do that you're responsible for most of what happens around here."

"I haven't done anything, *Jordan*." I couldn't help it. He was getting on my last nerve and was ruining a morning that had started out looking promising. "You're the one who was dumping water outside my door. You're the one who has been disruptive." I paused. "Did you ever get your drains fixed? I don't recall ever seeing a plumber."

J. Allen pulled Ginger close under his chin. She immediately started licking it. "Turns out I didn't need one," he muttered past her tongue.

"What was that?" I asked.

He turned to Olivia. "You can't allow her to do this to me."

"To do what, Mr. Leslie?" Olivia asked. "Did you have a problem with your drains or not?"

Quite suddenly, J. Allen looked like a man trapped. His eyes darted from left to right and his left foot started tapping at a rapid pace on the sidewalk. "You see, there *was* dog hair trapped in the drains, which caused them to back up. After some deliberation, I decided to fix it myself. It took hours for me to tug it all free. I got my hands dirty for this, all because Ash couldn't handle a little water outside her alleyway door."

"Were the drains completely clogged?" Olivia asked. Like me, she detected deception in J. Allen's tone.

He took a step back toward Bark and Style. "Define 'completely.'"

"Did the drains work or not?" Olivia pressed.

"They were running slow," he said. "It took *minutes* for them to drain, which meant I had to wait between sessions when I was busy. Dumping the buckets was quicker and allowed me to get to my clients sooner."

"But dumping the buckets outside Ash's door wasn't necessary, was it, Mr. Allen?" Olivia asked. "You could have dumped the water elsewhere, allowing for the both of you to conduct business without bothering the other, correct?"

J. Allen's jaw worked as he looked from me to Olivia and back again. Finally he found some of his outrage again and jabbed a finger at Olivia. "You are taking her side because of your family connection! The law has nothing to do with any of it. I want someone who will listen to me."

Olivia sighed. "If you want to make a formal complaint, feel free to call the station, but if your drains weren't clogged, and if we discover you lied about needing to dump the water at Ash's back door, then we'll have to cite *you*."

It was like she punched him on the chin. J. Allen staggered back a step, pulling Ginger in so tight to his body, it looked like he was afraid we might try to steal her from him. "You wouldn't *dare*."

Olivia shrugged, leaving him to determine what she would or wouldn't dare to do on his own.

He decided not to press the issue further. J. Allen made a frustrated sound and turned his back on us. "Let's go, Ginger. They were never going to listen to us anyway."

Both Olivia and I watched him march through the front door of Bark and Style and out of sight before she turned to face me with a heavy sigh.

"Thanks for your help," I said. "I can't believe he called you down here for this. He had to know you'd poke holes in his story."

"Actually, Ash, I'm not here because of J. Allen."

Uh-oh. "You're not?"

"No, I'm not." Olivia shivered, glanced toward the front door of my studio where it was warm.

"We can go inside," I said, taking a step that way. "Tyra's probably already there, setting up for the day. She won't interrupt us."

"No, this won't take long." She rubbed her hands together, shot one more look at the door, and then turned to face me. "It's about Dan's murder investigation."

Of course it was. "If Chief Higgins wants to talk to me—"

"It's the opposite, actually," Olivia cut in. "He's upset with you, Ash. He doesn't like that you're out there, poking around in his investigation."

"I'm not poking," I said, knowing that was exactly what I'd been doing.

Olivia gave me a flat look before continuing. "He appreciates that you contacted me and filled me in with what you learned, but he has requested that you cease talking to anyone involved with the murder victim until we have solved the case." And by requested, I'm positive the word he'd used was more akin to "demanded."

"I can do that. But . . ." I made a face.

Olivia closed her eyes, took a deep breath, and then let it out with a huff and an "Out with it, Ash."

"Did Chief Higgins ever tell you about a guy I thought might be stalking me and my family?"

"He did." She narrowed her eyes. "Are you telling me he *wasn't* stalking you?"

"Well . . ." I drew out the word, and then launched into how Mom had hired him, leaving out the bit about her running for mayor because it wasn't my place to say it.

Olivia listened, an incredulous look on her face. When I was done, she blew out a breath and shook her head. "You're telling me that this stalker you had us thinking might be our killer was actually a man hired by Cecilia Branson to keep tabs on her children?"

"Yep."

"You're sure about this?"

"Talked to him in Mom's dining room myself."

"That means he had nothing to do with Grady Richards's murder."

I made a seesaw motion with my hand. "I don't *think* he does. At least, I can't come up with a reason why he would kill him."

Olivia sighed and rubbed at the corners of her eyes. "Is there anything else you need to tell me before I go back to Dan? He's currently out looking for this guy you said was watching you, and when I tell him that he's on the wrong trail . . ."

I winced. "Sorry about that. I just found out myself."

I didn't envy Olivia having to tell Chief Higgins that he was following up on a bad lead. He was an intimidating man, though I'd often been told—and seen—that he's really not that bad of a guy. He was also good at his job, which meant he'd quickly get back on the right track in his murder investigation, despite my interference.

I hoped.

"All right," Olivia said. "I'll tell Dan. This might sound rude, and I don't mean it to be, but I really don't want to hear from you about any of this again, Ash. I know you're trying to help, but all you've done is cause chaos. A tip here or there about what you saw when you went to dinner was fine, but the rest of it . . ." She made a vague gesture. "It's not helping."

"I'm sorry," I said. I almost added, "I was just trying to help," but she'd already established that, despite my intentions, I was only making things harder on the police. It made me wonder: If I'd never gone to Higgins in the first place, would they have caught the murderer by now?

"I know you've got to get in there to get set up for the day, so I won't keep you any longer." Olivia started to walk away, but paused. "We need to get together soon. Alexi, Evan, the kids. It's been too long."

"It has," I agreed.

Olivia hesitated a moment longer before she nodded to herself and walked away. I headed inside where Tyra was already done getting the cats settled. She was out the door and on her way to school with a hearty goodbye within minutes of me entering, which meant another day and I'd still yet to ask her about making her job at A Purrfect Pose a more permanent—and more involved—one.

I tried not to think too much about Olivia and what my interference had caused as I readied myself for class, but it was hard not to. While most every other lead I'd given the police had turned out to be a bad one, my interaction with Kathryn felt more important. If Grady was indeed cheating on her—and since he'd agreed to a date with me, I found it likely—then she would be understandably angry. That was obvious with how she'd come after me in my own apartment.

If Leon hadn't been there, how far would she have gone with her attack on me? Would she have said something incriminating? Admitted to murdering her husband, perhaps? There's no way Chief Higgins could be mad at me about my interaction with Kathryn since I hadn't asked her to show up at my apartment door.

But if I were to seek her out and talk to her again . . .

I shelved the thought as I opened the doors to the Friday morning class. I was hoping to talk to George again to put any suspicions about his cousin Edward to rest once and for all, but much to my dismay, he didn't show. I even waited to start class, just in case he showed up late, before giving in and walking away from the door. It was strange not having George or Lulu there. They'd become such a permanent fixture to the Friday morning session, it felt almost blasphemous to start without them. The other students noticed as well, and what was usually a pretty upbeat class turned out rather bland.

He'll show, I told myself as I prepped for the next class. If there was one thing I could count on, it would be George Wilkins holding himself to his word.

George never showed.

I knew I shouldn't be worried, but I couldn't help it. A man had been murdered, a man who was peripherally connected to me. And now, another man I knew, a man who'd appeared during my dinner date with Grady, hadn't shown up for his usual yoga class, a class he'd promised he'd be at.

My mind started making connections it had no business making, and I was soon an absolute wreck, worried that the killer had gone after George because he knew or had seen too much.

I was glad that Friday sessions ended by noon because if I had to go through another class, wondering if something happened to George, I'd lose it.

As soon as the last student was out the door, I scribbled a note to Tyra, slapped it on the kitty room door, and then I all but ran home. I knew I was overreacting and that George likely had a perfectly good explanation as to why he never showed up, but I kept imagining him fighting for his life against a killer with a vendetta against me. First it was Edward. Then DK. Then Grady himself, somehow back from the dead.

As soon as I was through my apartment doors, I had my phone in hand. I checked George's number twice, and then called, fully expecting it to go to voicemail.

Instead, he answered on the second ring.

"Hi, Ash," he said, sounding mildly confused. "What can I do for you?"

I sagged down onto my couch as my legs went weak. Luna immediately took advantage and hopped up onto my lap. "George. You're okay."

A pause. "Why wouldn't I be?"

"You didn't show up for class and I thought . . ." I trailed off. What did I think exactly? Now that I was sitting down, talking to him, my worries seemed as irrational as I knew they were.

George could have laughed at me. He could have gotten irritated that I'd assumed that something had happened to him and that he couldn't take care of himself. The man had a life, one I wasn't privy to. As far as I knew, he'd had a date. Or perhaps a relative had fallen ill. Or . . . well, there was any number of reasons why he could have missed his yoga class, and yet I'd immediately thought the worst.

"I'm sorry," he said instead. "I should have called and let you know I wouldn't be there."

I closed my eyes, cursed myself for jumping to conclusions. "No, it's all right. I've had a week and I'm letting it get to me."

"I get that," he said. "I had every intention of being there, but Lulu called this morning and asked me to come over."

A new worry had me sitting up straight. "Is she okay?"

"She's fine. Everything's fine." Was that a smile in his voice? "I didn't think twice. We had a rather nice chat, to be honest. She was sad she had to miss class, and said so repeatedly, but did say that next week things will be back to normal." A pause, and then, "I'll be there too."

"That's good to hear." Curiosity had me wanting to ask why Lulu wanted him to come over, but I didn't pry. Not about that, anyway. "Did you talk to Edward, by chance?"

"I did." Relief filled George's voice. "He actually apologized to me, which is something I never expected out of him. We're getting together later tonight to talk things over."

"I hope you work everything out," I said.

"Me too, Ash. Me too."

I hung up a moment later, feeling like a fool. Grady's murder had me jumping at ghosts and if I kept it up, I was going to make myself sick with it.

"I think we should stay in and watch a movie," I told Luna, picking up the remote. "For real this time. Popcorn and treats and everything."

And that's exactly what we did.

I spent the next two hours with a movie that wasn't worth my time, but at least had kept me from irrational worry about my friends. Luna spent half the movie on my lap, the other half peering out the window from atop her perch, having gotten bored of the action flick long before it was over.

After the movie, I read. Then I played with Luna for a little while before reading some more. I kept expecting a call from Chief Higgins or Olivia at any moment, but it never came. I hope that meant he wasn't mad about my stalker not being the killer. Or maybe he was. Whatever.

I lounged around the house all day, and was considering calling it an early night when a loud voice echoed in the hall outside my apartment door. A moment later, Leon's door opened and a brief, muffled conversation took place.

I got up and moved to my own door, pressing my eye to the peephole. I'd recognized that voice, and was curious. I couldn't make out much more than a vague outline just barely within my peephole's range, but I knew who it was.

"You got what you wanted," Jake said. "We both did. Let's not waste this opportunity by sulking."

"I'm not sulking. It doesn't feel right," Leon said. "Not after—"

"Don't even mention him," Jake said, cutting him off. "Get your coat and let's go. I'm not leaving here without you."

Leon's sigh was audible through my door. "Fine. Wait here. I'll be just a moment."

Jake stepped back, gaze shooting toward my door as he did. Even though he couldn't see me, I leapt back.

What are they up to?

I knew I should let it go, that it was none of my business, but I kept thinking about how Leon had known Kathryn by name, how he'd been injured the night after the murder. Yes, it was very likely a coincidence, and that Kathryn herself was involved in her husband's death, but what if it wasn't?

I didn't even think about it as I pulled on my coat and grabbed my purse and keys. I returned to the peephole just as Leon exited his apartment, wearing black and carrying that big black bag of his. I waited until both he and Jake were heading down the stairs before slipping out of my own apartment. I gave them another couple of seconds to exit the building, and then I followed after them, praying I wasn't making the biggest mistake of my life.

Chapter 16

Tailing someone always looks so easy in the movies.

Jake didn't speed. He didn't weave in and out of traffic or run red lights. His pace was almost leisurely, and I could imagine him chatting it up and laughing with Leon as he drove them to wherever they were headed.

He approached a light and just as he went through it, it turned yellow. I'd left what I hoped was enough space between us so that Jake—or Leon for that matter—wouldn't notice my car behind them. That meant there was little chance that I'd make it through before the light was red, but I gunned the gas anyway and was somehow through the light just before it changed.

My heart was pounding so hard, I felt like I'd just robbed a bank when all I'd done was almost-not-quite run a red light.

"Olivia is going to kill me," I muttered, glancing down at my phone, which I'd tossed into the cupholder when I'd gotten into my car. Olivia's contact information was on the screen, and I considered tapping it and telling her what I was doing. No, I didn't know *where* we were going, but I could keep her apprised that I was up to something.

But what if I was wrong about Jake and Leon? Sure, Leon

knew Kathryn. And yeah, he went out on the night of Grady's murder and showed up the next day with unexplained injuries. Jake might also have said some things that could be construed as suspicious when I'd seen them together. And then there's the black bag and the nervous way Leon acted when I'd knocked on his apartment door and . . .

No, it wasn't yet time to call Olivia. I wasn't in danger, and I didn't plan on putting myself in a situation where I would be. If they parked at some out-of-the-way empty lot or warehouse, I'd drive on past, and *then* I'd call Olivia and tell her what's going on.

But I was finding the abandoned lot far less likely the longer Jake drove. He was sticking to brightly lit roads, and while it wasn't downtown Cardinal Lake, he wasn't taking me out into the middle of nowhere either.

What am I doing? I wondered as Jake slowed and coasted into a parking lot full of bright lights and cars. A neon sign above the door of the rectangular building proclaimed it to be The Letterbox. This wasn't some shady location where two killers would go to talk about their next victim. This was the kind of place two friends might go to have a couple of drinks and enjoy a show.

Jake pulled into an empty space and parked. I drove past, shoulders hunched in the hopes neither man would glance over as I passed, and found a place to park a few spaces down—and away from The Letterbox. I shut off the engine and slunk down in my seat and watched to see what the two men would do next.

Not surprisingly, they exited Jake's car, talking. Leon rounded it to the back, removed his black bag from the trunk, and then the two of them strode up to the front doors, still talking, and not acting the least bit suspicious.

If it wasn't for that black bag . . .

I spent the next few moments debating what to do. I knew

of The Letterbox by reputation, but had never been there myself. It was a small, locally owned club that hosted all sorts of musical and comedy acts on weekends, with an open mic for readings and solo artists during the week. I'd seen flyers for it around town, had heard from Henna that it was a little shady when it came to the quality of food and drink, but that's about it.

"I came all the way out here, so I might as well check it out," I said, just to break the silence, as I grabbed my phone and climbed out of my car.

Instant laughter hit me as soon as I opened the door and stepped inside the Letterbox. It was followed by the toot of a horn and more laughter. A hostess by the door gestured to a SEAT YOURSELF sign, too busy watching the woman onstage to pay me much more than a cursory glance. While The Letterbox was busy on a Friday night, I noted a couple of empty tables, one of which that didn't have empty beer mugs or the bony remains of wings sitting atop it. A trio of harried waitresses were zooming around the room as they attempted to take orders and clean up after their guests, all at the same time.

A quick glance around the room and I didn't immediately spot Jake or Leon, though it was hard to be certain with so many people packed so close together. Hot spices and spilled beer assaulted my senses as I snagged the clean table. I figured that if nothing else, I could scan the crowd easier if I sat—and I wouldn't stick out nearly so much.

A waitress rushed over to my table, dropped a menu and one of those little square drink napkins onto it, and then was gone again without much more than muttering a name I didn't catch. A man the next table over grabbed her arm as she tried to walk past him, said something to her, and then he released her as he turned back to his friends seated with him. The waitress scowled at him a moment, and then was gone, off to run whatever errand he'd asked of her.

Onstage, the woman finished her act, which seemed to consist of her barking out a few quick lines, tooting a horn, and dancing around on one foot. There was polite applause when she bowed, and then she retreated to the back. As soon as she was gone, nearly half the crowd stood, with a good portion of them heading for the bar, while the rest made for the restrooms at the far end of the room.

"Come on, Leon," I muttered, watching everyone's face as they passed. "Where did you go?"

There were a lot of men there, but none of them appeared to be Leon *or* Jake. It was as if they'd come in and then walked straight out the back door like DK had after our date. They weren't seated at one of the tables, and I hadn't seen them walk by. I spotted a door with an EXIT sign to the rear of the building. If they were conducting some sort of shady business out back, that is where they'd be.

But did I really want to go out there and check?

"Is there anything I can get you?"

I jumped at the sound of the waitress's voice coming from just behind my shoulder. "I'm sorry," I said, hand going to my chest where my heart had tried to leap free. "You startled me."

The waitress flashed me a strained smile. "Happens all the time. If you need a list of what we have on tap, it's on the back of the menu." She reached down and flipped the menu over for me. "Otherwise, we've got Coke products, water."

Patrons were filtering back to their tables. The back exit door remained closed. No Jake. No Leon.

This was a waste of time.

"Actually, I think I might just—"

I cut off as a man stepped out onto the stage. He had shoulder-length brown hair that was pulled back out of his face in a loose ponytail. He was extremely good-looking with sparkling eyes and a smile that was to die for.

Leon Fitzgerald.

Waitress forgotten, I sagged back into my seat, eyes riveted to Leon. He was wearing the same black outfit he'd left his apartment in, so he hadn't gotten changed when he'd arrived. He wore faint eyeliner that made those eyes of his really *pop*. His smile showed off his near perfect teeth, and when he stepped up to the mic, the entire room took in a collective breath and held it.

"Thank you so much for coming," Leon said in his raspy voice. "I'm Leon Fitzgerald."

Enthusiastic applause went around the room. It was so infectious, I found myself joining in.

Leon stood back, arms extended, and then bowed. He looked like a star, one who was accustomed to this sort of thing. He waited for the applause to die down, and then he stepped back to the curtain, reached into his black bag, which he'd placed just out of sight. He returned to the mic carrying a wooden puppet.

"And I'm Harvey, the real star of *this* show."

My jaw hit the floor as the applause hit new heights. *Harvey?* Leon was a ventriloquist?

Harvey the dummy had been made to resemble Leon, right down to the shoulder-length hair and winning smile. They were even wearing the same black outfit, though Harvey's had a little more sparkle to it, so that he twinkled under the club lights.

The applause died down. The banter began.

It was amazing to watch. Harvey's words flowed right into Leon's own, so much so, I was beginning to wonder if perhaps Jake was behind the curtain, playing the part of Harvey, but I could see Leon's Adam's apple bob when Harvey "spoke." This wasn't some amateur show, but the kind I'd expect to see on a talent show on TV.

I sat through the entire performance, mesmerized by Leon

and Harvey, to the point where I'd all but forgotten about Jake and Grady and everything that had been happening in my life as of late. The crowd laughed and cheered, and at times called out, as if they regularly saw the show and knew how to respond.

When he was done, Leon—and Harvey—bowed and vanished back behind the curtain to raucous applause. Unable to contain myself, I joined in, amazed by what I'd just witnessed.

Next to the stage, a door nestled in the shadows opened and the woman who'd been on before Leon exited. I was sitting only a few feet away, and on a whim, I popped up and hurried over. I caught the door before it closed, and ignoring the PERFORMERS ONLY sign, I slipped inside.

A short, dim hallway led to a room that I assumed was a green room or ready room or whatever they called those places where performers waited before going onstage. Two doors that led to empty dressing rooms were hanging open. There were only two people in the room with me: Jake Palmer and Leon Fitzgerald.

"Leon! That was amazing," I said, so excited by what I'd just witnessed, I didn't consider what they must have been thinking about me barging in on them like that. "Why didn't you tell me you were a performer?"

Leon tensed briefly before relaxing. "Thank you, Ash. I didn't know you were coming tonight or else I would have gotten you one of the good seats."

Beside him, Jake ran a hand over his mouth to cover a smile.

"I didn't know I was coming until the last minute." *When I followed you.* "Seriously, Leon, you were fantastic."

"Thank you." He used the side of his foot to tap the black bag containing Harvey. "Harvey here's the real star of the show. It's why . . ." He trailed off, expression going wistful.

"Why what?" I asked, unable to contain my curiosity.

Leon glanced at Jake, who shrugged at him in a way I took to mean, "Your call." There was a moment where I thought he might change the subject before he sighed and spoke.

"I've been performing for years," he said. "Like everyone, I started out small and unknown, but quickly gained a following in my hometown and the surrounding area. A year later, and I was doing shows in bigger cities to sold-out crowds. It happened fast, and while I'd like to take the credit, Harvey here was the one everyone came to see." Another foot tap of the bag. "There was even a Netflix special, plans for Vegas shows. I had it made."

I could feel it coming, so I said it for him. "But?"

"But, just as things started taking off, a scandal involving one of my assistants broke. I didn't have anything to do with it directly, but it affected me, nonetheless. I won't get into it here, because, honestly, it doesn't matter what happened, but it ended up getting my special pulled from Netflix and the Vegas deal was taken off the table. Within a week I was blacklisted and couldn't find a job."

"It was a crime what they did to him," Jake said.

"It's why I came to Cardinal Lake. I won't say that no one had heard of me, but I wasn't well known. Ian knew of the special, of course. It's why he was so eager to get me to move in." He chuckled.

Ian Banks, our landlord, had done everything he could to get Leon to move in. I'd thought it a little strange at the time, but now I understood. Leon used to be a big deal.

"He was a fan," I said.

Leon nodded. "At least, that's what he told me about twelve times over the first ten minutes that we spoke. It was nice to be recognized and not have what happened thrown in my face. It's why I like it here." He gestured to the room around us. "There's no pressure. The place is small enough that they cater only to local talent and local crowds. Despite my history, they are happy to have me and none of what happened before matters."

"Leon's presence has helped a lot of us out," Jake said. "Even Jayden can't deny that."

"Who's Jayden?" I asked.

Leon scowled at the mention of the other man's name. It was Jake who answered.

"Jayden Clay. He's a punk kid who used to perform Friday nights, but took it upon himself to make everyone else miserable. He got into it with Grady before he . . . well, you know."

I blinked at him. "Grady? Grady *Richards*?"

"The one and the same," Jake said. "Grady wasn't a regular like the rest of us, but put in appearances every few weeks. He was embarrassed by the whole thing. Never even told his wife what he was up to, told her it was for work."

My head was spinning so much, I desperately wanted to sit down, but that would mean walking away from them. I had so many questions that I couldn't figure out which one to ask first.

Thankfully, Leon took over without me having to prod. "Jayden didn't get along with anyone. The first time we got into it, he claimed it was because I was stealing his material—"

"Which was bull crap," Jake put in.

"—and when I refused to back down, he attacked me again. I'm not a fighter, so I didn't do much more than defend myself. Jake was the one who stepped in and kept Jayden from going too far."

"I went to management afterward," Jake explained. "Told them what was happening and said that both Leon and I would walk if Jayden wasn't dealt with."

"They moved Jayden to Saturday nights," Leon said. "Which isn't that bad of a deal, truth be told. He gets good crowds, and it keeps him away from the rest of us. I like weekdays, though I'll do Saturday shows if I'm needed." He frowned.

"Even though he was moved to a good night, Jayden nearly squandered it last weekend. He was late and Drake, the guy who runs the place, called me to ask if I'd fill in for him. By the time I got here, Jayden had arrived and he accused me of trying to steal his slot. He pushed me and I fell, which was how I got this." He raised his mostly healed arm.

Last Saturday. The same night in which Grady was murdered. "Do you think . . ." I couldn't even finish the thought, but Leon understood.

"I wish I knew. It's why I've been so out of sorts as of late. I can't prove anything, but Jayden is volatile. He didn't like Grady, and made sure everyone knew it. And then, when Grady ended up dead on a night in which Jayden was late for his gig . . ."

Suspicious would be an understatement.

"Why didn't he like Grady?" I asked. "Did he think he was stealing his material too?"

Jake and Leon shared a look, with Jake being the one to speak up.

"Grady was embarrassed by his act. It wasn't crude or anything, but he wanted to be a serious businessman. If people back home thought he was telling jokes and acting like a fool onstage, they'd dismiss him as such."

"And then there's Kathryn," Leon added.

"Who you know," I said.

Leon started to shake his head and say something, but Jake spoke up instead.

"I met her a few times," he said. "Grady and I ran in the same circles when we were kids, and I knew Kathryn from way back when, though I don't think she remembered me from then. We see each other every now and again and I've always thought about telling her what Grady was up to, but I didn't want to betray his trust."

"She thought he was cheating on her," I said. "Telling her might have eased her mind."

Jake rubbed at his chin and wouldn't meet my eye when he spoke.

"It may have," he admitted. "Hindsight and all that."

"Jayden is one of those people who doesn't get along with anyone else," Leon said. "He thinks of the rest of us as competition. When he found out Grady was hiding his performances from his wife, he threatened to tell her. They argued about it, but Grady always backed down. With the way he started talking, I think it was affecting his home life."

Secrets did that. Even ones that are seemingly innocent.

"I'm guessing Jayden said something to her," Jake said. "Must have told her that Grady was cheating, or at least, hinted that he might be. Maybe it was an anonymous phone call or email, because I don't know if Jayden ever met Kathryn, but whatever happened, it upset Grady. Dude was down and acted like he wasn't sure what to do with his life."

Which could explain why he'd been at Snoot's, talking to Sierra. If he thought Kathryn was going to leave him, perhaps he started thinking that he might as well give in and start looking for her replacement. No, it doesn't put him in the best of lights, but I could see why he would have done it.

"Shoot," Jake said, glancing at his watch. "It's my time to go on. I've got to get up there before the crowd gets restless. You take care, Ash, all right? Stay far away from Jayden Clay, Kathryn, and this whole mess. I wouldn't want you to get dragged into it. You seem like good people."

"Thank you. I will."

Jake hurried toward the door that led to the stage, leaving me alone with Leon. We stood there, awkwardly eyeing one another as if neither of us was sure what to say next.

"Sounds like this Jayden guy caused a lot of trouble around

here," I said after a moment. "Why would they keep him around if he's such a problem?"

"He's good." Leon bit his lower lip, then said, "If you want to see him perform, he'll be here tomorrow. And if you want to talk to him, I can make sure you get that chance. You're curious about him, right?"

Was I? Who was I kidding? Of course I was. He was connected to a murdered man. "I guess I am," I admitted.

"How about we come back here tomorrow night? You and me."

My heart gave a heavy thump. "Won't you showing up make Jayden angrier at you?"

"Probably." Leon frowned. "I don't know what was going on between you and Grady, and I'm okay if you don't want to tell me, but it seems like you have a stake in what happens here. I can't prove Jayden had anything to do with his death, but if he did, he shouldn't get away with it. If me showing up and asking him a few pointed questions gets him to admit to something, then it'll be worth it. With the two of us together, I'm sure we can get him to talk."

Thoughts of how Olivia and Chief Higgins were going to be angry with me if I agreed crossed my mind, but what if Leon was right and talking to Jayden helped solve Grady's murder? It's not like he'd admit anything to the police.

But if we were to corner him, make him think we knew more than we did? What was the harm?

"Sure," I said. "Let's do it."

Leon looked surprised when he said, "Really?" He cleared his throat, composed himself. "Jayden goes on at nine, so we should leave by eight. I'll drive."

"Sounds like a plan."

"Good." A stupid grin found Leon's face. "I'll see you tomorrow night, Ash."

"See you then, Leon."

I left feeling strangely unsettled.

Leon and I were going to confront Jayden Clay about Grady Richards and whether he had anything to do with Grady's murder. That's it.

So, if that was the case, why did it feel so much like a date?

Chapter 17

J. Allen ignored me the next morning as we both opened for the day. Actually, "ignored" was probably the wrong word. While I waved and tried to remain pleasant—we still needed to work next to one another, so why not try to be civil—he merely glared and muttered something to Ginger about not wasting her breath on me. Ginger, for her part, panted at me, just happy to be alive like dogs usually were.

I decided not to take his attitude personally. J. Allen would get over our spat eventually. Or he wouldn't. I'd like it if we could get along, but if he insisted on turning our businesses into a competition against one another, I'd have no choice but to bury him.

The first class of the day went smoothly, despite my concerns about my whatever I was doing with Leon later that evening—I didn't want to call it a date, but I supposed that was what it was. I knew I should call Olivia and tell her what I was planning to do. She'd tell me not to, that she'd take care of it, and that was all well and good, but then I'd feel bad about letting Leon down, even if it wasn't a real date.

The second class of the day was about to start when the door opened and someone I never expected to set foot inside

A Purrfect Pose entered. Ginny Riese was wearing tights and a tube top beneath a heavy coat that went down to her ankles. She paused just inside the door, spotted me, and then plastered on the biggest, most insincere smile I'd ever seen in my life.

"Hi, Ash." She said it loudly enough to be heard all the way to Branson Designs across the square. "I'm here for yoga."

I matched her fake smile with one of my own, already mentally scrambling to figure out how to diffuse the situation before it could even start. "Of course, Ginny. I'm glad to see you." A pause, then, "How would you like to pay? There's different rates, so if this isn't just going to be a onetime thing . . ." I motioned toward the price list.

She produced a slip of paper from her pocket and waved it around like it was a flag. "My friend gave me this voucher. That's okay, isn't it? You hand them out so people can try the place free of charge."

As if I didn't know what my own vouchers were for.

I crossed the room, smile frozen on my face. Ginny wasn't here for yoga. She was up to something and I was worried that whatever that something was, it was intended to make me look bad in front of, well, everyone.

I took the voucher from her and one look told me that it was indeed what she claimed it to be. "Great," I said, trying to keep the disappointment out of my voice. "Do you have a mat? If not, I have some for sale. Or we could always do this on another day if you want to find one of your own." Preferably when I wasn't already stressed out and could deal with her properly.

"No thanks. I'll just use the floor."

I almost argued with her. The hardwood floor wouldn't be comfortable, and was a health risk. She could slip and fall. She could . . . I shook my head and returned to the front of the class. "The cats are over there," I said, hooking a thumb toward the cat room. Yes, I should have told her, "No mat, no yoga," but why bother? It's probably what she was hoping for, just so she could cause a scene.

Ginny found a spot on the floor. She leaned toward her neighbor and whispered something, which caused the other woman to blush. Satisfied, she then raised her hand.

"Yes, Ginny?" Spoken through near gritted teeth.

"Do you think it'd be okay for us to bring our boyfriends with us sometime? A sort of couples yoga night?"

I blinked at her in mild surprise. Actually, that wasn't a bad idea. I could hold sessions, perhaps once a week, where couples could come in together for yoga. We could do partner poses. I could find someone to stand in as my partner and . . . a creeping dread worked its way through me as I asked, "Why do you ask?"

Ginny's smile widened as if I'd stepped directly into her trap, which I had. "You see, I have this boyfriend who just *loves* to spend time with me and it seemed like a good idea for us to spend even more time together. We could show everyone how close we are, how no one could ever get between us. I'm sure others feel that way." She glanced around the room, looking for support, before turning back to me. "Or do you think it would be a problem? You wouldn't be too upset if I were to bring Drew with me, would you? I mean, you *have* been trying to get with him for years now."

All eyes swiveled my way and someone sucked in a dramatic breath. Somehow I managed not to react with anything more than an "All right everyone, let's get started. Let's begin with the tree pose."

I made it through class, teeth clenched and a plastic smile stretched across my face, without snapping. Everyone in class knew that something was going on between Ginny and me, and they probably had some inkling as to what that something might be, considering Ginny's constant snide comments, but no one said anything. The cats were well behaved, which was a blessing, and Ginny didn't fall or slip, though I made sure we did quite a few floor poses that would leave her with sore knees, elbows, and, hopefully, a bruised keister.

"Thanks for coming," I said as everyone began filtering out. "Hope to see you again next time."

I expected Ginny to confront me directly once everyone had left, but she merely walked out the door, flashing me a dirty look as she went.

I ignored her. She'd had her say. I hoped that would be the end of it, but wasn't counting on it.

I was toweling off and considering whether to have a granola bar now or wait until after the next—and final—class of the day and get lunch at The Hop when there was a knock at the glass front door. My latest visitor wasn't dressed for yoga, but was in jeans and a sweater. He looked nervous as he peered in at me.

I opened the door and stepped aside, not quite sure what to expect.

"Hello, Ash," Solomon Justice said as he entered. "I hope I'm not interrupting anything."

"You're not. The next class starts at eleven, so I don't have long."

He glanced at his watch, nodded. "I won't take up too much of your time then."

I crossed the room, picked up my water bottle, and took a long drink. Solomon was trying not to appear nervous, but it was obvious he was. Did that mean Mom had sent him? Or was he here on his own volition?

Solomon took a deep, steadying breath and blew it out through his mouth. "I just wanted to stop by and tell you how sorry I am about how things played out. Following people around isn't normally in my job description, but when Cecilia wants something . . ."

"She gets it," I finished for him. I knew it all too well.

"She had good intentions," he went on. "It might not seem like it, but she truly did want what was best for the three of you. She told me that if I ever saw anything that concerned me, I was to step in or try to help in any way I could." He frowned. "Though, I suppose I'm not sure what I would have done if something *had* happened. I'm sure you can tell, but I'm not the type to get my hands dirty, if you know what I mean."

I did. "Did you ever notice anything concerning when it came to me?" I asked, curious.

Solomon rubbed at his cheek as he considered it. "Nothing that required me to play the hero," he said. "But I suppose there was one thing that stood out. I should have told Cecilia.... No, scratch that. I should have told *you* about it when it happened."

My stomach clenched. I crossed my arms over my middle when I asked, "When what happened?"

"I'm not sure that's the right phrasing," Solomon said, pacing away from me and back again. "Nothing actually *happened*, but I did see something that raised a red flag." A pause, and then, "I think somebody else was watching you."

I swallowed. "Somebody else?" As in, Grady Richards's killer, perhaps?

Solomon nodded. "I can't be certain that it was you they were after. In fact, they might not have been doing anything at all, and I was imagining things. When you sit around, staring at the front of a building long enough, you start to let your mind wander a bit."

"When was this?" I asked. It came out half-choked, so I took a drink of water.

"This would be..." His gaze went distant. "I can't recall exactly. I'd have to check my notes and I don't have them with me. It was at least three days ago, maybe four. I remember you were running all over town that day. You took me on a long drive out into the country, which was rather nice, actually. I was hoping to keep an eye on you without you noticing, but realized you might have spotted me—"

"On the day you followed Kiersten and me to the Holloway farm."

"That's the one," he said with a wince. "Sorry about that."

I motioned for him to go on. I hadn't quite forgiven him for stalking me, but I was getting there. It was Mom who was the one I should be mad at.

"Once I realized you were onto me, I decided to wait for you back at your apartment," he said. "I called Cecilia and asked her what she thought I should do, and she told me to stand pat, so I did. I wasn't happy about it, and I guess I kind of slacked off on my job. Sitting around in a car all day isn't my idea of a good time. I got some work done, and was only half paying attention to what was going on around me."

I mentally replayed the day. Kiersten took me back to the shelter, and then I'd gone back to A Purrfect Pose for the evening classes. From there, I went to Sierra's, and then the police station. I didn't get home until late. "You stayed there all day?"

Solomon's face colored. "Most of it. Like I said, I got some work done. I kept tabs on who went in and out. Was bored mostly."

"But you said you noticed someone else watching me?"

He made a face. "That's the thing. You weren't there at the time, so I might be wrong. They were in a car a few spaces away, closer to the apartments. They pulled in about an hour, maybe two after I'd gotten there, sat in their car without leaving for about forty minutes, and then they just drove off."

"They didn't get out of their car?"

"Nope. They just watched the complex."

If my mental math was correct, then this had happened before Sierra and I had gone to the police station to tell Chief Higgins about what we'd learned about the Grady I knew not being the real Grady Richards. That meant the police hadn't been the ones to send someone to keep an eye on my apartment.

But if not them, and if it wasn't Mom, then who?

"Why'd they leave?" I asked. "If the person in the car was waiting for me, why not stick around until I showed up? Did they spot you?"

"I don't think so," Solomon said. "It's possible they were waiting for someone else or realized they were early or . . ." He shook his head. "There's any number of reasons why someone might have sat out there. But with the murder and everything, and because I was there, waiting for you, that's what made the most sense to me: they were there doing the same thing."

"Was it a man or woman?" I asked.

"I couldn't see them well enough to be sure," Solomon said. He ran a hand over his face, sighed. "Honestly, it might be nothing. They sat there for a while, left, and, as far as I know, never came back."

I thanked Solomon and he left a few minutes later with another round of apologies, which I accepted. Yes, he might have followed me and scared me half to death, but at the same time, he'd been there in case something would have happened to me. He might not be certain that this other watcher was after me, but I feared they might have been. Solomon's presence might have kept them from making their move . . . whatever that move might have been.

But now that Solomon was no longer keeping an eye on me? I was on my own.

The final class of the day began a short time later. I went through the motions, barely cognizant of what was going on around me. My mind was elsewhere, but I managed to get through it without making too many mistakes.

Tyra arrived as we were finishing up. She waved from the hallway, and then headed into the kitty room to wait for class to finish. When we did, I was about to head back to talk to her about making her position permanent, when a third surprising visitor appeared at the front door.

The dread was palpable as I let Hunter in.

"Hey, Sis," he said, slinking his way through the door. His hands were shoved into his pockets so deeply, he looked like he was trying to reach his knees.

"Hunter." I looked him up and down, and noted that, other than his apparent nervousness, he appeared okay. "How's Lita?"

"She's good. Said she was going to talk to her dad today."

My eyes widened. "She's telling Chief Higgins that you're the father of her baby?"

"Yeah." He looked sick. I didn't blame him. Higgins was going to explode. "I guess he still doesn't know. Didn't know." He frowned. "Anyway, I figured I might hang here with you while she's doing it, if that's okay?" He glanced at me askance, like he feared I might tell him no.

"Of course you can stay here, Hunter," I said. "Do you need anything? A granola bar? Water?"

"I'm good." He scuffed a shoe on the floor, glanced toward the window as if he expected Chief Higgins to come flying through it at any moment.

"It'll be all right," I told him. "He's the chief of police. He's not going to hurt you."

Hunter looked as if he didn't quite believe me, but he nodded. "I guess you're right."

"Seriously. He might be mad, but if you've treated Lita with respect—"

"I have."

"Then you have nothing to worry about."

"Yeah, but—" His phone pinged, nearly sending him shooting to the roof when he jumped. He gave me a wide-eyed look, snatched his phone from his front pocket, and checked the message. "Oh."

I blinked at him. "Oh?"

"Oh. Oh no." Those wide eyes got even wider, to the point where they looked close to popping out of his head. "Oh, Ash."

I wanted him to stop saying, "Oh," because it was freaking me out. "What's going on, Hunter?"

"The baby." He stared at his phone, reread the message, and then looked up at me. "Lita." He swallowed. "She's having the baby *right now*!"

The hospital was packed when Hunter and I arrived.

Every Branson in town was there, nearly swallowing up the much smaller Higgins family. Hunter had made the calls while I'd driven, which meant his friends were also there. They were keeping well clear of the hulking form of Dan Higgins.

There was a moment of tension when we entered the room where I was positive Chief Higgins was going to fly off the handle. His eyes landed on Hunter and he reached for him with one of those massive hands of his. Hunter, for his part, didn't flinch. Much. That big hand came close to his neck, but instead of strangling him like I expected, Higgins merely squeezed Hunter's shoulder, gave him a sharp nod, before he jerked a thumb for me to follow him down a short hallway nearby.

"I assume you knew?" he asked when we were alone.

"About Lita and Hunter? I knew."

"It explains a lot." Higgins rubbed at his chin. "Can't say I'm over the moon about this whole thing, but it is what it is."

"That's very diplomatic of you."

A wry smile found his face. "What? Did you expect me to throttle Hunter? Maybe disown my daughter?"

The thought had crossed my mind, but I didn't want to admit it. "Hunter says Lita might move to Maine."

Higgins's expression fell. "She's considering it. I understand why she is thinking about it, but can't say I approve." The "she's all I have" was unspoken and made my chest ache just a little.

Dad crossed my field of vision as he walked past the hallway. To my surprise, both Kara and Mom were talking to one another right behind him. That will *never* look right to me.

He jerked to a stop when he noticed me, and then said, "Hey, Ash, Hunter's headed into the room with Lita. I guess she was asking for him. We'll be over there." He pointed toward the waiting room.

"I'll be there in a minute."

Dad hesitated, and then headed for the waiting room. Kara waved as she passed. Mom didn't so much as break stride.

"I won't keep you," Higgins said when they were gone. "I want to be there for Lita, even if it means waiting outside the door until she's ready." He wiped his brow, which was beaded with nervous sweat. "Your brother's not the reason I pulled you aside."

I suppressed a groan. "You talked to Olivia?" Who was somewhere out there with the rest of the family. I'd seen her when I'd come in.

"I did. Officer Chase informed me of . . ." He trailed off, as if reluctant to talk about the murder investigation in the hospital where his daughter was currently in labor.

I let him off the hook and said, "I wasn't trying to interfere. I also didn't want you chasing the wrong lead, so I told her everything I knew. I'm sorry I talked to DK and whatnot, but I was pretty sure he wasn't involved in the murder. I did it mostly because I wanted to talk to him about leaving me with the check." Mostly.

"I appreciate that, Ash, I really do." Higgins sounded almost contrite. "And I know I can be hard on you, but it's for your own good. Even if you suspect someone is innocent of a crime, it's still dangerous to go running around town, confronting people."

"I know," I admitted. "I'll be more careful. It's not like I want anything to do with half of these people. They sometimes show up on my doorstep and . . ." I trailed off when I noted his expression.

Higgins glanced down the hall, making sure no one was within earshot. "What do you know about Kathryn Richards?" he asked.

"She's Grady's widow."

"Which, as I'm sure you figured out, means he was married when he accepted that date with you."

"I know. But I didn't know he was married at the time of our date. Neither did Sierra when she set us up." Speaking of Sierra, I needed to call her and tell her about Hunter's baby. She'd hate me forever if I didn't let her know. "I didn't know she existed until she showed up at my apartment, yelling at me."

Higgins nodded slowly. "All right. I want you to be careful, Ash," he said. "Mrs. Richards has a reason to be angry." He clenched his jaw briefly. "If you see *anyone* who doesn't belong around your place, I want you to call me or Officer Chase immediately."

His tone had my heart thumping so hard in my chest, it was all I could hear. "Am I in danger?"

"I wish I could say no, but for now, let's go with: I don't think so."

"That's not very reassuring."

There was a moment when Chief Higgins looked like he might tell me something more when a ruckus down the hall caught our attention. Cheering and laughter, followed by Dad appearing at the head of the hall once more, grinning ear to ear.

"It's a boy!" he called, before following the flood of family and friends toward where I assumed Lita was currently holding that baby boy with Hunter at her side.

That was quick, I thought. Alexi's labor when she'd had both her kids had taken all night.

Chief Higgins clasped me on the shoulder, a stupid grin on his face and a tear in his eye. "A boy," he said it was a chuckle. "It's a boy."

"Congratulations," I said, mirroring his own grin.

And then, together, we hurried down the hall to welcome the newest member of the Daniels-Branson-Higgins family into the world.

Chapter 18

Christian Wayne—Higgins? Daniels? The preferred surname was never mentioned in my presence, so I'm not sure what Lita and Hunter decided upon—was born healthy and happy. It felt like all of Cardinal Lake showed up to congratulate the couple, and that included Sierra, Aaron, and the rest of my friends. I never got the chance to talk to Hunter one-on-one, nor did I learn what Chief Higgins was so worried about, due to the chaos.

But I was okay with that.

After basking in newborn celebrations in the hospital, I headed home to prep for my evening reconnaissance with Leon. I almost called the whole thing off so I could spend more time with my family, but Hunter didn't need me there. He was absorbed with Lita and his baby, as he should be.

On the way home, I spent an inordinate amount of time wondering if I wanted a family of my own. Drew and I had talked about it, of course. Back when we were dating, it was assumed that we'd get married, have the full family—son and daughter and requisite number of pets—and that we'd live happily ever after. But I wasn't fully invested in the idea, even when I was smiling and agreeing with everything Drew said. I *thought* I was, don't get me wrong. I never would have misled Drew about something so important.

Now, having seen Hunter's smile, after being there when Alexi's two children were born, I was beginning to wonder if it was time for me to take this dating thing more seriously and settle down. Not that I was a wild child, mind you. I was rather boring when you got right down to it.

Maybe that's your problem, Ash. Maybe if I was a little more exciting, I'd meet the right guy and things would start to work out. No more bad blind dates, for a start.

I pulled into the lot of my apartment complex, dismissing the thought as I did. I knew the only reason I was even thinking about a family and settling down was because of Hunter's baby. I swear, newborns emit some sort of weird pheromone that made everyone within range become strangely obsessed with children. It would eventually wear off and I'd be back to the normal old Ash again in no time.

I got out of my car and headed into the lobby where I checked my mail—bills only, of course. Oh, the joys of being an adult. I tucked the envelopes under my arm and headed up the stairs where Edna was waiting for me, just outside her apartment door.

"Ash," she said, tone serious. "Do you have a moment?"

"Sure, Edna." I joined her. "Is this about . . ." I nodded toward Leon's door, which was closed now, but would open in less than two hours for our evening out together.

"In a way," she said. "But mostly, it's about you."

"Me?"

Edna's lips pressed together briefly before she said, "I know Pavan and I have pushed you to give Mr. Fitzgerald a chance, but I've reconsidered my stance on the matter." She kept her voice low, just in case Leon was listening at his door. "I don't believe you should pursue a relationship with him any longer."

"You don't have to worry about that," I said. "I'm not interested in Leon; not in that way. We're just friends."

Edna made a sound I couldn't quite interpret. Disappointment, maybe? "I had the chance to speak with Mr. Fitzgerald earlier today. He's rather excited about your date this evening."

Oh. "It's not a date."

Edna cocked an eyebrow in obvious disbelief.

"Truly," I said. "We're going to the Letterbox to watch someone he knows perform."

"That sounds like a date to me."

I supposed it *sounded* like a date, but it wasn't. But how was I to explain that to her without telling her that the guy we were going to see might be a murderer? I didn't want Edna to worry about my safety. And if I was wrong, I didn't want to smear another man's name when I didn't have to.

"It's not," I said lamely, before asking, "Why the change? About Leon, I mean? You two seemed pretty adamant that I give him a shot."

Edna thought about it a moment before speaking. "It's not something I can pinpoint, really. Leon seems like a nice enough man and hasn't caused any trouble since moving in here."

I could feel it, so I asked, "But?"

"But you're not someone who should settle for 'nice enough.'"

I had no idea what to say to that, so I just stared at her.

"Don't look at me like that," Edna said with a scowl and wave of her hand. "I have a lot of free time on my hands. That means I have a lot of time to think about what's going on in my life, and the lives of those around me. And since you live right next door to me, and since I consider you a friend, you are on my mind more than most."

There was something in her tone that struck a soft spot. "Thank you," I said. "I think of you as a friend too, Edna."

"I wish you could see that you undervalue yourself too

much, Ash," she went on. "You care for your family. You try to make nice with everyone you meet. You love animals. You've done good for the community here in Cardinal Lake. I'll ignore the fact that you're a Branson." Spoken with a smile and a wink. "Pavan means well when he nudges you toward Leon, but I believe his intent is misguided. He, like me, doesn't think you should be alone. But we were wrong to try to influence you. This is something you need to figure out on your own. *You* are the one who has to live with the consequences of the relationship, not us."

My brain immediately made the jump from consequences to babies. I had a brief flash of coming home from a long day of yoga to a half dozen newborns screaming in my apartment. Luna was there, climbing the walls to get away from the noise. And a husband, be it Leon, be it someone else, doing their best to keep the peace during the hours in which I was away.

I suppressed a shudder as I said, "I promise you; this isn't a date. We're going out as friends and if Leon thinks of it as something more, I'll let him down nicely. After what happened with my last date, I'm not interested in getting serious with anyone right now." And after that last brain blast, maybe not ever.

Edna eyed me a moment before she nodded and stepped back toward her door. "I best let you go then," she said. "I hope you have a good time this evening, date or no date."

"I'm going to try."

"But think about what I said," she said, opening her door. "I want to see you happy." And then she stepped inside her apartment and closed the door softly behind her.

I remained in the hallway a moment longer before I headed inside my own apartment to get ready. Luna was waiting for me on her perch. She popped up the second I was through the door, jumped down, and started meowing as she threaded her way around my ankles, wanting to be held.

"Hey, girl," I said, picking her up and hugging her close. "We're okay with just the two of us, aren't we? We don't need anyone else."

Another tiny little meow that I took as an affirmative, and then I set her down and filled her dish.

"I'm going to be leaving soon. Keep an eye on the apartment for me, all right?"

Luna glanced at me once and then dug into her dinner. It wasn't an answer exactly, but it was close enough.

Since my outing with Leon wasn't a real date—no, really, it wasn't—I showered and dressed in warm, casual attire. Jeans and a sweater and a pair of shoes that weren't fancy, but weren't simple tennis shoes, either. I debated on putting on a necklace and bracelet, but opted against them. The fancier I appeared, the more likely Leon would think of it as a romantic date, not just a recon mission to scope out a possible murderer.

I reconsidered the shoes, checked my closet again for a different sweater, and then realized I was being silly. I was acting like it *was* a date, one in which I was trying too hard to make it look like it wasn't one.

Calm down, Ash. I took a deep breath, closed the closet without changing. Leon was a neighbor, a friend even. He knew what I wanted to do and wouldn't take advantage of the situation. Even if he *did* have romantic intentions, he wouldn't force them on me. I might not know everything about the man—what he did in his free time, where he worked—but I knew him well enough to know he wouldn't do that.

A knock at the door pulled me from my ruminations. I checked myself in the mirror, wished I'd done something more with my hair and makeup, and then I plastered on a smile and headed for the door.

Luna was watching from her perch, having already eaten her fill, and had one leg straight up into the air, caught mid-bathtime.

"Lovely," I told her with a laugh. It was oddly calming to have her in such a vulnerable state as I opened the door. If she wasn't concerned about my night out with Leon, then I shouldn't be either.

The door opened to reveal the man himself, dressed in what Mom would call his Sundays best. He was holding a bouquet of red flowers. Carnations, rather than roses, I noted.

Despite it not being a date, my pulse quickened at the sight of him. Leon Fitzgerald *was* a good-looking man. No, more than that, he was extremely attractive in a purely eye-candy way. I was certain that if I *were* to get to know him better, I'd find that he was just as attractive on the inside as the out.

Still, as pleasing as the sight of him was, the flowers, as well as his attire, made me worry that he was indeed taking the evening out too far.

"What? No Harvey?" I asked, hoping to lighten the mood before my own insecurities got the best of me.

Leon laughed. "No, he was afraid he'd garner too much of your attention and would leave me feeling like the third wheel."

The comment brought a flush to my cheeks that was mirrored in his own.

"Leon, I—"

"Don't say anything," he said, holding up his free hand. "I understand that we are going out so you can talk to Jayden. I always dress up when I go out with friends. And the flowers . . ." He held them out to me. "You can toss them if you'd like. Or take them with us and leave them in my car. I won't take offense. I wasn't sure what to do with myself and it felt odd *not* to get you anything. No strings."

I took the carnations, feeling mildly ashamed for making assumptions. "Let me put them away and then we can go."

Leon bowed his head and remained standing outside my door. I closed it so Luna wouldn't get out and then found a vase, filled it with water, and placed the carnations up high where Luna couldn't get to them. While they were only mildly toxic to cats, I didn't want her to get sick if she decided to give them a nibble.

Leon was waiting for me, hands behind his back when I returned with my coat on. "Are you ready for this?" he asked.

Was I? I didn't think I was, but answered with an "As I'll ever be."

Leon held out an arm. When I didn't take it right away, he repeated, "No strings."

I hesitated for a heartbeat more and then thought, *Why not?* and slid my arm through his.

The Letterbox was expectedly busier on a Saturday night than it was Friday. Not by much, mind you, but all the tables were packed and there were quite a few people standing at the bar, drinks in hand, as they chatted and watched the performers. Leon had the foresight—and pull—to have reserved us a table near the door that led to the performers' area in the back. The table was small, with barely enough room for the both of us to set our drinks down. It made our night out together feel a smidge too intimate for my liking.

"I'm really sorry about everything," Leon said once we were settled. "I should have told you I knew Grady once I realized what had happened."

"Don't apologize," I said, glancing around the room to see if I recognized anyone. I didn't. "How well do you know Kathryn?"

Leon sighed, looked down at his hands. "I don't." He noted my disbelieving expression and hurried to explain. "She never came to Grady's performances since she didn't know he was performing. And because she didn't come to his . . ."

"She never came to yours. I get it."

He nodded. "Grady would talk about her, so we all knew about her. He showed us pictures, which was why I recognized her when she showed up at your apartment. We'd never met before that day."

I thought about it and then decided that Leon had no reason to lie. "I didn't know he was married or I wouldn't have agreed to the blind date."

Leon reached across the table to pat me on the hand. The contact was brief, but it made me feel strangely warm, nonetheless.

"I know, Ash. This whole thing..." He shook his head. "It's hard to wrap your head around it when you only have bits and pieces of the puzzle."

The current performer—a woman with flaming red hair who'd fumbled through a few jokes before settling into her routine—left the stage to a smattering of applause. Leon tensed in his seat, glanced over at me. "Jayden should be next."

Conversation died away as we waited for him to appear. A waitress came by, but by now, my stomach was in knots and all I wanted was a Sprite to calm it. Leon ordered the same, and then we settled in to watch the empty stage, anticipation making us both fidget in our seats.

Our drinks arrived, and a minute later, a tall, lanky *kid* stepped onto the stage. He had one of those fuzzy mustaches of a teen who'd just started to be able to grow facial hair decorating his top lip. His hair looked like he'd put a curling iron to a mop and dropped it onto his head. He had the swagger of someone who thought far more of themselves than what was warranted, and I instantly disliked him for it.

Leon leaned my way and said, "He's older than he looks," before settling back into his seat.

After a moment of fumbling with the mic stand, Jayden Clay began his routine. I'd expected him to pull out a puppet like Leon had since Jayden had claimed Leon was stealing his material, but no puppet appeared. The jokes were crude at best. Downright obnoxious and sexist at worst. Yet there was charisma enough to Jayden that I found myself smiling along to a few of the jokes.

Leon and Jake were right; Jayden *was* good. Maybe not good enough to have a special of his own, or to ever break from the small-town scene, but he was good enough that he shouldn't have been worried about anyone else. If he'd just focused on his material, he probably would have been fine on his own.

When the routine ended, Jayden waited for his applause, absorbed it, and then hurried to the back, and out of sight.

"All right," Leon said. "You saw his stuff. What did you think?"

"Actually, it wasn't that bad. Maybe a bit crude at times, but good."

Leon laughed. "He's tamed it down some, to be frank." Leon stood. "Ready for a face-to-face?"

Was I? Chief Higgins's and Olivia's warnings about me not putting myself at risk floated through my head. Jayden might have killed Grady. If I was too blunt with him, he could end up doing the same to me.

But here? In public? With Leon at my side? He wouldn't try anything.

I hoped.

"Let's get this over with," I said, standing.

No one stopped us as we entered the side door, which made me briefly wonder about security. If anyone could stroll into the back like this, what was stopping someone from coming back here and attacking the performers? Not every performer told jokes, but I could see people getting angry about those that did, especially with the type of jokes Jayden told. And with alcohol involved, you never knew how someone might react.

Jayden was strutting around the back room like he'd just exited the stage to thunderous applause. His chest was puffed out and when he saw me enter, a wide grin spread across his face, as if he thought I'd been so overcome by his performance, I was going to throw myself at his feet.

The smile faded as soon as Leon strode in behind me.

"What are you doing here?" Jayden demanded, taking an aggressive step our way.

"We just came to talk," I said, drawing his eye before he could launch himself at Leon. And, because of his attitude, I decided to hit him hard. "It's about Grady Richards."

Jayden's intense stare moved from Leon to me long enough for him to ask, "What about him?"

"You had a problem with him."

"So?"

"So, he's dead." I adjusted my stance, forcing Jayden to pay attention to me, rather than Leon.

Jayden scowled, crossed his arms, and answered with yet another "So?"

"You don't see where I might be a little concerned?" I asked. "You fight with a guy, then he ends up murdered? What do you think the police are thinking right now?"

Jayden tried to hold on to his bravado, but my words seemed to finally slip through the cracks. "I didn't kill Grady." Nervous now, he took a step back. "I admit that I didn't like the dude, but that's not proof of anything. I don't like a lot of people who work here." He shot Leon another glare.

"You knew Grady was keeping his work here secret from his wife," I said. "You planned to use it against him."

I expected another "So?" but Jayden surprised me by saying, "I wouldn't have done that. That's not what our beef was about."

"Then what was it about?"

Jayden ground his teeth together as he regarded me. "Look, lady," he said after a moment, "I don't know what you think you think you know, but it's not what you think."

It took my brain a moment to catch up with that before I asked, "Then what should I think?"

"Grady and I butted heads over the same crap the rest of us did. He liked to 'borrow'"—air quotes—"my material, just like Fitzgerald over there. I called him out on it and he, like everyone else, didn't like it that I wasn't willing to take his crap lying down. It's not like we didn't have our moments where we got along."

"You didn't show up on time for your performance on the day Grady was murdered," I said. A little voice in the back of my head warned me I might be pushing him too far, but right then, I just wanted this to be over. If being blunt made Jayden reveal more than he intended, then so be it.

Jayden wiped his arm across his brow when a bead of sweat trailed down from his mop-covered hairline. "I'd had a rough night the night before. It had nothing to do with Grady. If you wanna pin this thing on someone, go talk to his wife. She's the one who had everything to gain by his death."

I considered asking him about what he meant by "rough night," but knew it would be pointless.

Jayden shifted from foot to foot, then motioned for me to get closer. I hesitated, half-afraid he might grab me, but all he did was lean forward and lower his voice.

"Grady and I didn't get along, sure, but we talked sometimes. He was feeling down about himself and I guess I was the only one around to listen at the time." He glanced around the room, but no one was paying us any mind. "He was worried his wife was having an affair. He said that the only reason she was still with him was because she didn't want to have to give up her lifestyle when they split their stuff."

Jayden snorted, shook his head. "I suppose him dying took care of that, now didn't it."

* * *

"Do you believe him?" I asked as Leon drove us home a short time later. "About Kathryn cheating. Jake said Kathryn thought Grady was the one who was cheating, not the other way around."

Leon was silent a long moment. He'd been quiet ever since we'd left The Letterbox. I wasn't sure if it was because of what Jayden had said, or if something else was going on, but I was definitely getting some odd vibes from him.

"Leon?" I prodded when the silence went on a beat too long. "Are you okay?"

His nod was jerky. "I'm just . . . confused, I guess. Do you remember that day when you came over to check on me?"

"There was a crash."

"It wasn't an accident like I told you it was. I knocked the stand over on purpose."

It was my turn not to respond.

"When Grady died, I was almost positive Jayden killed him." He fell silent as we waited at a light before he started moving again. "I was afraid that if Jayden killed Grady over his act, then what was stopping him from coming after me. I started getting paranoid and worked myself up over it. That day, I just sort of snapped and pushed the stand over and kicked it a few times for good measure." He laughed, shook his head. "It was stupid."

"You were scared and frustrated. We've all been there."

"I suppose, but it didn't do anything more than leave a mess. I didn't feel better, and now I have to buy a new stand to replace the one I broke. Hardly worth it." He sighed, turned onto another road. "When you knocked on my door, I thought it might be Jayden come to do me in, so I grabbed a hammer to defend myself. I felt stupid then, and feel more so now."

I remembered seeing the hammer sitting against the wall behind him when he'd answered the door. "You don't think Jayden killed him anymore?"

He thought about it. "I don't know. He didn't seem to be lying, but I'm not an expert. If Kathryn was cheating on Grady, but was afraid to lose everything if she left him, it would make sense for her to have killed him." A beat. "Or have him killed."

It did. But then, why come after me? For optics? Did she think that if she appeared distraught, then no one would suspect her? Maybe she hoped that the police would consider *me* a suspect, diverting attention from her and what she'd have to gain by Grady's death.

We reached the apartment complex a little while later. Leon and I walked up the stairs, each lost in our own thoughts. The hallway was empty when we reached the second floor. I had a feeling Edna knew we were there, but was letting us have this time to ourselves.

There was a moment of silence where we both just stood there, looking at one another. Then Leon cleared his throat and said, "Would you like to come in for a few minutes?"

Did I? We didn't have to do anything romantic. We could talk about Jayden and Kathryn and Grady and see if we could come up with a consensus on who we thought was the murderer and why. We could watch that Netflix special of his—I was sure he had it recorded somewhere, even if it was removed from the streaming service.

It wasn't an *un*appealing idea. Now just wasn't the time.

"Rain check?" I asked.

Leon smiled. There may have been a hint of sadness in his expression, but that might have been my imagination. "Rain check."

I approached my door, unlocked it. Leon did the same.

And then, in unison, we entered our respective apartments.

Chapter 19

My phone startled me out of a pleasant dream where I was doing yoga in a room full of available young men who all loved cats. They all had eyes for me—the men, not the cats—but I was stoically indifferent to their advances. There was a moment of disorientation where I wondered if I'd somehow fallen during a rather strenuous pose I'd been attempting, though I couldn't recall which—the dream was already fading. It took me a long moment to figure out how I'd managed to end up in bed.

Blinking sleep out of my eyes, and while trying to get some sort of moisture generated in my mouth, I fumbled for my phone, which I kept on a wireless charger on my nightstand.

"Hello?" I said. Or tried to say. It came out a mumbled mess.

"Is this Ash Branson? Did I wake you?"

My brain did a slow blink of its own. *I know that voice.* "This is Ash Branson." I glanced at the clock and was surprised to see it was half-past nine. I swung my legs over the edge of the bed, still not quite with it. There was a faint buzz in my head that wouldn't go away. "I guess I slept in. I need to get up anyway." A beat, and then, "Who is this?"

"Kathryn Richards."

I jerked upright, suddenly wide awake. "Kathryn?" I stood and nearly tripped over Luna, who must have been waiting patiently bedside for me to rise. She pranced back, then bumped my shin with her head. "What can I do for you?"

"I'm in town. Cardinal Lake. Can we meet?"

"Meet?" Yikes. I eyeballed my bedroom, not quite sure where to start. "When? Where?" Master of the one-word questions.

"I don't know. Where's a good place? I . . ." The cough that followed sounded fake, like she was masking her discomfort. "I'd like to apologize."

"For waking me up? Like I said, I needed to get—"

"Not for that," she said, cutting me off. There was a hint of mild annoyance in her voice. "I shouldn't have blamed you for what Grady did. You didn't know and I . . . Just, can we meet? I don't want to do this over the phone."

"Yeah, um . . ." I did a quick mental rundown of places we could go. Snoot's opened for breakfast, but by the time I would be ready to go, it would be too late. And since it was a Sunday, a lot of places were closed. "Do you know Shakes?" I asked, thinking that I could use a shot of caffeine right about then. "We can get coffee and talk."

"That works. I can find it."

"Give me an hour to get ready and I'll be there."

"I'll be waiting." She clicked off.

By the time I was showered, dressed, and ready to walk out the door, I was positive the meeting with Kathryn was a setup.

What kind of setup? I had no idea. But she could, and did, apologize over the phone. There was no reason for us to meet face-to-face. No matter what she said, I was still the woman who'd agreed to go on a blind date with her husband. She might have said she didn't blame me for it, but that didn't make it true. One look at my face and she'd be reminded of Grady and what he'd planned on doing.

And then there was what Jayden had said about her. If she killed Grady because she wanted to be free of him without risk of losing her lifestyle and she feared I knew, what then? This could be her chance at feeling me out. Or threatening me. Or . . . well, there's any number of things she could hope to accomplish if she was somehow responsible for her husband's death.

So, yeah, a setup. It's why I was dialing Sierra as I pulled on my coat. She answered on the first ring.

"Where have you been?" she demanded by way of answer.

"Same places as always?"

"You know what I mean. It's been like three days since we last talked!"

"I called you yesterday," I pointed out, patting Luna on the head before heading toward the door.

"Yeah, about Hunter's baby, which is the cutest damn thing I've ever seen, by the way."

Agreed. "So, technically we talked yesterday."

"But not about what's been going on with you, Ash," she said. "This whole Grady-being-dead thing affects the both of us, you know?"

"That's kind of why I'm calling now." Luna followed me to the door, still demanding attention. I picked up a nearby rattle ball and tossed it across the room so she wouldn't be tempted to follow me out into the hall. She gave chase and I quickly slipped out the door. "I'm meeting with Kathryn Richards at Shakes here in a few minutes and I was hoping you could come."

"What? Now? I'm on the way."

I was going to tell her to meet me outside, but Sierra was already gone. "Okay, then," I muttered, shoving my phone into my pocket. I jerked to a stop when I looked up and saw Jake standing outside Leon's door, watching me.

"Jake," I said, hand going to my chest. "You startled me."

His smile was slow in coming. "Sorry about that. I was stopping by to check on Leon." He jerked a thumb toward Leon's door before shoving his hands into his pockets. "Guess he's not home."

"Seems like that keeps happening," I said as I headed for the stairs. "You might want to start calling ahead first."

He laughed and followed me. "You're probably right."

I half jogged down the stairs, leaving behind Jake, who was moseying down them at a leisurely pace. I was okay with that. I didn't have time for small talk, not if I wanted to beat Sierra to the coffee shop so she didn't start in on Kathryn without me. Who knows what she would say in my absence.

I drove to Shakes, a nervous wreck. I kept waffling between thinking Kathryn was legitimately sorry for what she did to this meeting being a chance for her to throw me off her trail. She *was* the best suspect when it came to Grady's murder, and always had been. I mean, a cheating husband? Angry wife? Duh.

I parked just as Sierra pulled into the lot. I waited for her to park and then joined her at the side of her car. So far, there was no sign of Kathryn, though if she was inside, there wouldn't be.

"So, what's going on, Ash?" Sierra asked, squinting her eyes against the overly bright morning sun.

I gave her a quick rundown of my last couple of days, including my chat with Jayden Clay. "And then Kathryn called me up out of the blue this morning, and here we are."

"It's a trap."

"I figured as much."

"Did you call Olivia?"

I paused. "No. Should I have?"

"Should you have called a police officer who would come running to protect you at the first sign of trouble when you're about to meet with the widow of a murdered man, a woman who very well could be responsible for his death? I don't know, Ash, should you have called her? Let me think hard about this."

"We're meeting in public," I pointed out. "It's not like I'm going to her house or some abandoned warehouse on the outskirts of town. She's not going to do anything here with so many people around."

As if to prove my point, a large family dressed as if they'd just come from church piled out of a minivan.

"I guess you're right." Sierra sighed, made a face. "This seems weird."

"You're telling me." I eyed the coffee shop. "We should probably go on in."

"After you."

I led the way inside Shakes. Kathryn was seated at a window table, one that looked out over the parking lot, but was sitting back so that she couldn't be seen from the outside. She could have watched Sierra and me as we talked, but we wouldn't have been able to see her. Planned? Or by chance?

"Kathryn," I said, approaching the table. "This is my friend Sierra."

A tightening around her eyes told me Kathryn wasn't thrilled by the extra company. "I see."

"Sierra, could you get us a couple of coffees?" I asked. "Take your time."

She hesitated, then nodded. "Sure thing."

As soon as she was gone, I sat down. "Okay. What do you want to talk to me about? I doubt you only want to apologize for attacking me."

Kathryn, who apparently took her coffee black, took a sip from the open cup in front of her before responding. "I'm not going to get into my feelings about what you and Grady may or may not have been doing. You might say that you didn't know him, that he was nothing to you, and I won't believe you. And even if I did, I don't think I want to know either way."

The urge to tell her that it was a blind date, that I'd never actually met Grady Richards, was strong, but I kept my mouth shut. There was no point in pressing her when she had no interest in the truth.

"I've suspected Grady was cheating for a couple of years now." Her laugh was bitter. "Probably since before we were married, to be honest. He was secretive from the start. When I first met him, he was seeing someone else and he never told me. I found out about it on my own, but I let it slide. I knew better than to get involved with someone like that, yet I married him anyway. What does that say about me?"

"You loved him," I said.

"I guess I did. I was stupid. I let things go for a while, and then he started leaving for days at a time. He told me it was for work, but I knew that wasn't true. I talked to his coworkers and they knew nothing about where he was going, so what else was I supposed to think other than he was cheating on me like he'd done with that old girlfriend of his?"

She looked at me for answers, but I had none. All I could manage was a lame "I'm sorry."

She shook her head. "Me too." A sigh, and then, "Even though I suspect him of being unfaithful, I more or less let it happen. I mean, what else could I do? If I confronted him, we'd just fight and both be the worse for it. And I honestly didn't know for sure that he *was* cheating. I could have been wrong. Maybe he was doing drugs or was drinking with a friend and crashing at their place on those long nights when he didn't come home. There's any number of reasons why he'd stay out night after night without telling me what he was doing."

She swirled her coffee around, set it aside. "And then someone showed up and told me I was right; Grady was cheating on me."

My heart skipped a beat. "Someone told you about the date?"

She smiled, but there was no humor in it. "With you? No. I didn't find out about that until the police showed me the planner. This was before his . . ." She swallowed, coughed into her hand. "Before he passed. This happened months ago. He showed up at the house and told me that Grady was traveling out of town to pick up women. I was shocked. Angry. Humiliated. I didn't know what to do."

"You never said anything to him?"

She laughed, wiped at an eye. "I should have. Maybe if I had, he'd still be alive. Instead, I did something mind-numbingly stupid. I mean, Grady was cheating on me, right? So why not do the same to him?" She searched my face, almost pleadingly, as if begging for me to understand.

And I suppose I kind of did. She learned her husband was cheating on her. She was afraid to go to him about it because in doing so, it would upend her entire life. It probably made sense at the time for her to find someone of her own, someone who could make her feel wanted again. Or, if it wasn't that, someone she could use as a weapon against her husband.

Sierra returned in the silence that followed, carrying two coffees. She handed me mine and sank down into a chair without a word.

Kathryn sniffed, ran a hand over her face. I wasn't sure she'd continue talking with Sierra there, but after a moment, she did.

"This went on for a couple of weeks, maybe a month, before I realized I was making a mistake. It was nice at first, but soon, things started to get complicated. I was just looking for revenge, I guess. I didn't want it to get serious, if you know what I mean?"

"But it did."

She nodded. "The guy I was seeing started to get clingy. He told me I should leave Grady, that we should run off together and get married. I thought he was joking at first, but then he started pressuring me, saying that he'd tell everyone about us if I didn't comply. When that didn't work, he started getting angry, said I wasn't being fair to him." She leaned back in her chair, stared out the window. "In reality, it was me I wasn't being fair to. I was undervaluing myself, spending time with someone just because Grady had hurt me."

The wheels were spinning in my head. Someone went to Kathryn and told her Grady was cheating on her. Who would do that? Someone who knew where he was going, and someone who wanted to ruin his wife, that's who.

And who had threatened to go to Kathryn, and then, later, tried to paint her as the bad guy? Bad woman? Whatever.

Jayden Clay.

"Then, after I confronted you, I started to realize something," she went on. "It really started sinking in that something didn't quite add up."

"What do you mean?"

She made a face as she thought about it. "It's hard to explain. I was convinced Grady was going behind my back, so much so, I was willing to take anyone's word for it, just for validation. But . . . I don't know. Grady didn't *act* like someone who was cheating. He was being secretive, sure, but he came home and treated me like he always had. There were none of the telltale signs. No lipstick smears. No strange late-night texts or calls. And then I met you and you seemed so genuine that I started to wonder if maybe I'd been lied to."

"Grady wasn't cheating," I said. "Not in the way you think. He'd set up a blind date with me, but from what I understand, it wasn't because he didn't care about you. He was . . ." I tried to come up with a gentle way to put it and settled on "confused."

Kathryn stared at me, didn't comment, so I went on.

"He was performing at a club in town here. I never saw him. He was keeping it secret because he was afraid you wouldn't approve."

Kathryn's face scrunched up in confusion before she let out a laugh that sounded half like a sob. "Of course he was," she said, wiping at an eye. "That sounds like something Grady would do. Stupid, silly man."

"Whoever told you he was cheating, lied," I said. "Or was mistaken."

"They lied." It came out at a near whisper. She cleared her throat, tried again. "He lied to me. I should have seen through him right away."

"Who was it?" I asked as gently as I could.

Kathryn was silent for a long time before she abruptly stood. "I don't know why I came here," she said. "This was a mistake."

"No, please." I rose with her, took her hand before she could flee. "Who told you Grady was cheating?" Because if he was angry that Kathryn didn't run away with him, perhaps he thought getting rid of the competition would make her change her mind.

There was a moment where it looked like Kathryn might pull away and leave without telling me.

And then, squeezing her eyes closed, she whispered, "The guy's name is Jake Palmer. He told me he was Grady's friend." And then she pulled away from me and hurried out the door.

"That was *not* how I expected that to go," Sierra said as we left Shakes.

"You and me both." My head was pounding in time with my heart. Jake, not Jayden, was the one who went to Kathryn. Jake who was constantly hanging around my apartment, who was always looking for Leon.

Or claimed to be.

"What are we going to do?" Sierra asked. When I didn't answer, she nudged me. "Ash? Are you all right?"

"I saw Jake today," I said. "He said he was looking for Leon next door, but what if he was lurking outside *my* apartment?" I tried to remember whether I'd said anything in his presence about where I was going, but couldn't recall. "What if he knows I talked to Kathryn?" My eyes widened. "I need to warn Leon."

"We don't know for sure this Jake guy killed Grady," Sierra said as we reached our cars.

"I need to call Olivia," I said. "And talk to Leon and tell him about Jake, just in case. I . . ." I glanced around the lot. Looking for what? I had no idea. "I don't know if I should go home. What if he's waiting for me there? I can't look at Jake and *not* think that he killed Grady. He'll figure out that I suspect him and—"

Sierra put a hand on my arm. "Hey, look at me."

I did, and realized how wild I must look. I could feel my eyes bugging out of my head, and I was trembling.

"We're going to go to your apartment," she said, voice measured, as if talking to someone close to falling right off the ledge into the abyss. "You're going to go inside, grab some things, and then I'm going to drive the both of us to my place. You're going to stay with me, all right?"

I shook my head. "I can't leave Luna."

"Bring her with you. Herman could use a friend."

"He might eat her." The joke came out sounding flat, but Sierra smiled, nonetheless.

"She'll be fine," she said. "I'll call Aaron, Henna, and Bri. They can come over and we can all hang out. If you don't want to be left alone, you know we'll be there."

"Sierra, I can't invade your home—"

"Ash, yes you can."

"But—"

"Would you stop arguing and get into your car? It's freezing out here."

I stared at her, mouth working, but I'd run out of arguments. I was scared that Jake might be the killer. Jake knew where I lived. He knew I was asking questions. Why risk it when I had friends who were willing to make sure I was safe?

"All right," I said. "I guess we're doing this."

Sierra grinned. "Of course we are." She patted me on the shoulder and then climbed into her car. "I'll see you at your apartment." She closed the door, and in moments, we were both on the way.

Chapter 20

I called Olivia as I fumbled my way into my apartment, half convinced Jake would grab me while I was inserting the key into the lock. I missed three times in my haste, and ended up cursing in Olivia's ear when she answered.

"Sorry," I said, finally slotting the key in. "I'm in a hurry."

"Sounds like. What's up, Ash? You sound off."

I almost laughed as I closed the door and sagged against it in mild relief. Sierra was waiting in her car in the parking lot, though she wasn't happy about it. She'd wanted to come in with me, but I was afraid Jake would be outside Leon's door and I didn't want him to see her. I was paranoid and wasn't even sure I had a reason to be. Just because Kathryn told me a story, didn't make it true.

"I'm a little frazzled," I said, pushing away from the door. "I got an interesting call this morning. . . ."

As I rushed from room to room, grabbing what I—and Luna—would need if we were to stay with Sierra for more than a night or two, I filled Olivia in on what I'd learned from Kathryn about Jake.

"You think this Kathryn lady's boyfriend might be after you?"

"Jake Palmer. If he killed Grady, then maybe."

She sighed. "But you're not sure."

"She could have lied," I said. "Or she could be wrong. Either way, I don't feel safe."

Olivia was silent a moment before she said, "All right, Ash. You said you're staying with Sierra?"

"I am."

"Good. I'll come by your place and check it out. Might hang around a bit and see if anyone comes sniffing around."

"You don't have to do that." Though I was glad she'd offered.

"I think I kind of do. I'll fill in Chief Higgins and then I'll head that way."

"Thanks, Olivia. I'll be gone by the time you get here, but I'll see you soon."

"Stay safe, Ash."

I clicked off, dropped my phone twice, and then simply stood in the hall and breathed. *Calm down, Ash.* I was panicking and didn't need to be. I was safe in my apartment. Sierra was waiting for me outside. Edna was right across the hall. Even if Jake *was* the killer, he wouldn't try anything this early in the day. He'd wait until it was dark, and by then, I would be gone.

I bent over and with slow, deliberate movements I picked up my phone and pocketed it. That done, I retrieved Luna's carrier and set it on the floor. Seeing a new place to hide, she immediately jumped inside and started purring. That lasted right up until I closed the door, trapping her inside.

That's when the wail of the tortured soul began.

"You're going to be fine," I told her as I finished gathering our things. I didn't own a suitcase since I never traveled, so my clothes were crammed into a backpack and Luna's treats and toys were stuffed inside an old laptop bag I'd found on the shelf in my closet. I patted myself down, made a quick pass from room to room to make sure I hadn't forgotten anything, and was nearly out the door when I remembered the toiletries.

Luna *mrowed* at the top of her lungs when I set her back down. I all but ran into the bathroom to grab my toothbrush and supplies, silently cursing myself for forgetting them. I didn't expect to stay with Sierra for more than a night or two, but there was no way I was going to go without a toothbrush, and I was most definitely not going to use Sierra's.

"Okay, I think that's it," I told Luna when I returned. I tossed everything over my shoulder, picked up her carrier, and stepped out into the hall.

Pavan and Edna were standing outside Edna's door when I emerged. Edna had just handed Pavan a mug and they both turned to face me as I locked and double-checked my door.

"Going on a trip, Ash?" Pavan asked, gesturing toward my things with his free hand. "A grand adventure to the great outdoors?"

"I wish. I'm staying with Sierra." I considered asking them to keep an eye on my apartment, but that would lead to a hundred other questions I wasn't ready to answer. "I'll be back in a couple of days."

Edna's gaze flickered to Leon's apartment door and her lips pressed into a fine line, but she didn't press.

"Have a nice time," Pavan said. "I can just barely remember those days when I could drop everything and crash with a friend." He sighed dramatically. "But alas, I have to content myself with Seo-Jun's loving embrace instead."

"Poor you," Edna said, nudging him with her elbow.

"I'll fill you two in when I'm back. I've got to go." I waved as best I could, encumbered as I was, and then hurried down the stairs, and out the door, anxious to be on the way. Cold wind blasted into me, taking my—and Luna's—breath away.

The wails stopped and she moved to the back end of the carrier, nearly unbalancing me as she did.

Sierra was waiting for me in her car. "If I'd known it was going to take that long, I would have come in with you," she said, before turning her attention to Luna. "Herman's just going to *love* you." She reached through the metal bars on the door, but Luna wasn't having it. She remained pressed against the back of the carrier with her ears pinned back, and refused to budge, even for chin scritches.

"You don't have to drive us," I said, eyeing my car a few spaces away. "Actually, yeah, I really should drive myself." I started to reach for the door, but Sierra stopped me with a hand on my wrist.

"Trust me, Ash, this is better," she said. "If this killer guy shows up, he'll see your car and think you're inside your apartment."

"That's supposed to make me feel better?"

"No, but if he thinks you're home, he might try something. And if he tries something . . ."

"Then the police will catch him in the act. I get it." I sagged in my seat as she pulled out of the parking space and headed for the road. I didn't like it, but I got it.

"So, I probably should have told you something. . . ."

I suppressed a groan. "What?"

"I'm scheduled to go in to Snoot's tonight and help train a couple of new hires. I'm supposed to stay until we close. I could always call off—"

"Absolutely not."

"But—"

"No, Sierra. I'm disrupting your life enough as it is. Go to work. Herman will protect me."

She frowned, but didn't argue any further.

"I talked to Bri while you were in your apartment," she said after a minute. "She said she might stop by if she gets a chance. She's fifty-fifty on it. Aaron and Henna are doing Aaron and Henna things and I don't think any of us want to see that."

I made a face. "Isn't their anniversary coming up soon?"

"Which one?" Sierra laughed. "I swear those two celebrate every milestone like it's a wedding anniversary. Did you know they had a 'first-kiss' anniversary date a couple of months back?"

"They *didn't*."

"They did. They re-created the whole thing, right down to the clothing they'd been wearing at the time." She shook her head. "If it wasn't so cute, it would be creepy."

"Can't it be both?"

We arrived at Sierra's apartment a short time later. I took Luna, who'd given up complaining and was just lying there, glaring at me through the bars. Sierra grabbed the rest of my stuff and carried it to her apartment door. She, unlike me, slid the key into the lock on the first try, turned the knob, and popped the door open with her hip.

Herman was sitting in the middle of the room, watching us as we entered. His ears perked up at the sight of the cat carrier. He didn't get up, but Luna had grabbed his attention.

"Herman," Sierra said, tossing my bags onto the couch. "This is Luna. Don't eat her."

I set the carrier down close to him. His nose went into overdrive and he lumbered to his feet. He walked around the carrier, then pawed at the door, glancing back at Sierra as he did.

"I think he wants you to let her out."

"What do you think about that?" I asked Luna, who'd moved to the front of the carrier. She didn't appear freaked out, yet I was worried. "What if they get into a fight?" This to Sierra.

"As long as he doesn't lie on her, she'll be fine. Herman's a big baby, so if she swipes at him, he'll probably run and hide under the bed."

"I don't think he *can* run."

"Ha-ha. I'll have you know that he manages just fine. You should see him move when I open a can of food."

I imagined Herman waddling at warp speed and laughed as I opened the carrier door.

Luna hesitated before stepping out into Sierra's living room. Herman jerked back in surprise, and then started sniffing her. Luna returned the favor, and the next thing I knew, the two cats were circling around each other, trying to get a good sniff of the other.

"No aggression so far," Sierra pointed out.

We spent the next two hours watching the cats and getting me settled in. Once we were certain Herman and Luna were going to get along okay, we moved on to watching Netflix. Bri showed up, spent an hour with us, and then left again.

All in all, it was a perfectly boring afternoon.

"Call me if something happens," Sierra said a few hours later. She was dressed for work and looked unhappy about it. "I'll have my cell on. I'm just training, so Snoot won't care."

"I think I'll be okay."

She frowned at me before she walked out the door, muttering to herself.

"Looks like it's just us now," I told the cats before dropping onto the couch. It felt strange to be in someone else's apartment without having them there, even if Sierra was a close friend. I tried not to let it get to me, but within minutes, I started to get weirded out and wanted nothing more than to get into my car and drive home. Too bad my car wasn't there and it was too far to walk.

And what about work tomorrow? Sierra was either going to have to drive me or loan me her car so I could be at A Purrfect Pose for the first class of the day. We should have talked about that before I let Sierra bully me into letting her drive.

"That's it," I said a short time later. "I'm going to bed. You two coming?" Both Luna and Herman glanced at me, but neither moved. "Suit yourselves."

Sierra didn't have a spare bedroom, but had a bed big enough for an army, so we'd agreed to share like we used to when we were younger. One corner at the foot of the bed was coated in cat fur. A stool had been placed on the floor next to it so Herman could climb up. I decided to take the other side of the bed so I wouldn't crowd him if and when he decided to join me.

I lay down and then was immediately uncomfortable. Being in someone's apartment when they weren't there was weird. Sleeping in their bed was downright unbearable.

I tossed and turned for the next hour, unable to sleep. Herman climbed up ten minutes after I'd lain down and I swear I felt the entire bed tilt in his direction. Luna hopped up beside me five minutes after that, purring. I lay there, staring up at the dark ceiling, petting her, wishing I could just fall asleep so this odd experience would be over.

And then there was a click.

I was in a strange apartment, so I might have dismissed the sound as an unfamiliar, but typical noise, if it wasn't for how both Herman's and Luna's heads popped up. There was a moment of silence and then the faintest squeak. Then a near silent clunk.

Sierra's name was on the tip of my tongue, but in the dark, I didn't want to call out and alert whoever was there—and I'm sure *someone* was out there. Careful not to make a sound, I slipped from bed. My phone was sitting in the living room where Sierra kept her charger, a decision I was regretting.

I padded from the bedroom on bare feet, thankful the carpet muffled my footfalls. A floorboard creaked, but it wasn't because of me.

It had come from the living room.

I sucked in a breath and debated what to do. The lights were still off. If it was Sierra having come home early from working at Snoot's, she would have turned on a light. So, if it wasn't her, then who?

Who else?

The killer.

The bathroom was a few steps away. I could go in, lock the door, and wait.

But then what? If I was right, Grady's killer—be it Kathryn or Jake or even Jayden—would have me trapped. They could knock down the door and then where would I be?

And what if it was someone else? Like Bri. Or maybe Henna and Aaron come to play a trick on me. Then I'd feel like an even bigger fool.

But at least I'd be alive.

"I know you're there."

My breath caught in my throat. I knew that voice. And no, it wasn't Sierra or Henna or Bri or Aaron. It wasn't Kathryn Richards, either.

It was Jake Palmer.

"Come on out, Ash. I know you're alone. Let's talk." The living room light clicked on.

I stepped out of the hallway, into the living room, and there he was. Jake was dressed in the same clothing he'd been wearing when I'd seen him earlier that day, not in all black like I'd expected an intruder to wear. He was smiling, though there was a tension in that smile. He motioned toward the couch, which, yes, would put me closer to my phone, but if I sat, I'd be at a disadvantage.

I crossed my arms and remained in place. "I'm okay right where I am."

He shrugged in a "suit yourself" manner, then said, "I hate this; I really do." He took a step toward me and removed blue latex gloves from his back pocket.

"What are you doing?" I asked. And then, more importantly, "You killed Grady, didn't you?"

Jake sighed, pulled on the first glove. He didn't otherwise answer.

"You were the one who told Kathryn that Grady was cheating on her, weren't you? It wasn't Jayden, though you wanted me to believe it was."

The other glove snapped into place.

"Why do this?" I asked. I steadfastly refused to glance toward my phone. I wanted him to move to the hallway side of the couch, which would put him as far away from my phone as he could get. I was pretty sure I could reach it before he caught up to me, but could I call Olivia before he closed the distance? We were going to find out.

"You were getting too close," Jake said, turning his head to the side so that his neck cracked with a loud *snap*. "You talked to Kathryn. I don't know what she told you, but I can imagine. I watched you. And you"—he pointed at me—"are a persistent one, Ash Branson."

"You overheard me talking to Sierra on the phone."

He smiled, confirming it.

Jake took another step toward me. I tensed, but didn't move, though my legs were trembling for me to act. He wasn't where I wanted him quite yet.

Out of the corner of my eye, I saw movement from down the hall. Luna and Herman. While Luna remained at the bedroom doorway, peering out at me, Herman lumbered his way toward me, completely unbothered by the intruder.

"Why did you kill Grady?" I asked. If I kept Jake talking, then I hoped he wouldn't notice my phone or how I was subtly turning my body so I could make a run for it.

"Kathryn and I have something special," he said, this time cracking his knuckles one by one. "She refused to see it. Couldn't. Not with Grady still in the picture. I didn't mean to kill him, to be honest. But when I told him about Kathryn and me in the hopes that he'd let her go, he lost it. He attacked me, so it was self-defense, really."

He took another step.

Now.

I burst into motion, all but throwing myself toward my phone. Jake cursed, and like expected, came around the front of the couch to reach me. I didn't see him move, but I could hear him over the pounding of my heart.

I snatched up my phone and spun to face him just in time to see Herman, who'd just reached the living room, step in front of Jake. Herman is a big kitty, so I don't even think he felt it as Jake's foot caught him in the side. He just stood there, a dumbfounded look on his fuzzy face as Jake tripped over him, arms pinwheeling almost comically as he tried to keep his balance.

He couldn't, not with his momentum propelling him.

Jake pitched forward, overtop Herman, and crashed *through* Sierra's coffee table.

In the movies, that would have been it. He would have knocked himself out and I could call the police and they'd be there to arrest him before he came to.

Instead, Jake cursed loudly and stood up. His cheek was bleeding and he was favoring his left leg, but otherwise, he appeared unharmed.

I wasn't idle during those few seconds Herman had bought me. I tapped my screen, typed in my pin, and pressed the contact for Olivia. It rang and her voice came on the line almost immediately. "Ash? What time is it?"

"Jake Palmer killed Grady Richards. I'm at Sierra's apartment and he's here with me right now. Help!" The last came out as a panicked shout.

Jake sighed, brushed himself off. He didn't appear bothered that I'd just told the police that he was a murderer. In fact, he looked resigned, as if he'd always expected to be caught.

Olivia said something else, but I'd dropped the phone to my side and was backing away. The kitchen was nearby, as were Sierra's knives. I just needed to—

Jake made his move. He rushed forward, fluid despite his injuries, and came right at me. With an enraged shout, he angled himself so that he cut me off from the kitchen when I leaned that way. So, instead, I turned and ran for the door, but Jake was too fast. Before I could grab the knob, his fingers brushed my back, nearly catching hold. I spun away, and ran back around the couch, thinking we could face off from opposite sides and try this again, but he wasn't about to give me that chance. Jake kept coming, not slowing an iota as he trailed after me. I rounded the couch, just barely avoiding tripping over Herman myself, and made another pass at the door, but didn't have time to grab it. He was too close.

I ran past the door, thinking I might just keep going and wear him out.

Then a new sound. The rattling of keys.

And then the door opened.

Jake didn't have time to stop. He slammed into the opening door at full speed, hard enough to cause it to recoil back into Sierra's face. The impact caused Jake to lose his feet. He crashed down onto his back hard enough to knock the wind out of him.

Sierra staggered back a step, blinked at me in surprise, and then noting Jake was attempting to work his way to his feet, she reached into her purse and produced what I thought at first was pepper spray. She sprayed him square in the face with it.

A heavy floral scent filled the room as Jake screamed and tried to rub what wasn't pepper spray, but perfume, from his eyes.

And while he was thuswise occupied, Sierra stepped forward and kicked him right between the legs.

Jake went down with a strangled sound no human should make.

He didn't get up again until Olivia arrived with three other cops in tow. He was still whimpering as they took him away.

A childish scream was followed by a series of giggles as Evan chased his kids, Lily Rose and Philip, up the stairs, to their rooms.

I watched them with a smile.

We were at Alexi and Evan's house. Olivia was there, talking with Alexi, while Evan chased his kids off to bed. We'd had dinner and had spent a rather pleasant evening together void of talk of murder and cheating husbands and wives. It was nice.

"I saw Kara and Wayne yesterday," Olivia was saying as I turned my attention back to them. "Looks like those two have patched up whatever had gotten between them. They were with Hunter and Lita, cooing over Christian, like nothing had happened."

"Kara and Hunter were in the same room together?" I asked, butting into the conversation.

"Side by side." Olivia chuckled. She knew, just like everyone else in the family, that Hunter had avoided Kara ever since she'd started dating Dad, so this was a big development in the Branson-Daniels-Chase families.

"I hear Lita's reconsidering relocating," Alexi said. "She might not move to Maine after all."

"Think it's because of her dad?" I asked. So far, I hadn't heard a negative peep out of Chief Higgins when it came to the baby or how Christian was conceived. Hopefully, I never would.

"He didn't kill Hunter, so she probably feels safe enough to stay," Alexi said with a laugh that we all joined.

"What's so funny?" Evan asked, returning to the room, sans

children. "Did Ash trip over another murderer while I was gone?"

"Ha-ha," I said, smacking him on the shoulder. "And it was the killer who tripped over Herman the cat. I just ran away."

"You're lucky Sierra showed up when she did," Olivia said, growing serious.

Resigned that we were going to talk about it, I leaned against the counter and said, "She left work early. Just sort of walked out on her trainees and came home. I'm not sure what I would have done if she hadn't shown up."

Jake, having overheard me talk to Sierra, had gone to Shakes to watch us meet with Kathryn. He'd then followed us back to my apartment, watched as I loaded Luna into Sierra's car, and then followed us all the way to her place, where he waited until I'd turned out the light to make his move.

I'd like to think he was the guy Solomon had seen sitting outside my apartment complex all those days ago, but couldn't be sure. It might have been him, or it might have been Kathryn attempting to work up the nerve to confront me about her husband. I wouldn't know unless I asked her, but I had a feeling I'd never be talking to Kathryn Richards again.

"He's confessed to everything," Olivia said. "I guess he'd even had plans to do something about your neighbors. Mr. Palmer was growing paranoid and thought that everyone knew what he'd done. Guy might have turned into a serial killer if you hadn't stopped him."

We all ruminated on that a long moment before Alexi decided to change the subject. "So, Ash, are you planning any more blind dates we should be aware of? I think we should all be prepared if you are."

I stuck my tongue out at her before I said, "I think I'm done with dating for the time being. Especially now that Mom is running for mayor and I just *know* she's going to have Solomon dig through the history of anyone I go out with." She'd announced her intentions to the family last night. Not shockingly, her siblings weren't thrilled with the announcement, especially since they weren't handed the keys to the golden goose, as it were.

"That might be a good thing," Olivia said. "Considering your track record."

I made a face, and then we all had a good laugh. She wasn't wrong. From now on, when it came to my love life, I was going to make all the decisions. No more blind dates for me, at least for a very long time.

Until then, I was happy with how my life was going. I was alive, around family and friends who cared.

No one was ever going to get in the way of that. They'd have to kill me first, and thanks to those family and friends, *that* was going to be much harder than it seemed.

Visit our website at
KensingtonBooks.com
to sign up for our newsletters, read more from your favorite authors, see books by series, view reading group guides, and more!

Become a Part of Our
Between the Chapters Book Club
Community and Join the Conversation

Betweenthechapters.net

Submit your book review for a chance to win exclusive Between the Chapters swag you can't get anywhere else!
https://www.kensingtonbooks.com/pages/review/